# Hilarious

# Hilarious

Joey Truman

*Whiskey Tit*

NYC & VT

Published in the United States by Whisk(e)y Tit: www.whiskeytit.com. If you wish to use or reproduce all or part of this book for any means, please let the author and publisher know. You're pretty much required to, legally.

ISBN 978-1-952600-61-6



First Whisk(e)y Tit paperback edition.

*Editor*: Jess Barbagallo
*Design*: Michael Jung
*Art*: Jack Warren, George Truman

*To my brother Jade,
the wimpiest worm that ever crawled out of a mudhole.*

I can't say that I was surprised when the sound guy came into the green room to beat the living piss out of me. I was surprised that he threw the cash from the door on top of me afterwards. Normally you get stiffed when you pull shit like that. For good reason, I guess. It's not my fault the dude couldn't get the microphone working. I'm not a sound guy. What the hell do I know? I'm a joke man. A real hilarious dude. That is all that I know. But I do know that it isn't that fucking hard to run a cable and turn a fucking knob. Gah. Or ugh is maybe a better way to say it. I don't know, I need to stop drinking before I do these gigs. It is making me angry. It really doesn't help that they pay me in drink tickets and proceeds. Not really, at least. I have no problem using the tickets, and the door is usually crap anyway. Nobody comes to my shit. Just the jerks with nothing better to do on a Tuesday evening. Hoping to get laid or something. A place to sit for a couple hours that isn't their depressing apartment, or whatever. You know? A place that doesn't smell like frozen meatballs and ketchup soup. But whose fault is that? Not mine. Or at least I don't think so.

$42 dollars though. Not a bad haul. I counted the money when I could move again. The sound guy really did a number on my ribs. It took me quite some time before I could stand up. My lip was swollen. The top lip, I guess. Both of my lips were puffy. My nose was bleeding. I could still smell the sound guy's foot. Part dog shit, part soil. I guess he had a dog that he took to the dog park or whatever. On walks or something. He was really pissed when he busted through the door. He was more hilarious than I was. He was yelling at me. Saying shit like:

"How about I run this cable, right up your fucking ass!" Then he kicks me. Then he yells, "Sound check this, asshole!" Then he punches me. I couldn't stop laughing. Which made it worse. He then started yelling, "You think this is funny? How about this punch-line!" Which made it worse because he didn't think he was being funny. And I laid there absorbing his blows and his jokes. Eventually he gave up and threw the money on top of me and stormed out. I don't know. How do you put that on stage? I kind of wanted to go talk to him and ask him if he would do this again in real time, but he really did do a number on my ribs. Which made it hard to move around. So instead I just gathered up my shit, and left out the back door of the place. Another bridge burned. I got into my car. Which was parked in the alley. I reached into the glove compartment and pulled out my list. I had to turn the light on in order to read it. The alley was dark. I reached back into the glove compartment and grabbed a pen. I put the paper on the steering wheel. Underneath about ten other names I wrote: Tinderhooks Bar & Grill Oberlin Ohio shitty sound guy $42.86. I put the pen and the paper back in the glove box. Closed it. Tried to gauge if I could drive or not. Decided that I could not. I would probably get thrown in jail. Instead of driving I turned the car on. Drove up the alley, away from the dumpsters behind the venue. Parked next to a brick wall. Turned on the radio. A jazz station from the college, I guess. Debated if I should keep the car running. In the end I decided I should just turn it off for an hour or so. Let the radio play. Then turn it back on later. For the battery. Save gas. I guess. I pulled the seat lever and pushed the seat back. I was warm enough. Not too hot. Not too cold. It was May. The month of May. Good ol' May. Taking showers. Bringing flowers. I thought about this idea. That May was a person. Somebody that brings flowers, but also takes showers. For my routine. I listened to the college jazz. I closed my eyes and fell asleep, I guess.

I was very confused when I woke up to a knocking on my window. It was a cop. He was hitting it with a nightstick. It must have been around dawn, judging by the light. I didn't know what to do, so I rolled down the window. Just enough to talk to the guy. My car was old, a yellow Rabbit, with the manual window handles. I spoke first, hoping to disarm the dude. But it didn't work. I said:

"Hey man, what's up?"

"You can't park here, buddy. You have to move on."

"Yeah, okay."

I turned the key. The starter engaged. Then the engine started chugging, chugging. Then it made a clicking noise. I smiled. The police officer sighed. He shook his head. I watched him go behind the car. His cruiser was parked behind me. He got in. He pulled in front of me, and then did, like, a turn around. It was a wide alley. I marveled at how wide the alley was. He pulled up to the front of the Rabbit. Popped his hood. I popped my hood. I got out. Creaked the hood open and swiveled the puny rod that held the hood in place. He got out and thrust open his hood, he apparently didn't need a rod to hold his hood up. Our cars stood facing each other with their metal mouths wide open. My engine looking cracked, leaky, flaccid with age, clunkered and clogged up. His, a big, beefy, bulging, virulent machine, purring at my car with inappropriate intention. He said:

"You got cables?" I smiled. He sighed again. Went to his trunk. Opened it. Came back with jumper cables. Connected them. Looked at me. Smelled me, I guess.

Said, "You been drinking?" I said no. He said, "Are you sure? You smell like you been drinking." I said I was just doing a gig, so maybe the club was giving me smells. He said, "What are you a jokester or something?" I said, I don't know man, I am just a dude trying to take a nap." Then he said, "Yeah, okay, give it a try." I got back into the Rabbit and turned the ignition. The car started right up. I got back out of the car and went back to shut the hood. The cop said, "Alright, this is a warning, get the hell out of town." Sure thing, officer, I said. Slamming the hood down. I got back into the Rabbit. The cop put the cables back in his trunk and backed up. Drove away. I rolled up the window. The jazz coming out of the radio had turned into fancy college music. I turned it off. I felt like shit. Hungover, and thirsty. I was hungry now too. I drove out of the alley. Slowly. I was certain that the cop was still watching me. I wanted to stop at a gas station and get something to eat and something to drink, but I was nervous that I would get harassed again. I took a couple turns, and got onto the interstate instead. Not really knowing where I was going. This gig was the last gig on the tour I was doing. I had nothing more lined up. And now I was in the middle of Ohio with nowhere to go. I needed to piss, and I needed some coffee, and I needed something to eat. I got about five miles going west on I–480 before there was a sign that said, Next Exit 20 Miles. I looked at the amount of gas I had. Which was not good. I was driving on fumes. The traffic around me was cruising by at an alarming pace. The Rabbit was not meant for interstate travel. People were honking at me. I felt like an idiot. I was stuck now. But there was nothing I could do. The next twenty minutes were torture. Because the fastest I could go was 60 mph. And at any moment I would run out of gas. I really shouldn't be on the interstate. I kept telling myself. Over, and over. My mantra didn't make a difference though. I was on the interstate, and there was no way of getting off of it.

20 miles on fumes. What a bummer. I put the emergency flashers on. Said a little, I don't know, prayer? Dug my neck down into the steering wheel. Turned the radio up. The noise inside the car from the road was overwhelming. The music was really quite bad. Some of that funky groovy style tunes the kids like these days. A lot of drums, and a lot of fancy bass. Complicated stuff. Not that I could hear it. Not really. The road noise and the crappy speakers made it sound like tin cans bouncing off of balloons. Clink, thum, clink-clink, thum-thum. I don't really know why I was trying to even listen to it. I guess the idea was to keep myself distracted in this moment of crisis. But it was not making things better. The music. It wasn't really making things worse, it was just an added bonus of noise that I didn't really need. I guess I needed earplugs. If anything.

A mile went by. One of the signs on the side of the road went from 213 to 214. I guess this meant a mile went by. It seemed like a minute had gone by too. This was progress. About sixty seconds later the number 215 showed up, so I was right. Now two miles had gone by. This was indeed progress. Now there was only 18 miles to go. The Rabbit was doing good. Or so it seemed. The indicator for low gas was really getting on my nerves. I never understood that thing. It seemed like to me that if you knew that you were low on gas you could tell because the gas tank indicator would tell you by how close you were to the E side of the thing. You know, the empty? And this is when you should get more gas. I could never figure out why they needed to put a light there too. Like was it to mock you? To give you shame? To say, I don't know, I know you got no gas you fool, get some damn gas! I guess that is just something I will never understand. Not with my education and social skills at least.

Another mile went by. All good. Then one more. The complicated fancy college music turned into static. I didn't have the focus to find another station. I needed all my hope to be funneled into getting to the next exit. Cars, trucks, big rigs kept passing me. Some of them honking. The wind making the Rabbit wobbly. Pushing me to the side of the interstate. I did my best to ignore them. I held my hands at the prescribed ten and two position. My face close to the steering wheel. I was rocking back and forth. Back and forth. Trying to gain momentum. I didn't dare try and turn the radio off. I was convinced it was helping me keep going. Every new noise I was afraid was the sound of the engine making a last gasp. Sputtering to emptiness. Mile marker 220 came and went. 13 miles to go. The Rabbit was humming along. My pedal to the metal. There was no way to goose it more. I came upon a hill. I lost 10 miles per hour immediately. Now the cars and trucks and big rigs were approaching faster than before in the rear view. My focus turned from getting to the exit to doing my best to get up this hill. I was beginning to lose even more speed. I was rocking back and forth at a furious pace now. Hoping to get some momentum going. The Rabbit slowed down to 45 miles per hour. I passed a sign that read, Speed Limit 75, Min 40. I was moving so slowly that I could see details of the paint job on the speed limit sign. Also, how big the sign was kind of seemed weird to me. I guess you don't notice how big those things are when you are going full speed? But when you are doing a putt-putt, things change. I guess everything is perspective?

I was about to hit the top of the hill. Or so it seemed. The miles per hour were now down to 40. I was really rocking back and forth trying to get the momentum going. This wasn't helping. The cars and trucks and big rigs were scary now. Honking like crazy. Yelling things at me. But what could I do? Didn't they know that I shouldn't be on the interstate? I had my flashers on for crying out loud! I could feel the Rabbit giving up, when suddenly I crested the hill. A wave of relief hit me. I started to gain speed. 45 mph. 50 mph. 55 mph. 60 mph. I was really going now. Cruising right along. 65 mph. The Rabbit really shaking. The hill going up was now a hill going down. I was feeling pretty good. I gained another mile. 221. Then 222. I was really flying down the hill. I looked in the rear view mirror. Thinking I would be leaving all the traffic in the dust when I saw the blueberries and cherries on top of the dreaded black and white. Busted.

I didn't know what to do. I could see that a hill was coming after this hill was done. I really didn't want to lose my momentum. The cop turned on his sirens. I yelled, I know! I know! Can't you see what's happening here! The cop couldn't hear me of course, but I yelled it anyway. I kept driving. The cop sped up and came to the side of the Rabbit. The hill going down bottomed out. Then the next hill kicked in. I started losing speed. I looked over at the cop. The guy was pointing to the side of the road. I could read his lips. He was yelling, Pull over! I cranked my window down. He did the same. I could hear him yelling now, "Pull over!" I yelled back, I know! But this hill! He yelled, "Pull over!" I yelled, I know! This hill! Traffic was piling up behind us. I was going 50 miles per hour now. Slowing down fast. I saw the mile marker 223. We were going slow enough now, me and the cop, that I could hear him clearly. He yelled:

"Pull over!"

"I can't! I will lose momentum!"

"Pull over! Now!"

"It is not a good idea!"

"Pull over or I will pull you over for you!"

I will pull you over for you? What a weird thing to say. Alas, I was trapped. I would not be making it to the top of the hill the way I was thinking. I pulled over. The cop pulled over behind me. The traffic log jammed behind us took the opportunity to speed by. Someone yelled, "Get a real car you loser!" The side of the interstate was really bumpy at first then it was smooth. The shoulder beyond the white line. I put the Rabbit in park. I wasn't sure if I should turn the car off. Not because of the cop but because I was afraid that I wouldn't get it started again. I seem to remember that your car takes more gas to start than it does to run for 10 miles. I didn't know if this was just some urban legend or what not, but I didn't really want to find out. So I let the Rabbit keep running.

The cop was taking forever. Running my license plate I guess. I was legal, so I wasn't really worried about it. I was worried about running out of gas, and now that I was stuck on this hill, I was worried about that too. Eventually the cop came to my window. He had his hand on his gun. Stayed back and away. My window was still rolled down. He said:

"Turn your car off, sir."

"Ah, man, I can't man. I am running on fumes here."

"Turn your car off, sir." I turned the car off. The cop got closer. "License and registration." I reached over to the glove box and got the registration. I had to really dig in my pocket to get my wallet out. This took a second. I don't know why the cop was so nervous, but he never took his hand off of his gun. I could see this in the side-view mirror. I got my license from my wallet and handed him the documents. He went back to his cruiser. An annoying amount of time went by and he came back. Handed me the documents. He didn't have his hand on his gun anymore. He said:

"You really shouldn't be driving on the interstate in this thing."

"Yeah, I know, that is what I was trying to say."

"It's not safe."

"Yeah, I know, that is what I was trying to say."

"What are you going to do about it? It's not safe. You were going really slow on that hill back there."

"Yeah, I know."

"Well, what are you going to do about it? There are a lot of hills around here."

"I'm trying to get to the next exit and get off."

"Well, why don't you do that?"

"I am trying."

"Have you been drinking, sir?"

"You're the second cop that asked me that today."

"I will pretend I didn't hear that. You need to get off of the interstate."

"I'm trying, man! I got fumes in my tank!"

"Well, you got to get off the interstate."

"I am trying."

"There is an exit ten miles from here. You need to take it."

"I'm trying!"

"Okay, relax sir. I tell you what, I am going to give you a little escort, and you are going to get off the interstate, it's not safe."

"Okay, thanks."

"Okay, thanks?"

"Okay, thanks, with sugar on top?"

"What are you a jokester?"

"I try."

"Well, don't. Show some respect."

"I'm sorry, sir."

"You should be. You're lucky I don't give you a sobriety test driving this dumb thing on the interstate."

"I tried to tell you I was  trying to get off." The officer was waiting for me to finish my sentence. I frowned. He frowned. He cocked his head. "Sir." I sighed.

"What was that?"

"I said, thank you sir, you are very handsome." He sighed.

"Look, when you get to the exit stay off the interstate. It's not safe."

I cranked up the window. Did a little wish, or whatever. Started the Rabbit. Thinking about how much gas I just lost by doing this. Put the car into drive. Slowly started driving up the hill. The cop stayed on my trail the whole time. Helped me merge into traffic. My license and registration were on the passenger side seat now. As well as my wallet. I don't remember turning the radio off, but now that the cop was giving me an escort I wasn't so worried about running out of gas, so I turned the knobs until I found some cool jazz station that sounded okay. The cop's lights were flashing in my rearview. I adjusted my mirror so they didn't distract me. The next 10 miles were uneventful. The hills were not as dramatic as they were when I got pulled over. Nobody honked at me. The traffic that passed us was slow and respectful. Nobody honked at me or yelled at me. When we reached the exit the cop wailed his sirens and I went one way, and he stayed on the interstate. I rolled down my window to stick my arm out and flipped him the great big American eagle hoping there wasn't an exit soon that he could come back and give me the grief. I was too distracted by the cop that I didn't notice the signs for which way the gas station was. I had to pull over to take a look around because it wasn't clear. Just then the Rabbit made a gulping noise. Coming from the engine. I was out of gas. And it was an either or situation about which direction I should be going to get gas back into the car. Also, I didn't have a gas can. I was thirsty. Hungry. I needed to piss. My body felt achy and sandy because my hangover was really starting to catch up with me. I really didn't want to leave my car behind and start walking, I also didn't feel like dealing with another cop that would come along and give me the grief. I figured that if I was walking I would be left alone. I put my license back in my wallet. I put my wallet back in my pocket. I put the registration back in the glove box. I took the key out of the ignition. I got out of the yellow Rabbit. There was no reason to lock the doors because the locks didn't work anyway. I started walking away. In the most promising direction. I noticed that I had left the emergency lights flashing. They had been flashing the whole time it turned out. I walked back and turned them off. Running out of gas was one thing, a dead battery was another. I went back to walking towards what I believed would be a place to get gas. This was a pretty lousy morning, for the most part so far.

Walking was never one of my better traits. Not that I had very many good traits to begin with. I guess, if my ex-wife was to describe me, that is. In the years since we broke up, I won't lie, when I think of myself I do so in the terms that she used. Lousy, no good, greasy, smelly, stupid, boorish, did I already say lousy? Lousy. A wimpy worm. A wimpy worm that crawled out of a mud-hole. Spineless. Dickless. Hitler Junior. She always said I looked like Adolf Hitler. Greasy Adolf, she would say when she was really feeling the abuse. Monkey man. Because I had long arms, long torso, short legs. Which is one of the reasons walking sucked so much. I guess she really did a number on me. I swear. I guess. I mean, she would get up hungover, drink a couple of glasses of rot-gut, get nice and primed by noon, then the real insults would start coming my way. "Bouillon," she would say, "that should be your real name because you aint sauce you idiot, you are just a fake flavor." Then she would get really nice and fresh. Stab me with the Hitler insults. That is when I could tell she was about to pass out, when the Hitler insults came around. Then she would tank on the couch. A lit cigarette in her mouth. Waking up only when the smoke would fall on her lap and burn her, or when she pissed herself. Either way, she would blame me for these things. Wake up screaming. Throw things. Ashtrays, empty bottles, anything really. I guess. This went on for years. I still don't know how I took the abuse. I guess I was just as drunk as she was during these times. Trying to stay sober enough to get to whatever gig I was doing. Hoping the car would crash on the way home. Or that the house would be on fire with her in it.

That never happened. I guess we just grew apart in the end. That, or the cops showed up one day, told me to pack a bag, escorted me to my car, and said, "Don't come back, if you do, we will arrest you on sight." I don't know. I guess I did something wrong that night, but I don't really remember. I do remember getting thrown in jail when I showed up a little while later trying to retrieve my shaving kit. I guess I didn't expect to see the same officer that threw me out to show up at the front door when I knocked. There was a police cruiser parked in the driveway. I don't know why I didn't keep driving. I guess I just thought that nobody aside from myself would take the kind of abuse she was handing out. I mean, I walk into the place and the scumbags shoving his nightstick up my ex's solitary confinement on the couch and I'm the bad guy? I guess I was the bad guy, because the dude knocked me out cold the second he saw me. His huge love cannon bouncing like a diving board. I woke up in jail. And that was the last time I was anywhere near that maniac. My ex, not the cop that knocked me out. I guess both things apply to both of these jerks, but I really couldn't care less about the cop. And, as much as I wanted to be done with my ex, it didn't help that she served me divorce papers in the county jail. Which, I don't know, seems illegal, but whatever. And then the trial when the judge issued the divorce, and ordered me to pay alimony, that seems illegal too. I didn't have a lawyer, and my ex wasn't even in the courtroom. But whatever. All of it, whatever. All I know is that if I ever go back there, to that town, I don't think I will live to come back out. There are too many cahoots against me. And that is just fine by me. If you want to know the truth. And she can come try and find me if she wants that alimony, but you can't wring blood from a stone, you know? As the saying goes. So, I say good luck, good luck to her and her cop dude. I hope he likes cleaning up shit soaked panties from the bathroom floor. Because I sure the hell didn't. And to tell you the truth, I was impressed that he could get her to do anything like what they were doing in the middle of the day on the couch like that. Or at all, really. Maybe his nightstick had something to do with it, but still, she was sloppy drunk by noon. Not sometimes, but every day. Every single day. And by the time I walked in on them, it was the time in the afternoon when things got pretty sketchy, if you know what I'm talking about. Not pretty.

I walked and walked for what felt like hours. The road was deserted. I had no idea where I was. Not really. I knew I was in Ohio. Twenty miles from Oberlin. Or so. There were trees and birds and stuff, but nothing good to look at. The sun was getting up in the sky. It was warm enough. I kept hoping to see stuff on the horizon, but all I could see was more road and some grasses. I came to a stop sign. I didn't understand what the stop sign was doing. I guess. I mean, there was a crossroads that went in a different directions, but there was no traffic to make it seem necessary, you know?. I looked to the left, nothing. I looked to the right, nothing. In my mind that meant that I should keep going straight, even though there was nothing in that direction either. I guess. But I am glad I did this because about ten minutes of walking later I saw a gas station.

The gas station was pretty janky. It had a pump, and

a sign that said, Gas. The station part was just a little hut that had a door made of wood. No windows. A paper sign that said, Please Kncock, written in what seemed like charcoal. I knocked. There was some rustling around, then a loud stumbling, then the door opened. I don't know what I expected, but it was just a short little guy, with gray hair. He was square and slim. He said:

"Yel-low? Can I help ya?"

"Yeah, you got gas?"

"Yeah, you got a car?"

"Yeah, it's down by the interstate. You got a can?"

"I don't, you need a car."

"But the car is down by the interstate, I need a can."

"I don't have a can."

"Can I buy a can? I need gas."

"You need a car."

"I have a car, it's just down by the interstate."

"Bring the car, I will give you some gas."

"But I need a can to bring the car to get the gas."

"I don't have a can."

"Do you have a truck to bring my car to get the gas?"

"I have a truck, but it won't bring your car."

"Why not?"

"Because it is not what you need, what you need is a car."

"For what?"

"To get the gas."

"But I can't get the car because I need the gas."

"No, you need the car to get the gas."

"But what about the truck?"

"The truck isn't a car."

"Does the truck have gas?"

"The truck has plenty of gas."

"Will you drive me back to my car and pull me back here?"

"I can't do that, I have to watch the pump."

"Is there a number to call? For somebody to bring my

car over here to get gas?"

"Do you have any money?"

"I mean, maybe, how much money do I need?"

"Enough to get your car here."

"What do you mean?"

"It depends."

"On what?"

"On the situation, you gotta cork in your nappy?"

"No reason to get personal, man! I just need some gas or someone to pull my car over here to get some gas."

"Good luck with that."

The square and slim guy with the gray hair shut the door. I heard him knock around a little bit. Then there was silence. I stood there looking at his charcoal "Kncock" sign. He was a pretty big jerk about specifics for somebody that spelled knock that way. I started walking back to the yellow Rabbit.

When I got to the yellow Rabbit I got into the car and turned the key. Put it in neutral. Turned the steering wheel to the right. Got out, and started to push from the back. The door wide open. My wimpy worm short legs getting a little bit of traction.

The yellow Rabbit didn't want to move at first, but then it got going. I had to stop once the corner was turned. I got back in. Cranked the wheels straight. Got out. Started pushing again. Luckily the car was small because otherwise I don't think I would have the strength to gain any sort of momentum. The car veered off and I had to stop pushing so I could adjust the steering wheel.

This sucked. Pushing. Adjusting. Pushing. Adjusting. Steering wheel. Back of the car. Steering wheel. Back of the car. It was exhausting and sucked. When I got to the stop sign I took a break. A truck pulled up as I was standing there catching my breath. He honked his horn. I held out my arms and shrugged. The good old universal, "What the fuck do you want from me?" He honked again. Pointed to the driver's side door that was open.

I shut the door. He stopped at the stop sign. He yelled through the open window, "Get some gas, you idiot!" He threw an empty beer can at me, and then he drove off. I stood there irritated. The guy was a jerk. I watched him drive down the road. He stopped at the gas station. The square slim guy with gray hair came out and gave him some gas. I found this very annoying. The guy in the truck said, "Hey Mack, can you fill up those gas cans in the back? Watch out for the tow ropes so they don't get tangled." Mack. The square slim guy with the gray hair was named Mack. "You got it, Joe." The guy in the truck was named Joe apparently and neither of them wanted to help me. I was so close to the gas station that I could hear them and neither of them wanted to help me.

Joe drove off. I kept pushing the yellow Rabbit down the road. It took me forever, but I eventually got to the gas station. I pushed the Rabbit next to the pump. Waiting for Mack to come out. He never came out. I walked over to the door with the Kncock sign. I kncocked. Nothing. He didn't answer. I yelled, "Hey, Mack! I got the car! You can give me the gas now!" Silence. I waited. I kncocked again. There was the sound of things moving around. Then some loud steps. Then the door opened. Mack opened the door. He said:

"Yel-low? Can I help ya?"

"I need some gas."

"Yeah? You waiting for an award, Hollywood?"

"What do you mean?"

"The pump is right there."

"But?"

"But what?"

"What about Joe, I watched you pump his gas?"

"You want me to pump your gas for you?"

"Well, no, I mean, I don't know, I guess, I just saw you pump his gas, and I assumed..."

"Did you also assume that I would come out and give you an award for being a jackass?"

"Jesus, no reason to get personal, man."

"I would prefer it if you didn't take the lord's name in vain."

"Which vein? The main vein?"

"I don't follow."

"You know what I mean. Like the, you know, the whatever."

"What, are you like a jokester or something?"

"I've been known to fling a few yucks."

"Toss them in the trash while you're at it, Hollywood, pump your own damn gas"

Mack watched me pump my own damn gas. I opened the gas flap. Unscrewed the cap. Placed it in the holder. Put the gas spigot in the hole. Pulled the lever down. Pumped the gas. I watched the price go to $20 dollars and stopped. I put the lever back up. I put the cap back on the gas hole. Shut the gas flap. Took out my wallet. Handed him a twenty. He took it. Mack started walking away. I said, "Hey, buddy! I'm a little lost here, you got a map I can buy or something?" Mack frowned at me and pointed, "That way is East." He went back through the door marked Please Kncock. I could hear him moving things around.

I got in the yellow Rabbit and checked the mirrors. I looked at myself. I really did look like Hitler. Which was not good. A hungover Hitler, is that any better? Bouillon? I can't say I hated the name exactly. Even if it came out of the worst mouth I knew. Sometimes I called myself that if it made sense. She wasn't wrong, I guess. If getting beat-up and run out of town in Oberlin, Ohio, and then running out of gas on the interstate meant anything, I was a slimy greasy worm.

I really can't understand why my ex-wife had such a hold on my emotions, but there she was, screaming at me in the mirror. "You are a dirty gross worm! You're a slimy worm! How can you be so stupid and slimy? Who the hell runs out of gas in a piece of shit car like you drive? You could fuel that hunk of shit with a wet fart! I really wish you weren't such a stupid fucking moron!"

I turned the car on. It took a second. The gas needed to get back into the tubes, but it eventually got there. I don't know why, maybe it was because of the cycle of abuse in my life, but I got back out of the Rabbit and yelled, "Mack! I hope you choke on your gas! And spoiler alert! Jesus doesn't make it past the first chapter!" I got back in the car and slammed the door. Both upset and feeling clever. I spindled off towards the west trying to remember the Bible. Worried that my joke about Jesus wouldn't land correctly.

I drove along for a while. Feeling okay. Thirsty, but not parched. A tank of gas. Looking at trees. Seeing some birds flying around. I came to some houses. The speed limit changed. I didn't change with it. I was already going the speed limit. The speed limit changed again. Back to what it was before the houses. I kept going the same speed. Thinking about my next move. I really needed to figure out where I was, but I didn't feel like pulling over. I knew that my map wouldn't help me. It was one of those big ones that had all the states in it. But not the best nuance. And I knew, or assumed that I was heading West. At the speed I was going I wouldn't get very far. I guess. What I mean is that I wouldn't get very far away from the interstate. The interstate was probably heading in the direction I should be going. And maybe I was driving parallel to it at the moment. It didn't really matter. That last gig was the last gig on my agenda. I was still surprised the dude paid me after he beat me up. My ribs still hurt. But whatever. Same pain, just at a different angle, as my dad used to say, right before he would hold out his hand to "show you something" and then give me a swift punch from his other hand. Then he would laugh. "Same pain from a different angle, you idiot." This usually meant he was drunk, so he would go into the bedroom and do the same thing to my mom, who would scream, and I would run outside so I didn't have to hear the noises. Half the time I would come back in and hear sex noises, which were just as confusing as the beating noises. I guess men are brutes. My poor mom. I wonder what she is up to?

I drove for another thirty miles. There was nothing but farms and fences. A random house here or there. A sign bragging about fresh eggs. The sun shifted in a way that I knew I was indeed heading West. Which was good. For me. I suppose. I came to another crossroads. This time it was stop signs in all directions. Which made me feel better than the one by Mack's Kncock Please. At least everybody had to deal with the stupid signs, not just half the people. I sat there at the sign, reached into the back of the yellow Rabbit. Grabbed the vague road map that had all the 50 states in general, unspecific. Took a look at Ohio. I don't even know what was what at this point. I couldn't remember the last time I was this lost. I did have a general idea of where I was, but there was no reference to tie it to. I knew I was north of the interstate. Or so I thought. And I knew I was heading West. Because of the sun. And I knew that I was roughly 30 miles from Oberlin. But that was it. I mean, I don't recall seeing a single highway sign. And these stop signs just made me think I was on a road that was not a highway, even though the speed limit suggested I was. I mean, it seemed like I could just flip a coin and end up right back where I started. Nexus-style. Like the Ohio Bermuda Triangle. Things looked the same in every direction. I mean, I kind of thought I should go West, but my gut told me to go North, and my emotions told me to go South. The only way I didn't want to go was back. Which was East. I don't know why, maybe it was the pull of Canada, or something, but I went with my gut. I threw the map in the back seat, and turned right. Heading North. Same pain from a different angle.

I thought about my dad as I was driving. I didn't want

to, but I did. I gave myself a little chuckle thinking about the time he sat me down on my seventh birthday and gave me a present. He was holding this train thing that he was certain I would love, I guess, and he was so proud of it that he didn't even wrap it, he was just holding the box, smiling. His eyes bright as welding rods. He said:

"Son, I know you are a little turd, and your mom loves you, so I want to give you this promise, no listen," I was backing away from him because this is usually how he talked to me right before he gave me the same pain from a different angle speech. He said, "No, listen, it is your birthday, and I know you really want this train thing, and I promise, from here on out, I won't lay a hand on you on your birthday. Is that okay?" I didn't know what to do. He asked me again. I stood there. He pounded on the table. He was sitting at the table in the kitchen. I was standing. Really wanting to grab the train and run away to my bedroom to be alone. He could see me looking at the train. He asked me again, "Is that okay?" I said, yes. He said, "Okay good, now go along and play." I took the train in the box and ran to my room. When I got there I was about to open the thing but I heard him go into the room where my mom was and start screaming. Then I heard my mom screaming. Then I heard silence. I put the present on my bed and waited. I knew that I couldn't open it. A few moments later he came into my room. Grabbed the train in the box. Cocked his head to the side. Smacked me with the back of his hand. I fell to the carpet. The back of my head was on fire. I had turned my face to the side I guess. He stormed out of the house. I heard the car start. Then I heard the car peel out. Then I heard a clanking noise. I got up from the carpet and walked into my mom's room. Her face was not right. I went back to my room and played alone with myself. Waiting for my dad to come back. He never came back that night. I guess I fell asleep. In the morning the train in the box was sitting on the kitchen table. Next to a cake that said, Seven. I don't know if this was a joke or what, because I didn't see my mom for three days after that. The only food I had to eat was that damn cake. And as much as it was sweet it tasted like shit. I threw the train in the box in the trash. Three days later my mom came back. She was hungover and her eyes were broken. She didn't say anything to me, just went straight to bed. The next day she made me some mac and cheese, pretending that nothing had happened. That was my last good birthday, I suppose.

I don't know why I chuckled about this. I guess I do know, the irony of my dad telling me he won't beat me on my birthday from here on out, and then beating me on my birthday. But it is kind of funny. Empty promises that end up in violence. Driving down the road in who the hell knows where Ohio. Deciding to go to Canada for whatever reason. I don't know. It's not not funny. Who am I to declare what is funny or not? I am just driving around America with a chip on my shoulder getting kicked in the ribs by some sound guy that doesn't like my jokes. I mean, I could go anywhere. I am versatile.

I drove for a long time. Nothing changing. Birds, trees, roads and farms. I must have made some progress because the sun eventually started to set. I was hungry and thirsty, but I didn't mind so much. I was kind of enjoying the pain. I guess it was nice to feel like your body was so sensitive. That you could punch yourself from the insides as well. I guess, I mean, I don't even know, but I drove slowly up the road to Canada for hours. Thinking about my next move. I don't know what got me, but I had to pull over and take a nap. When I woke up I was as dirty as everything. I could barely move my mouth. I got back on the road. It was dark now. I was feeling kind of desperate now. I wanted water, and I wanted food. But there was nothing on the horizon. I guess there was no turning back now, though. It took a whole bunch of focus to keep driving. And so what? I did think about just giving up, waiting on the side of the road until somebody came along. That would save me from my dumb ideas. My dumb driving. My wimpy worm approach to living. My bouillon nature. I saw a sign that was itself a sign. And I don't even know what to say about it. It said:

COME HITHER

And if you think my joke about my father telling me he won't beat me on my birthday and then beating me on my birthday is hilarious, then you will really love this next one liner; as I approached the building it was actually called: COMEDY SMITHEREENS. The SM in Smithereens was broken and looked like an H. The "eens" were blacked out. The COME was just the beginning of the word COMEDY. The "DY" blacked out. I pulled into the parking lot. There was a motel next door that was called Mumbo Jumbo Motel. Which didn't have any lights on. I guess, but I don't know, but I guess this was some sort of sign. There were no other lights on, aside from the big one. And I was a little burned out, so I sat there looking at the sign, trying to decide if I should go in or not. The parking lot was empty. I guess I knew I would always go in, but for a moment I hesitated. A guy came out of the door of the comedy club and puked next to a trash can. This made me feel at home. Maybe people just parked in the back? I don't know. I guess. I mean, you don't just come out puking from a club that is empty, right? I checked my wallet for some reason. I knew I had some cash. I could get a drink or two at least, quench my thirsty lips, hit the road after, or something. Maybe get the lay of the land. It was a comedy club, right? I might even fit right in.

I got out of the Rabbit and walked towards the entrance of the club. I stopped at the guy puking and said, "Don't worry, brother, you will be okay." The guy held up a thumb. He was still bent over. Continuing to puke. I felt bad for him, he wouldn't be okay. He was drunk as shit. I walked into the club.

The club was empty. Not a single person milling around. The place was circle shaped. There were booths and tables with chairs around them. Candles burning. The bar was shaped like a horseshoe. The lucky part, or where the luck drains out, however you want to say it, the top of the U as it were, was pointed to a sign that said, BATHROOMS. There was a stage. Not a large stage. Not a small one either. Yellow drapes around the back. A single microphone standing in the middle of it. A spotlight pointed on the microphone. The floor was wooden and creaked as I walked up to the bar. There were stools. All empty of course because nobody was there. The regular amount of booze bottles behind the bar. There were no sounds. I suppose there were some sounds. The sound of the ice machine. Some humming from refrigerators. Maybe an air conditioner somewhere. I pulled a stool out. Sat down. Waited. It was early, I suppose. Not too early for a drunk to be puking by the front door, but early enough. I kind of envied the guy. I was in the mood to be that drunk at the moment. It had been a long day. A long week. A long month. A long year. A long life. A good old fashioned puke in front of the club kind of drunk would really hit the spot right about now. I sat there waiting. Getting a little nervous, I won't lie. The vibes in this place weren't very easy. A little spooky even. I thought about getting up and hitting the skids when the door opened. The drunk guy came stumbling in. Stumbled left, then right, then left, then right again. He went around the bar, went back into the BATHROOMS area. I heard a door open. A clanking. A toilet flushing. A door opening again. The drunk stumbled behind the bar. Picked up a rag, came over to me, wiped down the top of the bar. Said:

"Whatool you haves?" He did not look well. His eyes were pussy and pink. He was drooling a little bit. Some food was stuck to the side of his face. Ketchup maybe? His face was bright red. He had done a horrible job shaving. There were quite a few long hairs sticking out. Also spots of dried blood. His eyes made me nervous though. I didn't know if he should be making anyone any drinks. I don't know if it was pink eye or what, but I was second guessing my idea to get really shit faced. Second guessing my idea that I should stick around this joint.

"Um, you okay, man? You're not looking so hot, bud."

"Oooh, you don't dare worry about me [pause] pardner, I am right as rain, I'll hhhhoooks you up real good." Just then someone yelled from the back.

"Randy! Get the hell outta there!" Randy looked up at me, startled, scooted around from behind the bar and disappeared back to the BATHROOMS sign. This time I heard a door open but it wasn't the same door because it slammed with a loud thud thing. The sound a door leading outside would make. I guessed that there was an exit back there. I don't know where Randy was going, but it did seem like he hit the skids himself. For a second time I envied him. My instincts failing me yet again.

I heard some soft footsteps behind me. I turned around. When I didn't see anything I turned back to the bar. Suddenly there was a guy standing there. I jumped, not expecting it. I said:

"Jesus!"

"Oh, don't you worry about him, that's just Randy, he

means you no harm."

"I wasn't worried about, hey wait!" The guy was playing with the rag that Randy had just been wiping down the bar with. "I wouldn't touch that if I was you, I think Randy has pink eye."

"Randy? No, he always looks like that, it's in his genes from what I understand. Whatool you haves?"

"A bucket of bleach."

"Coming right up!" The guy turned around and went looking for a bucket of bleach.

"Hey man! I was just joking. Just give a rum and Sprite, easy on the ice, maybe with clean hands?"

"Sure thing Boss." The guy started washing his hands. Whistling. Wiped them down with the same rag that Randy used to wipe down the bar. Made my drink. Put a square napkin on top of the bar. Put the drink on the napkin. I looked at the drink. Then I looked at the guy. He smiled at me. His hair was slicked back. He wasn't showing any teeth. With his smile. His eyes were slightly off-center to his face. I couldn't tell if he had a mustache or if there was a strange trick of the light. I looked down at the drink again.

"Um, okay. How about a straw?" The guy started to reach for it. "No wait, I got it." I grabbed a straw from the little station that held the napkins and olives and limes. I took a napkin. Wiped down the straw. The side of the drink. I put the straw in the drink. Grabbed another napkin. Wrapped it around the glass. Sucked a drink in. It was nice. The warmth of the booze relaxed my body. The liquid really wetting my whistle. I looked up at the guy again. He was still smiling. I nodded at him.

"You still want that bucket of bleach?"

"Buddy, I told you I was joking."

"I know. Now I am the one that is joking, ha!" The guy walked away. Pretending to mind his own business. I drank on my drink trying to figure this place out. As far as I could tell it was in the middle of nowhere. I suppose. Outside

Oberlin. I guessed I was still in Ohio. There was nothing that told me I wasn't. I drank the drink quick. The sound of me sucking the last drink made the guy come back over. He raised his eyebrows. I nodded. This time he just poured the booze and the Sprite in the glass without touching anything. I was glad about this. I stirred the drink. Sucked a drink. Felt better by the minute. The guy stayed nearby. Pretending to do stuff. I could tell he wanted to talk. But he was waiting for an invitation. I didn't give it to him. I was in a silent mood. Sometimes it is better to keep your mouth shut when you are in such a mood. But two drinks later I was feeling really good, and the mood had lifted. A couple drinks after that I asked him a question.

"What is this place? Where is everybody?"

"Oh, nobody comes in here anymore. You're the first customer we have had in years. I'm a little confused as to what you are doing here."

"Well, why you light the candles then? That's a little odd."

"I got a business to run, don't I? People like candles, don't they?"

"Yeah, I suppose they do, but if nobody comes in, I mean."

"You came in."

"I suppose I did. You own the motel as well?"

"Randy runs the motel. You got a problem with the motel?"

"I don't, not really, the name is pretty racist. Mumbo Jumbo."

"It didn't used to be racist."

"Well, it doesn't work that way. He should maybe think about changing the name."

"Okay, you can tell him later when you check in. That's not up to me."

"What makes you think I'll be checking into the hotel, man?"

"It's either that or your car."

"What makes you think that? I'm just a guy having a drink, bud, I could easily hit the skids at any moment."

"Those five rums and Sprites make me think otherwise. You know what I think? I think you will drink five more and Motel Mumbo Jumbo will be looking pretty good after that. I know you have no place to go."

"Oh, you don't know shit. Give me another and I will tell you what I think about your thoughts, Nostradamus."

The guy poured me another drink. Then another. Then another. I was well in the tank when I brought up the stage.

"You do things here? Stage stuff? You like a comedy place or something?" I was quite drunk now, and as much as I wanted to be clever, words just fell out of my mouth like marbles.

"We used to. Back when people used to show up. Now it's just lighting candles mostly, and hoping somebody shows up. You're the first customer we have had in years. I already told you that."

"Yeah? You used to get some funny guys coming around?"

"We had some fun times."

"Anyone I know of? You ever get that guy that does the car noises? That guy is hilarious!"

"One time we got this one guy that could do voices, that was pretty funny. I mean, we did used to get some talent. But then the interstate came through and nobody thought about us anymore. There is that Laugh Factory down South that everybody loves, or so they say, where all the Big Comedy goes now. I used to open the shows. Sometimes I still pretend that people are around, you know? That love Small Comedy. Like in the old days. Where it all wasn't just fart jokes and take a look at this and that kind of stuff. Back before all the lesbians thought short haircuts were funny. You know what I mean?"

"Yeah, I know. Jokes used to be funny. Back when you could say shit and nobody else could say nothin'. Make me another drink won't ya, and go do your thing! I want to see what you got! Make me yuck, man!"

The guy got excited. Made me a drink. Walked out from behind the bar. Walked onto the stage. Stood in front of the microphone. I clapped. Very drunk at this point. I yelled, Give it to us! He tapped on the microphone. Said:

"Is this thing on?" The sound was very loud. I had to cover my ears. There was feedback. The guy went backstage. Came back. Tapped on the microphone again. "Is this thing on? Ah, much better. You can never tell with these Mikes these days, David's, I tell you what, you can always tell with the Davids." I hooted. Drunk at the bar. "Now don't get me wrong, I love Jesus, I mean, he was a real cool dude, but why were all his buddies such lame weirdos? I mean, Jesus was like doing all this cool shit and his friends were like, How about instead of hanging out with this cool guy, why don't I sit around and write some shit in my diary? Dear Diary, my name is like Mike, I had a good time with Jesus today, he turned some water into wine, what a weirdo, me and Dave and Luke were thinking that we should go over to Sodom and get some hot tail, but Jesus was all like, I don't know guys, I don't think my dad will like that. What a loser. But then Jesus was like, here is one loaf of bread let me turn it into a million, and his buddies were like, I don't know Jesus, you are kind of making us look bad, working so hard to help the poor, I thought we were going to make this book and you are making us work harder than we need to. What's in it for us? And then Jude was like, Fuck this, I am going to go tell the Guidance Councilor and you're gonna be in trouble, and Jesus is all like, So what, dudes, what they gonna do? Hang me? And then they hanged Jesus, and his buddies were like, Oh, fuck, what do we do now? And then they went back to making the book pretending like nothing happened. And then the soothsayer was like, Beware of the ides of March, Caesar, and then religion went from being really weird to being really specific, and for the next two thousand years shit got fucked up. History? Am I right?"

The guy finished his set. I didn't know what to make of it. I wasn't sure if it was just stupid or what. It wasn't a history lesson, that was for sure. I didn't clap when he finished. He came back. Stood behind the bar. Said:

"What do you think? Pretty good, yeah?"

"I don't know, man, you were kind of all over the place."

"Yeah, I know, nobody liked it when we were popular, I'm sorry. I just have this thing with the Bible, it makes me mad sometimes, I can't get over it. It puts a craw in my side. I think about it a lot, but nothing ever goes anywhere. You got any tips? Help a buddy out?"

"I don't know, buddy, I think you got a bunk one, I don't really want to talk about it. The Bible is a hard sell."

"Yeah, I know. But I brought Caesar into the mix! Doesn't that change things? Like the Romans?"

"The Romans are the least of your problems. I think I might go talk to Randy about taking one of his racist rooms for the night. I guess you were right, Nostradamy, I don't have it in me to sleep in my car. What do I owe you?"

"Ah, you can pay me tomorrow, you're not going anywhere."

"Ah, nah, that is bullshit, I aint that drunk."

"It's not that you're drunk. There are other things. Things you haven't considered. Just go out the back door. Randy will take care of you."

"Randy, right. With his pink eye."

"It's not pink eye, it's genetic."

"If you say so."

"I do."

"Okay, buddy, you did me a good one, I'm gonna go get some sleep."

"Well, good. You really think my set was bunk?"

"It's shit, hate to tell you."

"Well, damn. Okay. I will take your word for it."

"You should. It started out funny, but it did not end funny."

"Alright, no reason to rub it in. Name?"

"For what? Your jokes? Petering, I guess?"

"No shit, really? What's your name?"

"Oh, ha! I don't know, hey! Give me a couple beers for the road, you don't mind?" The guy gave me two beers. I put them in my pants pockets. He looked kind of upset that I didn't like his set. He asked me what my name was again.

"What's your name?"

"Bouillon"

"What, like the spice?"

"It's not spice, mister, it's a flavor."

I got up from my barstool. I had to take the beers out of my pockets because when I stood up they didn't work in my pockets anymore. I nearly dropped them, but I didn't. Small miracles. I looked at the bartender. He smiled at me, kind of. I still couldn't tell if he had a mustache or not. If it was just a trick of the light. I nodded. Said, "Don't take any wooden nickels." He picked up the rag that Pink Eye Randy had used to wipe the bar down with. He started wiping the bar down. Where I had been sitting. Drinking. He stopped for a second and wiped his eye. I grimaced. Mumbled to myself, "Oh, boy." He looked at me and kind of smiled. I walked around the side of the horseshoe bar. Passed the sign that said, BATHROOMS. Holding the beers in my hands. I walked past the bathrooms and out the door that Pink Eye Randy had used earlier. It slammed behind me with the same noise from before. Which meant I was on the right path.

I crossed the dirt parking lot that led to the racist Motel Mumbo Jumbo. The lights were on in the office. I could tell it was the office because the door said, Office. The lights of the motel sign were also on. As far as I could tell nobody was staying at the motel. There were no cars parked in front of any of the rooms. There were six rooms that I could see. None of them had lights on inside. I found myself standing at the office door looking in. Holding the beers in my hands. I was having second thoughts for the third time. The vibes I was getting from this place were not easy vibes. Pink Eye Randy was nowhere to be seen. I was about to turn around and get in my car and take my chances with the highway when Pink Eye Randy popped up behind the office desk. Looked at me with his puss soaked eyes. Drooled a smile in my direction. Made a waving motion that meant come on in. Against my better judgment I put both beers in one hand and used my free hand to turn the knob. This made me sink a little. I was feeling drunk, but also exhausted. I didn't want to get pink eye, and now I had to remember to not touch my eyes with my right hand. Also, I now had to keep carrying both beers in my left hand. As well as the fact that I couldn't touch anything else if I was to keep myself free of pink eye. I really didn't buy the bartender's explanation that Pink Eye Randy's condition was genetic. A bell sounded when I opened the door. I slowly walked up to the counter trying to pay attention to what my body was doing. Where my hands were. What I was touching. I was drunk, and exhausted, so this was very hard for me.

Pink Eye Randy was standing there looking the same as he did when he was behind the bar. Except now he wasn't trying to wipe down the top of the bar. He was holding a pen. The light was harsher. Synthetic, if that is what you would call fluorescent lighting. I suppose I would, but maybe that is not the way to describe it. Because, isn't all light that isn't sunlight synthetic? His face was still not good. The ketchup stain next to his mouth was still there, except now it kind of looked like a canker sore. He smelled quite drunk. He also smelled like throw–ups. He said:

"Whatool ya haves?"

"I need a room, Randy."

"You got it pardner. A single? Double? The

HoneyMoon Suite? A-haha! Hunk-a-hunk-haha! My jokes, my jokes! We only got one kinda room. You can have one room."

"Okay."

"Okay."

"Okay, well?"

"Okay, well, what?"

"Can I have a key or something?"

"Oh, right! Come with me!" He opened a drawer and rustled around. It sounded like keys that were hooked to plastic things. I grimaced a little. Thinking about him touching all those keys. He took one out. Held it up for me to look at. The number 4 was written in black marker on a red diamond. "Four okay?" Okay. He walked out from behind the office counter and went out the door. I had to move quickly so I didn't have to touch the nob before the door shut. He scurried down to room 4. Opened it. Left the key in the knob. Turned the lights on. The door stayed open. He walked into the bathroom and turned the light on. Came back out. Said:

"Good, okay?"

"I guess."

"Okay, good. I'll let you sleep it off."

"What does that mean? Sleep what off?"

"The booze. That is what I do at night, sleep off the booze. What did you think I meant?"

"I didn't think you meant anything, really. I guess. It's just a weird way to say it."

"Good then."

"Okay, good."

"Okay."

"Okay, shouldn't I give you some money or something? For the room."

"Oh, right. Okay, later. Maybe tomorrow."

"Yeah, okay, Randy, you take care."

"You too, little buddy. I will see you tomorrow. Towels are in the bathroom. The lights work."

"Thanks, okay."

"Okay."

Pink Eye Randy left. I stood there holding the two beers in my left hand. Trying not to touch anything on my face with my right hand. My face got itchy because of this. I ignored it for a second. But it became too much. I put my face into my elbow and tried to scratch it that way. It kind of worked. I was thinking about just putting the beers on the bed. Going into the bathroom. Washing my hands. Getting back into my yellow Rabbit and driving away. But that sounded exhausting. I was exhausted. And drunk. And it had been a really exhausting day. I put the beers on the bed. The covers looked greasy. The whole room looked greasy. There was a queen sized bed. A night stand with a lamp. The lamp looked greasy. The night stand was definitely greasy. A greasy television. Greasy green carpet. A greasy drawer thing under the greasy television. A greasy remote control next on top of the greasy drawer thing next to the greasy television. The room was greasy and I decided to stay.

I walked over to the door and removed the number 4 key from the knob. I shut the door. I walked into the bathroom. There were towels. A bar of soap wrapped in plastic. Little miracles. I unwrapped the soap. Turned on the faucet. Washed the key. My hands. I scratched my face with my wet hands. I went back out, leaving the water running from the faucet. I washed the beers. The water was very hot. I opened one of the beers and took a drink. It was warm now. Foam poured out of and over the neck. I sighed. I was exhausted, and drunk, the beer was annoying, and I just wanted to sleep. I took the beer with me into the room. I hadn't noticed a refrigerator. There was not one. I put the beer on top of the night stand. Pulled the lamp's greasy cord. No light came on. I reached for the lightbulb. To test it, I guess. There was no lightbulb. I stood there thinking. Was I warm? I looked at the greasy bedding. I pulled the covers back. There were little brown stains running up and down the white sheets. I had seen this before. It was bed bugs. I put the covers back. I really didn't want to stay here, but I really didn't want to get back in the Rabbit and drive. I was drunk and exhausted. I thought about it. As much as I could, with the idiotic drunken state I was in. I thought, I am warm enough. The room seems warm. I can just have a quick lay-down. Sober up for a few winks, and then hit the skids. I mean, the bed bugs won't get me on top of the covers, right? they usually just hang out in the sheets, I mean, the last time I dealt with them that is how it worked, if I remember right. And as long as I stay on my back, I won't have to put my face on the pillows, and get whatever it is that is living on them inside my eyes. I mean, I suppose. My drunken logic was flawless.

I managed to lie down on the bed without touching anything. My shoes on. Feeling warm. I looked at the ceiling and realized that I had forgotten to turn the lights out. I got off the bed. Walked into the bathroom. Saw the towels. Grabbed them for covers. Turned the light off Turned the light off in the room. Checked that the door was locked. Got back on top of the bed covers. Did my best to stay on my back while covering myself with the towels. I was warmer now. Kind of comfy. Cozy even. There was a great deal of silence. Some crickets outside. I laid there for a little while. I was about to fall asleep when it became apparent that I had to piss. I got up again. Fumbled myself into the bathroom. Had to lift the toilet seat to piss. I pissed for a year. I had drank a million drinks and hadn't pissed once. My liver must have sopped all the drinks up. The toilet flushed itself there was so much piss that came out. Just joking. I didn't flush the toilet out of exhaustion, but I did force myself to wash my hands again. I got back on top of the bed, under the covers of the towels. Everything was now itchy, but I ignored it. I was warm enough. I could catch a couple Zzzz's and hit the skids a few winks later. None the worse for wear. I was exhausted and drunk. Sleep came pretty fast after that.

In the morning I couldn't open my eyes. I was stiff as a board. Shivering. My eyes were so itchy that I felt sick to my stomach. There was crust covering them. I couldn't believe it. I thought I may have been poisoned or something. But I knew it was pink eye. Pink eye plus a new horrible hangover. I rubbed my eyes with my fists. The danger was over now. I suppose. I mean, I couldn't be in any more danger than I already was in. The damage was done. I rubbed enough boogers out of my eyes that I could see enough to make my way into the bathroom. I turned the shower on. Took my clothes off. My shoes included. Got into the shower. Ran water over my face for as long as I could stand it. As hot as I could stand it. Eventually I could see okay. I got out of the shower, picked up the bar of soap next to the sink, and washed my face, over and over and over and over. This helped. Kind of. I decided that this was as clean as I could get myself. There was no amount of washing that would get rid of the pink eye. I turned the shower off. I stood there naked, squinky-eyed. Dripping wet. The towels were on the bed. I didn't want to use them to dry off. Both because they were my blankets, and because I didn't think I should be wiping my body down with pink eye towels. I stood there dripping. With absolutely no clue how to move forward. I was in no shape to drive now. As far as I could tell the sun was coming up. My eyes were very sensitive. I needed some medicines or something for my eyes. But the maniacs that were running this place seemed to be in denial about how scummy the place was. But maybe they knew a doctor or something? I mean, this was bad news. Really bad news. My hangover felt like shit. And my eyes sucked. I was hungry and irritated. Wet and dripping. I put my clothes on. This made me feel as greasy as the motel room. I felt cold now. Damp. My socks took the biggest hit from being wet when I put them on. My feet seemed muddy. Squishy. Now with a hint of itch. I suppose I should have just dried my body with the towels, but I didn't. For all I knew they had scabies or something on them. It wouldn't have surprised me. I wasn't exactly thinking clearly.

I squinted my way out of the motel room. Leaving the door open. It was morning. That was very clear because the sunshine hurt my eyes. I squinted my way into the Office. Pink Eye Randy was standing behind the counter. He was different than before. In a sense. I guessed because he wasn't drunk yet. Because he slept it off, as he had said last night. He looked at me, I suppose, I mean, I could barely see anything. He said:

"Well, yello! You sleep alright?"

"No, I did not sleep alright, your motel room is an anathema!"

"You don't look so good, sir."

"You think?! I need a doctor, you maniac, I think your room did me in!"

"Oh, you got the itchy eye? Yeah, I got that too, you just need a little rest, then you will be right as rain."

"I don't need rest, I need a doctor! Get me a doctor!"

"You don't need a doctor, you just need some squirts and some rest, let me show you."

Pink Eye Randy came around the front desk like a deer. Part grace, part lumbering. He put me in a headlock. Pried my eyes open. One by one. And squirted something inside. I tried to get away. He held me tight. Said, "Stop struggling! This is for your own good!" I tried to punch him but he was too strong. The vulnerable drunk puker with the ketchup cold sore on his face from last night was gone. The eye drops felt good. I was able to see straight again. He let me out of the headlock. Said, "Go back to your room, I will bring you some soup. You look hungry."

I was stunned. I stumbled back to my room. I got back on top of the bed. Under the towels. I was feeling sick. It seemed like a fever was setting in. I blinked a bunch. Then I fell asleep. There was a certain smell of sickness that I could feel. Or smell. It somehow invaded my dreams. I was standing on stage, giving a monologue to a Senior Center in Santa Fe, New Mexico:

"And then the Judge said, Do you promise to pull the tooth, the whole tooth, and nothing but the tooth?" The geezers didn't laugh. I was losing them. I pulled out my best material. "Speaking of the medical profession, I went to the doctor the other day, hoping to get some help with my hair loss. I said, Doctor, you gotta help me out! I am losing hair like nobody's business, I need a cream or something fast! I don't want to be bald. And the doctor took a look at my scalp. Picked up a prescription pad and said, I am going to write you a script for Rogaine. You just rub it on your head twice a day until your hair starts coming back. And I said, Rogaine! I thought you were a doctor, not a personal trainer. I don't need to be rowing no boats, I need help with my hair! What is there to be gained by rowing something? Am I right?!" The geezers just looked at me. I tapped on the microphone. I said, "Is this thing on? Maybe you should turn up your hearing aids." Then the geezers yelled, "Booooo!" A nurse came up to the stage and put his hand over the microphone. Said, "Okay, guy, you are making everybody upset, it's time to go."

I woke up to Pink Eye Randy putting a spoonful of soup in my mouth. He was holding a pan. Sitting on the side of the bed. His nose was dripping into the soup. I had a moment of repulsion, but the soup tasted really good. I couldn't remember the last time I had eaten. The soup was chicken noodle. I had a couple spoonfuls. Then he put a Saltine cracker in my mouth. I bit down. It was like a crunchy heaven. I sucked down the whole pan of soup, and a few more crackers. Pink Eye Randy said, "Now, that's a good boy." He was drunk now, I could tell. I didn't care. I was sick. I fell asleep after the meal. Dreaming more about the old folk's home. They were a tough audience. Which surprised me. I knew my Rogaine joke was garbage, but I really did think I could sneak it by those geezers. It was weird to be wrong about something like that.

I don't know how long I was asleep for, but it was night again. The room was dark. My eyes felt a little better. I was really itchy though. I was naked. But under covers. This alarmed me and I jumped out of bed. I went over to the door where the light switch was. I turned on the light. The light was very fast and very bright. I squinted down at my naked body. I was covered in bites. I guess Pink Eye Randy had stripped me naked and put me under the covers. He had folded my clothes and put them on top of the greasy drawers the television was on top of. He even folded my socks. He had left the pink eye medicine on the nightstand as well as something in a brown paper sack. I walked over to it. Not sure if I wanted to find out what was inside. I looked down at the bed. The brown stains from the bed bugs gave me some shivers. I grabbed the pink eye medicine and took it into the bathroom. I turned the light on which hit me fast and bright. I squinted at myself in the mirror. My wimpy wormy body covered in bites. My eyes as bright as maraschino cherries. I made sure the lid from the medicine was on tight. Then I turned on the hot water and scrubbed the outside of the bottle until the water was too hot to take. I rinsed the bottle in sections. Letting the steaming water hopefully kill any germs that were on the outside. I turned the water off. I shook the bottle. Took the lid off, and squinted into the mirror getting really close with my face. I put a couple drops in each eye. Then I became alarmed because I didn't bother reading the instructions on the bottle. I squinted at the bottle. Half expecting to find out I had just squirted super glue into my eyes. But it was indeed pink eye medicine. And I should put two to three drops in my eyes every six hours. I twisted the lid back on. Put the medicine on the counter. Went back into the room.

The paper sack had a sandwich inside it. And a bag of potato chips. I sighed and opened the plastic bag the sandwich was in. I wanted to eat it. I was very hungry. But all these germs, everywhere, germs, there were too many germs. I decided I had whatever there was floating around this place by now. I was covered in bed bug bites, I had pink eye, I suppose that there probably wasn't much damage that could be done by a sandwich. But I couldn't do it. I couldn't eat the sandwich. I put the sandwich down. I opened the bag of chips. Clean food. I ate all the chips standing there naked next to the bed looking at the bed bug striations. There was a knock at the window. I looked over. I guess the curtains were open because I could see Pink Eye Randy standing there smiling at me, waving. I waved back and made a motion for him to come in. He came in.

"Yer up." He said. He seemed very drunk.

"Hi Randy, I'm up."

"You must have been sleepy. You slept a long time."

"I suppose so, I do feel pretty awake now."

"Did you see your sandy? I made it myself."

"I saw it."

"And there was chips too."

"I saw the chips." I held the empty bag up to him.

"Oh, good. I also folded your clothes over there."

"I saw that."

"Oh, I wasn't sure because you are naked."

"Yeah, I know."

"Don't you want to get dressed?'

"I haven't decided."

"Oh, okay. I guess I was just checking in. Let me know if you need anything."

"You got any clean bedding? Maybe a plastic cover for the mattress?"

"Oh, did you have an accident? That happens. It's nothing to be ashamed of."

"No Randy, I did not have an accident. You have a very horrible case of bed bugs here. Like maybe the worst I have ever seen."

"Oh, okay."

"Do you not understand?"

"About what?"

"The bed bugs."

"I understand about bed bugs, I just don't understand what you think I can do about them. That's between you and Jesus."

"How is that between me and Jesus?"

"That is how Jesus lets you know it is time to get up, when the ticklies wake you up. Don't you know science?"

"Randy. Science? Can you get me an extra comforter and maybe a sheet of plastic? I'm going to go have a drink."

"Don't you want to eat your sandy? I see that you didn't eat your sandy."

"I'll eat it later when I get back." Which was probably the truth.

"Oh, okay, good idea. You should probby put some clothes on, the bar has a dress code."

Randy left. I was interested in what he was going to come back with. I figured that if he at least came back with another blanket I could take the shower curtain down and put that on top of the covers on the bed. Cover the shower curtain with the towels, and sleep under the blanket. Which might prevent another attack. That, or I could just sleep on the greasy floor. Either way

I grossed myself out thinking about it. I put my clothes on. Rubbed my eyes and walked across the parking lot to the bar.

The bar was the same as when I had left it. Candles burning on the tables. No one around. The guy with the tricky mustache was nowhere to be seen. I sat down at the same stool I had sat on the last time. Waiting. I heard some feet shuffling. I turned around. Nothing. I turned back around. The guy was standing there. I jumped. He was a Houdini, this one! He said:

"Whatool you haves?"

"Rum and Sprite. Easy on the ice, bud."

"Coming right atcha."

The guy made the drink. Put a napkin down. Put the drink on the napkin. Made a hand motion for the straws. I said:

"Nah, I'm alright. The damage has been done, sir."

"Very well."

"How's business? I don't suppose the candles drink much?"

"Not booze at least, plenty of wax though, haha. I wish the candles drank. Hey, there was a guy in here earlier looking for a guy that kind of fit your description. I told him I don't know nobody like you, but he didn't believe me, I don't think. He seemed pretty preoccupied with your car out there. I saw him poking around. Reading your plates and stuff."

"What? What did he look like?"

"Oh, I don't know. Kind of like an egghead if you ask me, like a nerd, I guess is what I would call him."

"What did he say exactly?"

"Um, let me think." Tricky Houdini did some face things that indicated he was thinking. "Um, he said, Did you see a guy that looks like you? And then I said, Yeah, I seen the guy, but he moved on. Then he said, Okay, thanks. Then he went out to your car and poked around and then drove away."

"And he looked like an egghead?"

"I don't know, he seemed like an egghead, real smart kind of. Like a scientist or something. I guess, I mean, he had a notepad and a pen or like a clipboard and a pen. I think he wrote down what I said."

"Did he say he would be back?"

"He didn't say anything. Just said, Okay, thanks. Then went and poked around your car for a while and drove off."

"Who the hell is looking for me?"

"I don't know, this guy I guess."

"Yeah, but why?"

"I don't know, but he seemed to have his reasons. I mean, he had a clipboard and a pen."

"That's kind of scary, don't you think?"

"Oh, I don't know, he seemed kind of nice. Maybe he will come back soon, bring some friends and whatever. Drinking friends, not like these lousy candles, haha."

"Yeah, I guess."

"You don't want people to show up here? What do you have against this place?'

"Oh, no, nothing like that, pal, I mean, I'm just a little worried about why anyone would be looking for me is all, right?"

"Well, I guess if you put it that way."

"How would you feel if somebody came around looking for you?"

"I'm always here, so probably pretty good, I guess?"

"Yeah, alright."

"You want another?"

"Yeah, alright."

I sat there drinking. Thinking about who would come looking for me. I suppose I maybe owed people money, but not enough money that they would send out a private butthole to come hunt me down. I was certain I didn't have any unknown kids floating around. I don't remember the last time I got laid was. It wasn't yesterday or a week ago or a month ago or a year or even whenever I don't even know. I was kind of a Quick Shot McGraw, a two pump chump when it came to the humping department. Two pumps and I was done. But always on the outside. And with condoms because I knew I wouldn't last. The idea was always to make the loins less sensitive. But it never worked. It was always, one in, try not to move, then one out, then another in, try not to move, then I would pull out because I couldn't take it because it felt so good, then pop goes the weasel, fun times over, sorry lady, next time, I promise. I suppose the condoms never fit anyway, you know? But still, they never had a chance to fall off because I never pumped more than twice. So what was it? Did the cop that pulled me over tell someone about the joke I made about how this was the second time someone had asked me in the same day about whether or not I had been drinking? I mean, are there menace laws around these parts? Is that a thing? This was Ohio, I wouldn't be surprised if the cops kept tabs on everyone that seemed like trouble.

There was nothing I could think of that would drive anyone to come looking for me. I didn't owe any taxes. It has been a while since I paid any taxes, but the last three years I had made maybe $20,000 dollars total. I was way below the poverty cutoff. If anything the Government owed me taxes. I was really at a loss. My student loans were paid off. Useless money that was. Art School. Just thinking about the words, "Art School" made me feel like an idiot. Who goes to Art School? Idiots and dolts, that's who. And to think of all the years I spent working those lousy jobs to pay that shit off? My best years. The young years, back when I cared. When I had energy to care. To spend it all, my time, my feelings, working for goons just to pay off a loan for something that I should have never bought in the first place. I suppose if I would have been rejected in the first place, I don't know, maybe I would have gone on to do something with my life. Run for city congress or something.

I had to stop thinking about the reason the guy was looking for me and what it meant. I ordered another drink. Then another. Then a couple more. I tried to get Tricky Houdini to drink with me, but he said he had a thing. What the thing was, he didn't tell me. But the way he said it made me think he either lost his spleen in a biking accident in Paris, or he was a recovering alcoholic, either way he didn't want to talk about it so I let it go.

I drank until I was ready to try to go back to sleep again. To wait for Jesus to wake me up with the tickles as Pink Eye Randy had said. Let me know it was time to wake up. By the time I was in that head space I was so drunk that I could barely walk. I had to hold onto the horseshoe bar all the way around to the end of it. Then I had to stumble to the wall. Then I had to push against the wall until I found the exit door. I could barely open it. But I managed somehow. Pink Eye Randy was bent over puking outside the office of the Motel Mumbo Jumbo. He looked over at me. I kind of waved. Then fell over. I don't remember anything after that.

I woke up on top of a plastic sheet, naked. Lying in a puddle of piss. My head felt like cotton. My eyes were nearly swollen shut. I was thirsty. There was a pressure behind my eyes that made me want to vomit. My teeth felt huge. Scummy. I hadn't brushed them in forever. My tongue was swollen. I felt exhausted. I looked over at the night stand. The sandwich was still there. Dried out now because I never put it back in the plastic bag it came from. I reached over and took a bite. Bologna. With Miracle Whip and American cheese. I chewed the bite slowly. It was dawn. I could tell by the light coming in from the open curtains. I forced myself out of bed. Went into the bathroom. Drank some water from the faucet. I looked in the mirror. Luckily it was too dark to see the state I was in. I was wet from piss. But no bed bug bites. I sat down on the toilet and pissed. This led to some other things coming out. Wet things from the back. Followed by some noises. I did my best to wipe. Took another drink of water. Went back into the room. Pulled the blanket up over the plastic sheet. Laid down on top of the blanket. Felt the piss soak into the blanket. Sighed. Got up, looked around for the towels. They were nowhere to be found. I took another bite of the sandwich and got back on the bed. I found a dry place that wasn't too scratchy. I stared at the ceiling chewing. Before I knew it, I was asleep again.

A few hours later I woke up. I got out of bed. I put my clothes on. I went out to the Rabbit. It was bright as hell. My eyes were so squinty that I thought, I may go blind. I got into the driver's seat. Had to wrestle with my pants to get my keys out. The Rabbit turned on without issue. I drove it to the space in front of my room. Got out. Went to the back. Opened the hatch. Took out my suitcase. Closed the hatch. Which was very loud. I squinted my way back into my room. Put the suitcase down. Took another bite of the dry sandwich. Took off my clothes. Got back on top of the covers. They were only damp now. I reached over and pulled the other half of the blanket over myself. I thought that I should put more squirts of pink eye medicine into my eyes, but I didn't, I was not in the mood. My headache was getting worse. I pulled the covers over my head and went back to sleep. Hoping the headache would go away and I wouldn't wake up puking all over the place.

I woke up puking all over the place. I suppose I woke up and then puked all over the place but who is splitting hairs here? And by all over the place, I mean mostly on the greasy carpet. I got out of bed and went into the bathroom. Yacked some more into the toilet. What came out was yellow and had little chunks of what looked like coffee grounds. It was kind of a miracle though because after that my headache was gone. I tried to think if I had somehow eaten some coffee grounds at some point in my drunkenness. I couldn't remember. It wouldn't surprise me though. Either way I was convinced that the coffee grounds were what was giving me the headache and not the lack of food, or excessive drinking, or the lack of water in my system, or the pink eye or the bed bugs. I felt great all of the sudden. So good in fact that I decided to get myself cleaned up and go back to the bar. I took a shower. Combed my hair. Brushed my teeth. Put on some clean clothes. I was a new man. I even whistled a little ditty. Which got dark pretty quick when I realized it was the same tune my dad would whistle right before he beat me up. And not really being in the mood to revisit the past, I turned out the lights and ditched my room. Hoping for a distraction, any distraction would do.

The Comedy Smithereens was hopping when I walked

in. Well, I suppose that is what you would call it, I mean, comparatively speaking. There was a couple at one of the tables having drinks. There were even tunes playing through the speakers. Crinkly old-timey music, but music as compared to the normal silence. Tricky Houdini was behind the bar. Smiling at me. I still didn't know the guy's name. I didn't want to ask what it was. I don't know why. Or I couldn't tell you why. Just that I felt that if I did, this whole place would go up in flames or something. I suppose it had some mysterious vibes. Which is something I picked up by osmosis or something. I suppose Pink Eye Randy would survive if everyone went around naming things, but the rest of us, we had something to hide or something. I mean, I don't know why I told Tricky Houdini why my name was Bouillon. That was not my name. That wasn't even my stage name. It was just the name that my ex-wife used to call me. And why Tricky Houdini never told me his name, I couldn't tell you. I suppose I never asked. I sat down at my usual stool. I said:

"Busy night!"

"It is! It is! Maybe your nerd scientist brought us some luck! Whatool you haves?"

"The usual, bud, easy on the ice."

Tricky Houdini made me a rum and Sprite easy on the ice. I drank it slowly. I wasn't in the mood to get wasted. Not yet at least. I suppose I knew how these things started and how they ended, so I wasn't in any real hurry about things. I nursed my drink and listened to the crinkly music. Taking in the scene. I nursed the drink pretty fast and ordered another. Then I nursed that one even faster. I was starting to feel pretty loose. I asked Tricky Houdini if he was going to give us some entertainment. He said:

"Nah, not tonight. You made me feel pretty bad about my stuff the other night, I guess I got some retooling to do."

"It's a tough biz, bud. Don't take it personal."

"You can say that, Bouillon, but I'd like to see you try.

You seem like a funny guy."

"Don't threaten me with a good time, bud."

"Oh yeah? Hey Randy!" Pink Eye Randy came out of nowhere. He wasn't looking so good. He didn't look drunk though.

"Yeah, boss?"

"Go up on the stage and introduce this guy, I want to see his chops."

"You got it, boss." Pink Eye Randy walked over to the stage. Got on to it. Tapped the microphone. Said, "Ladies and Germs, give us a hand for the guy that sleeps in room number four!" The couple clapped. Kind of. They clapped, it is true, but they didn't seem to mean it too much. I swallowed my drink and walked up onto the stage. I tapped the microphone:

"This thing on? Thanks Randy. A round of applause for Randy! The only guy I know that gets treated like a fancy painting, or a stripper in Vegas, don't you dare touch, cause if you do, you'll regret it!" I heard Randy yell off in the distance, "Hey! That aint cool!"

"I joke, Randy, just jokes. Randy is a good guy. Generous. He gave me pink eye and made me a sandwich, which also gave me pink eye. I mean, the guy should be a chef. I swear, I mean, listen, I wrote a recipe for what kind of stuff the guy is giving out. It's called, Pink Eye Randy's Recipe For A Good Time:

Take one part bologna sandwich with Miracle Whip, add two parts bed bugs and pink eye, combine that with what is probably super glue, piss yourself in the night, and wake up with a migraine and you got racist Motel Mumbo Jumbo soup!"

For some reason this made the couple clap like I was actually hilarious. One of them hooted even.

"Now, I know that working in the kitchen is hard work. I used to be a dishwasher. I tell you, it's tough all over. I mean, why did the dishwasher get taken off the football field? Because he had a dish-located shoulder.

Why did the dishwasher have so many quarters? Because he wanted to make a long-dish-tance phone call. Why did the dishwasher get kicked out of his apartment? Because he couldn't pay his rent."

This last joke really riled up the crowd. "More! More!!" The couple yelled.

"Well shit, I wasn't expecting such love from this crowd tonight, had I known I would have written some new material. But whatever, I guess I got a couple more. Why couldn't the art school student pay his rent? Because he went to art school. What's the difference between going to art school and not going to art school? One hundred thousand dollars of debt and being dish-owned by your parents. Why did the dishwasher go to art school? Because he was already dish-owned by his parents. Why did the dishwasher drop out of art school? Because he realized he would make more money being a dishwasher. Thank you! Good night! Don't go to art school!"

The couple clapped and hooted. Tricky Houdini clapped and hooted. Pink Eye Randy clapped and hooted. I rubbed my eyes and walked back to the bar. There was a fresh drink waiting for me. Tricky Houdini was smiling. His tricky mustache was playing light tricks. Pink Eye Randy was doing some bar back business, looking kind of upset. Making noises with the glasses. I could tell he had something to say to me. I nursed my drink for a few seconds. Tricky Houdini went over to do some stuff down on the other part of the bar. I said:

"Randy! I'm sorry, those were just jokes."

"You hurt my feelings."

"I didn't mean to."

"I made you that sandy in private. You shouldn't just yuck it up all the time about things like that."

"I know, I am sorry."

"I don't like it, it's not nice."

"I am sorry, Randy, I won't do it again."

"Okay, promise?"

"I promise."

"I made you another sandy, and I cleaned up your pukes and hosed down your plastic sheets for later."

"Randy, you're the best, I really..." Just then the couple came up and interrupted the conversation.

"Pure gold!" The guy in the couple was shaking my hand. "Buy this guy a drink! On me!"

"Well thank you."

"Art school! I never! Keep it up!" The gal in the couple smiled at me. Tricky Houdini placed another drink in front of me. The guy in the couple paid. The couple went back to their table. I looked at Tricky Houdini.

"See! You just need to know your audience is all."

"You really hit the spot tonight, Bouillon! I think you got something special!" Tricky Houdini shook my hand. It seemed like a contract, like an audition had just happened. That is, as long as I could lure them in, I was now doing a residency at the Comedy Smithereens. Staying in room 4 at the racist Motel Mumbo Jumbo. I was feeling pretty high. Things seemed to be working out just right. I sat there drinking rums and Sprites easy on the ice. Patting myself on the back. Getting drunk enough to be okay with going back to my room. Trying not to think about whistling the same tune my father used to whistle when he would beat me.

When I got to the point that nothing would touch me, I stumbled back to my room. Ate the sandy that Pink Eye Randy had left for me, while I stood swaying next to the night stand. I made sure I went and took a piss before hopping into bed. When I got back I put a couple squirts of pink eye medicine in my eyes after I stripped naked. I looked out the window. Pink Eye Randy was watching me. I waved. He waved back. Then he doubled over, presumably to puke. He always seemed drunk, but I never saw him drink. What did that mean? I turned off the lights and pulled the blanket back. I got into bed. The plastic crinkled. I thought that maybe I should shut the curtains at some point. Maybe get a lightbulb for the lamp on the nightstand. But those problems could wait until tomorrow. I opened the bag of chips that Pink Eye Randy had left for me. Potato chips. Plain. I fell asleep eating them. In the dark. Under the blanket. The crunching lulling me to sleep. The plastic sheet making sweat wherever my naked body touched it. I was warm and cold at the same time. But avoiding the bed bugs was worth it. And I would probably have to get up to piss at some point during the night, so I could drink some water when that happened. I suppose, to replenish my fluids. Before I knew it, it was lights out for me.

In the morning I woke up to a banging on my door. Pink Eye Randy was yelling:

"Mister Bouillon! Mister Bouillon!" I got out of bed and opened the door. Pink Eye Randy said, "Mister Bouillon, you're naked!"

"Yes Randy, I am. What do you want? It's the crack o' dawn."

"It's eleven ay em." Randy seemed drunk already. He was drooling. His eyes had streams of mucus held together by his eyelids that stretched when he blinked. I rubbed my eyes and tried to look away. A little sick to my stomach about it. For some reason I thought about licking his eyes. This made me so nauseous that I had to bend over. But then I wasn't in the mood to puke, so I stood up as straight as I could. Trying to avoid eye contact. I was so distracted that I didn't hear what he said. He turned around and left. I stood there trying to get the image of his snot-soaked eyes and eyelids out of my mind. I couldn't do it. I just couldn't get the image out of my mind. I shut the door and went into the bathroom and got into the shower. I let the water get as hot as I could stand it. This didn't help, so I turned the knob to make the shower as cold as it could get. This shocked me. Thank god. I let my body be shocked for as long as I could take it. This distracted me enough to kind of forget the image of Pink Eye Randy's eyes. I turned off the water and got out of the shower. I still had no idea where the towels were, so I drip-dried on the greasy carpet next to the bed. I got dressed. There were chunks of floor things  on the bottom of my feet when I put my socks on. I had to wipe the bottoms of my feet off like I was at the beach or something, like it was sand, but it was not sand. I was starting to find this motel room very exhausting. It was something I would have to deal with at some point. Maybe one of these days when I didn't wake up with a hangover. I put my shoes on. Went into the bathroom and combed my hair. I was going to brush my teeth but I still had Randy on the brain. I just needed to get away. Clear my mind for a second. I made sure I had my car keys and my wallet and went out to the yellow Rabbit.

I got into the car and looked in the rearview mirror. My eyes were pink and swollen. Not gummy thank god, like Pink Eye Randy's, but it made me nervous enough to go back into the room and squirt a couple of drops of medicine in each eye. I put the medicine in my pocket. Just in case. Grabbed the room key that I had left behind before. Made sure the door was locked and got back into the yellow Rabbit. I backed up and turned around. Drove out of the parking lot and took a right. I didn't have a plan as to where I was going, maybe find some food that wasn't infected with pink eye, maybe a cup of coffee or something.

It was a nice day. I rolled my window down. The air smelled pretty good. The trees were pretty green. The landscape was pretty looking. I was driving in a direction that seemed like it might lead me somewhere okay. After a while I turned on the radio, trying to catch some news or something. I couldn't find any news. The only station I found was just some jerk yelling at me about illegals stealing my food stamps or something. I turned the radio off. I drove for a while longer and came to a small town. Maybe a few hundred people or something. I saw a diner down the road. Just past the one stop light in town. It was called Parky's or Porky's or something in between. The way the word was written it was hard to decipher. I wasn't so good with cursive. For all I know the place was called Sparly's. The name didn't matter. The diner was open. I could tell because they had a big neon sign that said OPEN. I pulled into the parking lot and parked. I went inside. There was a post with a sign that said, Please Wait To Be Seated. There was nobody sitting down. I could hear noises in the kitchen. Aside from that there was no indication that anyone knew I was waiting to be seated. I stood next to the post telling me to wait. I felt like an idiot. I was about to yell out to see if someone would seat me, but I didn't. I didn't want to be rude. I waited some more. Eventually a very buxom and nonpurulent woman came out of the kitchen. She was adjusting her clothing like she had just been molested. She took out a compact and smiled her lips into the mirror. Made some adjustments to her face. Shut it. Looked up at me. Kind of shocked. Or so it seemed. I suppose she didn't know I was standing there. She said:

"Oh, hello hun, take a seat anywhere." I found a seat by a window. It was a booth with good light. I could keep an eye on the parking lot. And it gave me a direct look into the kitchen. Where I supposed the molester was cooking up the hash. I sat down. Scooted into the booth. The waitress brought over a glass of iced water and a menu. She said, "Nice day we are having. Coffee?" I flipped my coffee cup over. She poured some coffee in the cup. There were four place mats made of paper. She took three of them away. As well as the silverware rolled up in napkins that were on top of them. She left the place mat in front of me alone. As well as the silverware. Then she walked away. I looked at her buns as she walked away. It wasn't really a sexual thing. I suppose. I was just kind of interested in what was happening in the kitchen before I came. And this was some useful information somehow. I suppose. Or I was just looking at her buns, but it wasn't anything sexual. Necessarily.

I read the menu carefully. Looking up now and again at the yellow Rabbit in the parking lot. Making sure nobody was breaking into it. Not that I thought somebody was about to break in, just an old habit I had learned from being on the road as long as I have been. It's easier to be paranoid than to deal with the aftermath of being a fool. That was another bullshit thing my dad taught me. Just like the same pain from a different angle thing he was always abusing me with. However, this juicy piece of horrible advice came after I caught him stealing money that I hadn't hid well enough from him, money that I had earned doing odd jobs during the summers for years at that point. I was saving money to buy a car. I was 15. I walked into my room to find him counting the money that I had hidden under my mattress. He counted out what looked like a hundred dollars in twenties. Put them in his pocket. Put the rest back under the mattress and then turned around. I didn't say anything. He shrugged at me. Smiled like the asshole he was. Said:

"Well, son. You caught me. Let me offer you a little advice, it's easier to be paranoid than dealing with the aftermath of being a fool. Let this be a lesson to you." He walked out the door. I was hot, trying not to cry. When he left I ran over to my hidden stash. Counted the money. Counted it again. That fucker had stolen over half of it. Hundreds of dollars. I was heartbroken. I sat on my bed tearing the rest of the money in half. Tears welling up behind my eyes that I refused to let come out. When all the money was torn in half I wadded it up into my hands. Went out into the back yard. Made a mound of it. Lit it on fire with the matches I carried in my pocket because I had just started smoking. I watched it burn until it was ash. I turned around and went back inside. My father was standing in the kitchen. Drinking a glass of cheap vodka. Extra ice. He had watched me do this through the window. He smiled at me like the asshole he was. Said, "Well, does that make you feel like a big man now? Burning all your money to stick it to your old man? What do you need all that cash for anyway? You thinking about moving to Wall Street or something?" I said:

"I was planning on buying a car."

"Ha! You buying a car. You can't even drive, you idiot."

"I'll be sixteen next month."

"I'll be sixteen next month, I'll be sixteen next month." His voice was high and squeaky. He was mocking me. "We'll see about that. Come here a minute." He put his drink on the counter. I could see his hands were turning into fists. His beckoning was hypnotic. I started to move towards him knowing he was about to knock me around. Same pain from a different angle. Just then the Waitress showed back up. She said:

"Whatool you haves?"

"Oh, give me the Juicy Lucy, over easy if you don't mind. With bacon and white toast, please."

"You got it, hun." I handed her the menu. She turned around and walked away. I didn't look at her buns this time. I took a drink of coffee. Realized I meant to add milk. Poured some milk from the metal container by the sugar packets. It had a lid that clanked when I was done using it. I stared out the window. Not really looking at anything. Trying to forget the episode with my asshole dad and Pink Eye Randy's snotty eyes. This morning was not turning out so good.

When the waitress brought me the Juicy Lucy, which was just eggs, hash browns, bacon, and toast, I felt a little grossed out that I had got the eggs over easy. I dumped salt and pepper on everything but that didn't solve the fact that the eggs were runny and reminded me of Pink Eye Randy's eyes. I was hungry enough that I was able to do a suspended disbelief thing until everything was gone, but I didn't feel much better when the meal was over. I felt as greasy as my motel room on the insides now. The waitress came back and refilled my coffee cup. Laid the check down. Asked me if everything was alright. I nodded. She walked away. I watched her go back into the kitchen. Finally the molester came into view. He was a very hairy man, with mutton chop sideburns and a hair net. Black hairs sticking up on his shoulders. Wearing a white tank top and a white apron. The waitress walked by him. He smacked her ass with a spatula. She let out a yelp, JayJay! stop that! I smiled somehow. It was the first time I had smiled sincerely in days, if not weeks, if not years. It felt odd. It didn't hurt or something stupid like that, it was just odd. I didn't mind.

I took the bill to the counter to pay. The waitress came out of the kitchen. Did some stuff on the cash register. Told me what I owed. I gave her cash. Tipped her two dollars. She said:

"Just passing through?"

"Yeah, I guess, staying down at the Mumbo Jumbo I suppose."

"No shit! Excuse my lenge-wedge, I thought they closed that joint down?"

"Not that I know of, I been there a couple days, I sure hope they didn't close down. I got my stuff there still."

"The Smithereens still open then?"

"As far as I know, I mean, we did a jokes thing last night, there were people there and everything."

"What do you mean? You a jokester or something?"

"I've been known to sling a few yucks now and again."

"No shit. Huh? Maybe me and JayJay will come have a look-see. Nothing happening around here since the interstate came around."

"Well, come on over, I mean, why not?"

"I suppose so. You doing your thing tonight?"

"I don't see why not."

"Well, okay. It's a date."

I walked out to the yellow Rabbit feeling better about my life, but not feeling so good about my insides. The Juicy Lucy was going straight to my exit door and I was starting to feel a little rushed. I got into the car and took off. Trying to sweat it off. Hoping to sweat it off. It was now a race against time. I drove as fast as the little car could go. Looking in the mirrors, hoping to not see any cops. When I got back to my room I had to run to the door. Cursing myself for letting myself be paranoid that somebody would steal my shit. The way my asshole father had instilled in me. I got the key in the key hole. Burst through the door while leaving the door open. The key dangling. Dropping my pants just in time for the brown sneeze that came out of my backside. Fucking JayJay and his damned greasy eggs. My eyes were on top of their sockets when I sat down. As things rearranged, my eyes went back to their normal position. I sat there panting. Looking at the key dangling in the key hole. The number 4 mocking me. A breeze came by and made the red plastic diamond swing a little. The smell wasn't so nice. And the toilet paper was cheap. But in the end I was able to stand up again and pull my pants up. Not so clean as a whistle, maybe as clean as a snail or a slug, but clean enough.

I closed the door. Taking the key out first. I put the door key and my wallet and my car keys on the nightstand. I took the medicine out of my pocket and squirted a couple drops in both of my eyes. I screwed the lid back on. I put it next to my other stuff. I kicked my shoes off. Got under the covers. On top of the plastic sheet. Closed my eyes. I could feel the medicine slide around under my eyelids. I let out a sigh of accomplishment. The day seemed successful already.

That afternoon I was sitting on the edge of the bed, staring off into space, trying not to think about anything. Waiting for something, I suppose. I was feeling a little raw. Frustrated, maybe. My life was starting to stagnate. I just wanted some peace. Something to look forward to. Maybe there was something a little depressing about being a middle aged failing comedian sleeping in a bed bug infused motel room with pink eye. I was feeling very soft, tender even. Without much spirit. The light coming into the room seemed as flaccid as I felt. The light beams were lazy. Instead of bouncing off of things in sharp angles, the light just kind of flopped around, hitting some of the stuff in the room, not really bothering to shine into the dusty and greasy folds of the room. The light wasn't really white, or sharp yellow, or orange even, it was some kind of dirty brown greenish hot yellow thing. But not. But something hard to describe, like boiling chicken noodle soup from a can. There was a greasy film on the top of the light with like wimpy skinny noodles that were an off white or maybe even bright white when they came to the surface, but then engulfed in some sort of super salty rolling boil that obscured your vision. But then a chunk of light would come into focus, something that looked like a chunk of chicken fat or something, but then it would disappear and foam would start to collect over everything. The light kind of made me hungry. Not hungry like hungry hungry, but hungry like when you are sick for a few days and you can finally eat something and that thing you can finally keep in your stomach without throwing it right back up is chicken noodle soup from a can, and maybe some white toast with butter on it. I mean, I suppose me and the light and the room were having some symbiotic relationship. Like I was the room and the light or something, or like the room and light and me were the same thing? A certain clarity hit me. I had a vision of the perfect joke. I didn't have a pen or paper, so I had to make sure I would remember the joke. I paced around thinking about it in its nascent state, but it wasn't working though. I could feel my memory fading, like waking up from a dream and trying to remember the dream. The harder I thought about it, the faster it went away. I ran out the door. Down to the office of the racist Mumbo Jumbo Motel. The bell rang when I walked inside. There was no Pink Eye Randy to be found. I found a pen on the counter and wrote, "Pee Wee Pulitzer" on the back of my hand. Put the pen back and turned around. As I was walking out I heard Pink Eye Randy talking:

"Hi, Mr. B. How are you doing?" I turned around slowly, trying to keep my eyes from looking at his face. I couldn't take any more shocks to my system today. Pink Eye Randy looked drunk from his neck down. He was swaying behind the counter.

"Hi, Randy. I'm doin' alright, how are you?"

"Oh, no complaints. Same ol', same ol'. Did you talk to those guys?"

"What guys are you talking about?"

"The guys I told you about. The ones from before."

"The ones from before?" I remembered that I had forgotten to process what he was saying earlier because I was so distracted by his eyes. I was trying to remember the interaction without remembering the actual interaction. It was difficult.

"Yeah, the science guys that were looking for you."

"Oh, shit. That guy came back?"

"What guy? There was two of them. They had notebooks."

"There were two guys?"

"Yeah, I already told you. They had notebooks. They were looking for you."

"Notebooks, or notepads, or clipboards?"

"What's the difference?"

"Yeah, I don't know, Randy. I don't know why I asked you that. Did they say what they wanted?"

"I already told you, they were looking for you. They had notepads. Or notebooks. Or clipboards. Now I am confused."

"Okay, thanks, Randy."

"Thank you! Mr. B." I turned around again. Glad I didn't look at Pink Eye Randy's face. I went back to my room.

I spent some time working on the perfect joke that struck me in my meditation. The wording was hard, but I thought I got it just right. I was excited about it. It is not often that you get new material just handed to you from the heavens. I was feeling pretty lucky. I did some practice runs with it. Working it into my routine. I gave myself a few chuckles in the process.

The sun went down. The room got dark. I turned the light on. Soon I would be able to hit the bar again and have some drinks and get loose for the show. Plus the waitress and JayJay were supposed to show up. Maybe the couple from last night would come back? Maybe the science guys with their notepads or notebooks or clipboards? Maybe some other new people? I wasn't feeling like such a loser for once.

I held out as long as I could. The anticipation fueling me. I was waiting for a clue from the universe. A sign. Any sign. It came pretty fast once I asked for it. A crow cawed in the distance. That was it. That was God's way of telling me I should go get some drinks and try the new joke he sent me from heaven.

The Comedy Smithereens was the same as I had left it. Candles burning on the tables. Crinkley music floating through the air. A couple drinking at one of the booths. The waitress and JayJay weren't there, but it was still early. Tricky Houdini was behind the bar. No sneaking up on me this time. I sat down at my usual stool. He smiled at me. Wiped the bar down with his disgusting rag covered in pink eye. He said:

"Whatool you haves?"

"Rum and Sprite, easy on the ice my good man."

"Coming right up!" He made the drink. Put a paper napkin down in front of me. Put the drink on top. I was so excited that I almost drank the whole thing in one gulp. "You seem excited today, Mr. B. Get some good news or something?"

"Oh, maybe. I guess we will see. Good crowd!"

"Oh, yes. There is some electricity in the air."

"I think I got us some more people coming. The couple down the way that run Handy's."

"Handy's?"

"Pandy's? Porky's? I don't know, the diner down the way there. They got the sign with the cursive."

"Oh! Shandy's! I know that place. They make the best Juicy Lucy in town."

"Shandy's? Are you sure?"

"Yeah, Shandy, she owns it. I've known her since high school."

"You're from here?"

"Born and bred."

"Really. Hmmm."

"Surprised?"

"Not really, I guess I need to learn how to read. I could have sworn the name was Parky's or something, you guys got some odd signs around here I noticed."

"Yeah, I guess. The sign says Sparky's, it's just Shandy that owns it now. I don't think you reading the sign wrong is her fault though." This conversation was going nowhere. I ordered another drink. Drank it slower than the first one. I didn't want to blow my load quite yet. I was kind of waiting for the waitress, Shandy, I guess, and JayJay to come. I wouldn't mind an audience for what I was about to unleash. Tricky Houdini left me alone. Wiping down things around the bar with his dirty dish rag covered in pink eye. I didn't know the politics of pink eye. Whether you could get it again and again and again. I was hoping I was immune now. That I wouldn't need to worry about it anymore. But who knows. I once again fell into the trap of trying to not think of Pink Eye Randy's gummy red eyes blinking in the sunlight. And it was tough. Too tough. Because I couldn't think about his eyes, I thought of a mouthful of snot instead, sickness snot, chewing on snot, the snot sticking to the teeth, the jaw moving up and down, the tongue licking the snot, the snot getting stuck to the lips. The image I conjured in my mind was so much more grotesque than what Pink Eye Randy's eyes looked like that I was able to think of his eyes with nostalgia, I supposed it was the kind of nostalgia you get from looking at a dead rat after seeing a pile of dogshit on the sidewalk. Pink Eye Randy's eyes seemed to be in a state of stasis at least. They weren't at the beginning of their decline, or so it seemed. They weren't like a dead rat. They wouldn't continue to rot. To stink. At least with dog shit you just need to avoid the fresh piles. Soon it's just gross instead of disgusting. Or not. Pink Eye Randy's eyes did not seem to be done with what was happening to them. I didn't know why I was trying to pretend that was true.

I managed to stop my brain from thinking about Pink Eye Randy. A while went by. I looked around. The couple sitting in the booth seemed to be engaged in some nice conversation. The crinkly music was nice for the mood. I had another drink. Going over my set in my mind. Kind of feeling nervous about it. Self doubt creeping in. A little while later JayJay and the Shandy came in. They took a seat at a table kind of close to the stage. I could hear her say, "The place is hopping tonight!" JayJay was dressed up. Cowboy boots. Stiff shirt with lots of colors and buttons. Black jeans. Shandy was wearing a flowery cotton dress with pink flamingos on it. She looked as nonpurulent as she'd looked before. Maybe even more so. Or maybe that was because I had just been fixated on Pink Eye Randy and his eyes, but she seemed like the only one around here that didn't have something wrong with them. She also seemed to be excited to be here. I watched JayJay nod his approval while accessing the bar and its surroundings. His hair slicked back. His muttonchop sideburns looked well trimmed. He pulled a chair back. Sat down. I watched Shandy walk over to the bar. She saw me and said:

"Oh hey! You're the jokester from before! I hope you got some good yucks for us tonight! Maybe a zinger or two to top it off?"

"I'll do my best." I was embarrassed. I got a pit in my stomach thinking about my new material the second she spoke. Shandy interacted with Tricky Houdini and got a couple of drinks. As she was walking away she turned to me and said:

"Break a leg!" I opened my lips revealing my clenched teeth. I couldn't look her in the eye. Tricky Houdini put a new drink in front of me. I watched Shandy take the drinks back to the table. I watched her buns swishing back and forth in her cotton dress. This time it was sexual. She had nice buns. I must have been wearing my wimpy worm on my face because when she sat down I turned to Tricky Houdini who was rubbing the tip of his tongue along the hair-ends of his phantom mustache. He said:

"She's a hot one, that Shandy."

"Yeah, no lie."

"So you are going on tonight or what?" Tricky

Houdini's face suddenly was serious. I reflected his seriousness. He reflected his own seriousness right back to me. "Why are you so serious?"

"Why are you so serious?"

"I was afraid you wouldn't go on tonight."

"I was afraid you wouldn't want me to go on tonight."

"Why would you think that?"

"Why would you think that?"

"I don't know."

"I don't know either."

Both of us looked back at Shandy and pretended the conversation didn't happen. He made me another drink and then went off to wipe some stuff down with his horrible rag. I watched Shandy and JayJay drink and have what looked to me like good times. A while went by.

After a while a couple guys came in wearing suits carrying clipboards. I tried to make myself hidden. Hiding behind my drink. Hoping they didn't see me. But of course they did. They went into one of the back booths. By the bathrooms. They didn't come up to the bar. They just sat there. Tricky Houdini went to their booth. Came back. Said to me in a whisper that was so loud that the entire bar could hear it:

"Those are the guys!" I didn't bother responding. He brought them their drinks. Tricky Houdini came back. He said:

"You ready to go on?"

"I'm ready, where's Randy?"

"I don't know. Oh, there he is!" Pink Eye Randy stumbled up onto the stage and knocked on the microphone. "Hello, hello, hello." The people in the Comedy Smithereens clapped. "Okay! Glad to hear it! Have we got a treat for you tonight! Give it up for the greasiest easiest joke in town, the Mamma Mia in your diarrhea, the hot dog in your Time's Square, Missss-ter Bouuuuuillon!" Everyone clapped. Pink Eye Randy stumbled off stage. I could see him puking behind the curtains. He was on his hands and knees, his butt sticking out, as I walked onto the stage. My nerves were something else. I was holding my drink for some reason. I chugged it as I got on the stage. I threw the empty glass at Pink Eye Randy's exposed buns. He farted. The crowd thought this was quite something. Somebody whistled. I felt bad for Pink Eye Randy. I also felt ashamed. I had broken the promise I made to him before. There wasn't anything I could do. Comedy is a thinking man's game. Nothing is off limits. I went to the microphone. Looked out. I looked at my hand. The words "PeeWee Pulitzer" were still there. I started my act:

"Randy, everyone! Give it up for, Randy!" The crowd shouted and hooted. "Randy, I love your work, it's good, quite good, but there is one aspect of it that is hard to take, it stinks!" I waved my hand in front of my face. I waited for the applause to calm down. Poor Randy kept puking and farting in the wings. "I mean, I don't mean to make him the BUTT of my jokes, but Randy, come on!" Randy looked over at me with hate in his eyes. I could see him blinking snot at me. Puke running down his chin. He was in pain. I should have gone over to help him, but I didn't. I kept going:

"Well, good to see everyone here tonight. We should all consider ourselves lucky, well maybe not everyone, earlier today I made the mistake of going to Shandy's for breakfast, I mean, I just flew in from the bathroom, and boy are my ass-cheeks tired! I haven't shit like that since God put me in charge of the Nile River during inundation three thousand years ago. Am I right? Why is my ass like an ancient Egyptian Pharaoh? Because they have a toot-in-common! King Tut. Remember that guy? He had so many pyramids that he put Bernie Madoff to shame. Remember that guy? He stole ALL the money! And what is up with all those mummies? I mean, why did they spend so much time making jerky? Didn't they have 7-11's back then? I mean, c'mon! Where are the nachos, dudes? Am I right? How hard is it to get the cheese flowing? You know what I mean? Ancient Egyptians make cheese like I make sense, never and by accident! An obelisk is right twice a day, am I right? Let me get my measuring tape out." I pretended to measure the pretend shadow from the pretend obelisk. "Looks like it's about tooth-hurty. What are we in China all the sudden?!"

"I wonder if the ancient Egyptians had dishwashers. I really do. And what the hell were they like? I mean, were they standing there washing big pots made of clay and some dude was behind them whipping them, yelling, Wash the tubs you slimy jerk! And the dishwasher was like, Hey man! Stop whipping me! I am trying to work here! And the whipping guy was like, Wash faster you dirty worm! And the dishwasher was like:

"I can't get any work done because you've dislocated my shoulder!" And then all the other workers had a great big laugh, and then the guy with the whip was like, "I don't get it?" And then the dishwasher had to explain it to him, and then the guy was like,

'That's not funny! Now back to work!'"

"Whatever. I don't mean to talk shit about things that happened thousands of years ago, but I will. Because shit is pretty fucked up now. I don't know. Things are tough all over. I just heard that Pee Wee Herman is in the news. Anyone else hear about this? Yeah, I mean, he has finally gotten the credit he deserves. Are you sure you haven't heard about this?" I waited for a response. Somebody yelled, "No!" I said, right after looking down at my hand. The joke that was an epiphany in my motel room just hours before:

"Well, after all of this exposure coming from the porn industry, and what it means to be a celebrity in the age of attention from the paparazzi it turns that Pee Wee Herman is getting an award:

"It is the, Pull-It! Surprise! Get it? Pull-it, Surprise!" I made a wanking motion. "Thank you, good night!"

The crowd clapped and clapped and clapped. I slunk

back to where Pink Eye Randy had left his pukes. Trying not to step in them. I thought my jokes went good. Maybe not as fresh and tight as they could have been. I realized the PeeWee joke, as much of an epiphany as it was, was kind of out-dated. I was kind of drunk, and didn't want to talk to anyone. I did, however, want to have a few more drinks before I went back to my bed bug room, so I hid there behind the curtains watching people leave. The couple in the booth were the first to leave. Then Shandy and JayJay left. Eventually the Scientists became inpatient and left. After that I snuck out from behind the curtains and went back to the bar. Tricky Houdini was very happy with the performance. He got me drunk. Talking about what the future held. I let him get me drunk and eventually stumbled back to my room.

I wasn't so happy with my set afterall. My jokes seemed clanky. But the crowd seemed to like them. I supposed that I would need to process this before I went back on stage. But whatever. The night seemed like a success. I stripped naked and got into bed. The plastic sheet reminded me I should take a leak before I fell asleep. I didn't bother to go into the bathroom. I just pissed on the greasy carpet. I mean, if they didn't care, I didn't either. I fell into the bed after I did this. Hitting the snooze button the second I pulled the blanket on top of myself.

I woke up pretty fresh the next morning. Scrubbed the scum off of my teeth. Smiled my banana Laffy Taffy's in the mirror. Combed my hair to the side. I really did look like Hitler. It wasn't funny. I don't know why this bugged me so much, aside from the obvious. It's not my fault I look like Hitler, you know. But still. Nobody wants to go around looking like Hitler. Well, not in this day and age. Maybe back when the Nazis were looking like they might have a chance at ruling the world. But even then. Hitler wasn't a handsome guy. And by default, neither was I. I was feeling pretty lousy after these thoughts, so I tried to forget about them. I went out and got into the yellow Rabbit. It started right up. All these years I have been driving this thing around and for whatever reason I took it for granted, but the thing must have been  40 years old. And I guess in the back of my mind I expected it to shit-out one day, leaving me stranded wherever the hell I was at the moment. With no savings, no prospects. I mean, the only thing that kept me from being a hobo was this car. Yet for some reason, even with all my neglect, it ran like a charm. I must have been sending it good vibes or something, because whenever it started I always gave out a sigh of relief.

I drove down the road to Shandy's place, or Sparky's

as the sign would have you believe. It was a nice spring day again. Things were looking pretty good. The air was smelling nice. I pulled in and parked. Got out. Went inside. This time Shandy was behind the counter filling salt shakers. I waved at her when she looked up. She smiled.

"Well look at this! Hey, JayJay, come look at this!" JayJay poked his head out of the kitchen. "Well look at that!" Then he sucked his head back into the kitchen. I could hear some clanking. "Table for uno?"

"Por favor." I said. Not knowing why we had switched to pseudo Spanish. I walked to the same booth I sat at the day before. Shandy met me there with a menu and a glass of water with ice. Then she turned around and went back to get the coffee pot. I sat down and took a look at the yellow Rabbit making sure I wasn't getting robbed. Shandy came back over. I flipped my coffee cup over. She poured some coffee. Took the three other sets of silverware and the paper settings. Looked down at me.

"Damn good one last night! Me and J there had a blast-off! Been ages. Won't lie, things got kinda frisky when we got home." This gave me a boner as soon as it left her lips. Like a really strong boner that embarrassed me. There was no need to hide it because she couldn't see it under the table, not to mention other reasons, but it was there. There in a way that I hadn't felt in a long, long time. I was astonished by what was happening. I was trying my hardest to stay focused. "You going on again tonight?"

"Um, yeah I think so. Don't see why not." My mind was nearly white with carnality. I mean, I kind of just wanted her to keep talking, I suppose. My heart started beating really fast. It was all very confusing.

"Well, good. Not sure if we will make it, but there's a chance, hun. You know what you want?"

"Um, yeah, I guess the Juicy Lucy again. Over easy, with bacon and white toast."

"Coming right up." She took the menu from me. Her hand brushing my arm as she reached down. I won't lie, I lost it. Like really lost it.

"Unghh." I mumbled without control.

"You okay?" Shandy had a peculiar look on her face. Which meant that I must have had one too.

"Oh, yeah, sorry, I just, uh… late night is all, I can really use this coffee." I fumbled with the metal container holding the milk. My hands shaking. She must have thought I was an alcky the way I was acting. Which, I suppose was better than her thinking I had just shot a load in my pants because her hand brushed my arm. I suppose I didn't want her to think either of those things, but thinking I was a drunk was the better option. She made a different weird face and walked away. I was too embarrassed to look at her buns because I thought that that would be some sort of violation, so I stared out the window trying to ignore the load in my drawers that was probably seeping through as I sat there. This would be a problem when I got up to pay. I did what I thought was a smart thing and put my napkin down my pants. Hoping to soak up the load. But this left me without a napkin, and that would seem suspicious, so now I had two problems to deal with. The one where I secretly clean up my loins with the one napkin I had, and also the problem of making it look like I didn't clean up my loins with the one napkin I had.

A while later Shandy brought me my breakfast. Poured some fresh coffee in my cup. Said:

"Everything look alright?"

"Looks delish!"

"What, did you eat your napkin? That hungry, eh? Ha! No worries, hun." She handed me a couple more napkins from her apron. I couldn't tell if she was messing with me, or what, but at least I solved one of my problems. I would have to deal with my other problem later, assuming that I had successfully covered up the fact that I shot a load in my drawers, however, that meant that Shandy probably thought I was a drunk who eats napkins.

I ate my breakfast slowly. Assuming with good reason it would be the only thing I ate that day. It was pretty good. Basic. But good. And luckily I didn't think about Pink Eye Randy's eyes when I was eating it. I suppose time does heal all wounds. Shandy came back when I was finished. Took my empty plate. Maybe counting the napkins I used. Maybe knowing that I had put one down my pants. Maybe, or maybe not. Maybe I was being paranoid. I drank the cup of coffee. Looked at the cup of water with ice. The ice was gone now. Melted. I had a few drinks of that too. To keep hydrated. I did a funny maneuver to get out of the booth in a way that I didn't immediately expose my crotch. So I could check to see if anything had seeped through. This meant that I had to back out of the booth. For no good reason. I suppose. I mean, if anyone was watching me. I pretended that I was looking for something in the booth. Like my wallet or something I dropped. I looked down. My crotch looked dry. The load was really itchy now. The napkin was stuck to it. I could feel it. It took all my focus not to scratch my crotch. I took the ticket up to the counter to pay. Shandy was busy and wasn't very playful anymore. I noticed she looked a little tired. I mean, I don't mean to presume, but I think she was doing some business numbers and business didn't seem to be doing so good. These last two times I was in the diner I was the only customer. I felt bad about that. Kind of. I suppose I tipped her an extra dollar thinking that that would help somehow. She seemed grateful, in the way you can seem grateful for a meaningless gesture, but grateful nonetheless. I told her I hoped to see her at the Comedy Smithereens tonight. She barely registered my comments. Said, "Okay, hun. Thanks!" I guess all my worry about my wet crotch was for nothing. Which was kind of frustrating because I was really wracked with worry about it. But I suppose a failing business is more important than some middle aged dude shooting a load in his pants right before breakfast. But I think because I find myself so self-involved all the time, I kind of wanted to drop my pants and say, "See what you did to me! Don't feel bad about nothing, toots! You still got the goods!" Or something. Like that would help somehow. I didn't do it though. I walked back to the yellow Rabbit and got into the car. Turned it on. Let out a sigh of relief and drove out of the parking lot.

I got about halfway to the racist Motel Mumbo Jumbo before the runny eggs felt like somebody had fired a wet cannonball at the inside of my butthole. Luckily I had shot that load earlier so my prostate was feeling strong and I didn't shit my pants, but it was a sketchy ride from there on out. I got to the motel, parked as fast as I could. Ran into the room. Went into the bathroom and sat down just in time. The results were action packed. Explosive and violent. Like the Revolutionary War. Two if by sea, if you know what I mean. When everything calmed down I realized I was out of toilet paper. Annoyed I just sat there, breathing in the stink. Then I realized I still had that napkin stuck to my earlier load. I leaned back and peeled it from my hip. Wiped as best as I could. Dropped it into the tank. Stood up. Pulled my pants up. Looked down. Frowned. Flushed the toilet. I saluted the toilet thinking it was funny. But the joke didn't last very long because just then there was a knock on the door.

I yelled, "Hold on, Randy!" Washed my hands. Looked in the mirror. My eyes were looking better, but still pink. I took the medicine out of my pocket and squirted a few drops in each eye. Put the lid back on. Put the medicine back in my pocket. Walked to the door, thinking Pink Eye Randy was on the other side. When I opened the door I was very confused. Not because I was confused at what I saw, but because it wasn't Pink Eye Randy and for whatever reason me and Pink Eye Randy had an understanding, like we understood each other, and I was comfortable with him. But the two guys standing outside the door made me nervous as shit, and I was suddenly very self-conscious. I didn't want them to smell the shit I just let out. So instead of being cordial, I pushed myself out of the room, closing the door behind me. This made the two men back up. And I don't know if I am being paranoid or not, but I think the smell coming from the bathroom came with me, because they both had looks on their faces that suggested that they were smelling something unpleasant. I kind of sidled to the side, and backed away from the door, luring them towards the yellow Rabbit that felt like comfort to me. I suppose I was trying to get them away from the smell, but I was also trying to gain some perspective that they weren't giving me because they were standing so close.

Both men were wearing suits. Carrying clipboards. The Science Guys as Pink Eye Randy had called them, or the Science Nerds I think Tricky Houdini had referred to them as. They didn't look like scientists to me. More like reporters or something. But from the Government. Like gum-shoes or something. What's the word? Spooks? I mean, that sounds racist, but maybe it is the term. G-Men? I mean, they seemed like FBI guys or CIA guys. They were wearing cheap suits. Had cheap haircuts. They weren't not white. But they seemed white. Like institutionally white. Their hairs were like wires on top of their heads. They weren't either attractive or unattractive. They were just normal guys. If that is a thing. Normal guys with cheap suits and cheap haircuts but with some sort of thing behind themselves. I mean, I could tell they were from the Government, but what that meant exactly, I couldn't tell you. The shorter guy, because one guy was taller than the other guy, but the shorter guy looked down at his clipboard and paraphrased:

"Are you so and so? Born in such and such? Married to this and that? Son of his and her? Born on this specific day?"

"I suppose."

"You don't know?"

"I mean, that is my name, and that is where I was born, and that is my ex, and those are the names of my parents. And I was most likely born on that date. I have a license that says as much."

"Can we see it?" I took out my wallet. Then I stopped. I put it back in my pocket.

"Who the fuck are you dudes?"

"That's not important. We just need some information, sir."

"Like hell you do. Show me a badge or something."

"Well, we can't. You just have to trust us."

"Really? Really? You knock on my door and interrupt me taking a shit just so you can get some information and you won't tell me who you are? That's a little rich, don't you think? I mean, you already know too much about me."

"Well, we just need you to know that we have information that you would want. It is in both of our best interests."

"Yours, yeah, mine, I don't think so. Do me a favor and get lost." I walked over to my room door. Somehow I had locked myself out. I walked over to the yellow Rabbit and got in. My keys were in my room. I got back out. The government goons just stood there like they were never going to leave. I walked over to the Office of the racist Motel Mumbo Jumbo. Went inside. No sign of Pink Eye Randy. I yelled his name a few times. Nothing. I walked back out. Went over to the back door of the Comedy Smithereens. The door was locked. I looked back at the government goons. Just standing there. I thought about going around the front and running off into the hills. But this seemed exhausting. I was in no mood for running. My ass was sore from my shit, and my crotch was itchy from the load I launched earlier at Shandy's. I gave up and walked back to the Government goons.

"Okay, well played, you got me. What the hell do you want?"

"We just want to talk to you is all." The taller guy was talking now.

"But you can't tell me who you are?"

"It is not important who we are. I think you will understand soon enough."

"Okay, fine." I let out a large sigh.

"I think you should sit down."

"Well, you saw that my room is locked and I don't have the key. The bar is closed, and the motel office aint got shit to sit on."

"Perhaps your little car here?"

"The Rabbit? Are you insane? I can barely fit in there alone."

"I really think you need to be sitting down."

"Well, okay."

I got back into the yellow Rabbit. The short guy somehow slunk into the backseat from the passenger side of the car after the two guys figured out how to make the seat pull forward. He had to move a bunch of stuff to have room to sit. A pair of unused running shoes, a box of cereal that I kept meaning to throw away, a stack of Field & Stream magazines that some drunk who loved my set a few years ago had insisted I take with me, a long plastic bag of Nag Champa incense sticks. I didn't help. The tall guy got into the front seat. Pulled the lever to make the seat move back, but his knees were still pressed against the dashboard. He shut the door for some reason. This made the space seem even more cramped. He did roll down the window though. I don't know why but I closed my door too. My window was already rolled down. I adjusted the rearview mirror so I could see the shorter guy half-lounged in the back seat. Looking like a cramped turtle. This made me chuckle a little. The whole scene was absurd. It was a joke. More than a joke. The taller guy started talking. Which made the shorter guy get really serious. I mean, what the fuck could these assholes have to tell me that they would hunt me down in some racist motel in the middle of bullshit Ohio that I needed to be sitting down to hear? I mean, they weren't doctors. They weren't going to tell me I had AIDS or some such bullshit. I mean, I am sure I had whatever already. This life I had been living for so long was bound to catch up with me. But this thing that was happening now? Like maybe it turned out I was the President all along and the votes just finally came in and I had to decide to nuke North Korea or something? It was all just so absurd. I was really feeling entertained. Because there was nothing, not a single thing they could tell me that would change anything in the world for me. I mean, unless they were about to give me a bunch of money, which, judging by the way they were acting, was the last thing they were about to give me.

The taller guy started talking:

"I don't know how to say this, so I will just say it, you're a clone."

"Hey, c'mon, man. I might be a hack, but that is some rough criticism, dude. I mean, I know my jokes are derivative, but you were there last night, you heard my PeeWee joke, that shit was transcendent."

"No, you, yourself, are a clone. You were adopted by your parents and raised as their child. You were part of a secret mission to study sociopathy by the government. I don't know how else to say it. You are the exact replica of somebody else."

"Yeah, that's ridiculous."

"Yeah, I don't know what to tell you. I'm sorry. We're both sorry. The government is sorry"

"Why are you telling me this? That's ridiculous. How can I be somebody else?"

"You're not somebody else, you are yourself, it's just you are the same as the other person you are the exact same person as."

"Who put you up to this? The Lizard?"

"The Lizard?"

"You know who I mean."

"I assure you, we don't"

"You don't know who Liz is? You know everything about me from the second I came dribbling out of my old man's needle dick up until yesterday and you don't know who my ex wife is? Give me a fucking break. Everyone out. We're done here."

I got out of the yellow Rabbit and slammed the door. It took a second for the government goons to extract themselves. I watched. When they were both out I glared. The tall one said:

"This isn't the last you will see of us."

"Ask me if I care." They stared at me. "Go on, ask me." They said nothing. I yelled, "Ask me!" This startled both of them. The tall one spoke.

"Do you care?"

"No, I don't." I watched them walk away. I walked to my door and tried to turn the knob. My room was still locked.

Pink Eye Randy was just standing behind the counter of the Office of the racist Mumbo Jumbo Motel. Staring off into space. It took him a second to turn his head towards me when I walked in. I did my best to not look at his face. He was swaying. I don't know, maybe he was drunk. I couldn't understand this guy. I actually liked him, he seemed like he had a great big heart, and I never saw him drinking but he did seem drunk all the time. What with the puking and all. But I never did see him drinking. Maybe there was some other drug he was doing. Like huffing gas or something. Or maybe the pink eye had just eaten part of his brain away. Or maybe it was in his genes like Tricky Houdini had told me. Either way, I liked him, but I didn't like his eyes. I was avoiding his eyes at all costs. I couldn't go through that again in real time. I already had to suffer the memory.

"Hello, Mr. B, how the hell are ya?"

"Hi, Randy, I am doing alright. I got a question."

"Yes, Mr. B?"

"I locked myself out of my room."

"That's not a question, Mr. B."

"I know, Randy, do you have a spare key?"

"That's a question, Mr. B."

"I know, Randy. Do you?"

"That is also a question, Mr. B."

"Randy!" Pink Eye Randy reached into his pocket and handed me a key with a yellow diamond. The word SKEL written on it in black marker.

"That's a skel key, Mr. B, I am going to need it back."

"Thanks, Randy, of course. Also,"

"Yes, Mr. B?"

"I need some butt-wipe and towels in my room."

"Oh, that is something I can do!"

"Okay, well good, can you do it soon, possibly? It is kind of an emergency."

"I can do it whenever you want, Mr. B, that's my job, I am good at my job."

"You are great at your job, Randy. Is there any chance you could do it soon?"

"Well, yes, I suppose I can. You make a good point, Mr. B."

"Okay, thanks Randy."

I walked back to my room holding the yellow key. I was trying not to think about anything at all. I went inside. Sat down on the bed. Looked around at things. The greasy carpet. The lamp. I realized that I forgot to ask for a light bulb. I was getting up to go back and ask Pink Eye Randy for a light bulb too when there was banging at my door. I opened the door to a giant box of toilet paper. On top of the box of toilet paper was a mound of towels. Pink Eye Randy must have kicked the door with his foot because he could not be seen. I opened the door as far as I could and moved to the side. He brought the box toilet paper and towels in. Put them on the bed. Made a noise that meant that he was relieved from the weight of the things he was carrying.

"I brought buttwipe and towels, Mr. B."

"This is great, Randy. I'm sorry, I meant to ask before, but can I get a light bulb too, for the lamp?"

"Sure thing, Mr. B. Coming right up. Can I say though…?"

"Yes, Randy?"

"The yellow skel would be delightful." I didn't know what he meant so I repeated his words back to him.

"The yellow skel would be delightful? Is that the code for asking for a light bulb? Okay, one yellow skel would be delightful, please, Randy?"

"No Mr. B, the yellow skel key." I had forgotten about the skeleton key he had given me. I felt like a fool. The government goons had really knocked me off of my game. I handed him the key and told him I was sorry and thanks. He glared at me through his gummy eyes like I had intended to steal his key. I would have said sorry a second time, but I was whiplashed by the pink eye. Pink Eye Randy grumbled to himself as he scooted off.

I left the door open thinking he would be right back. Minutes went by. Then more minutes. Then half an hour of minutes went by. I guessed he wasn't coming back so I closed the door. I put a fresh roll of toilet paper on the spring loaded tampon. I put all the towels in the bathroom on the counter next to the sink. I put the box of toilet paper on top of the drawers that held the television. I didn't want to find myself pissing on the box later that night. Which was a pretty good possibility. And I didn't want the greasy carpet to seep into the box. And for some reason the bathroom seemed like the worst place to store it. So I put it next to the television.

I stood there looking at the box of toilet paper. Then the television. Then out the window onto the parking lot. The yellow Rabbit wasn't being molested. I thought about shutting the drapes, but I was enjoying the light turning into evening. There wasn't much to look at, but I was okay with that. I wondered if the government goons would come see my set tonight. If Shandy and JayJay would show up as well. If anyone would show up. Maybe the place would be a ghost town and I could just get drunk by myself and not have to perform. I thought about the trick my ex had played on me earlier. I was a little angry about it now. She was such an asshole. I wondered why she chose to fuck with me at this moment. Maybe she knew that I was gaining traction again. I mean, I had single-handedly increased the attendance at the Comedy Smithereens by like 1000%. That was nothing to sneeze at. And my jokes were hitting like hammers and nails these days. Even if I was feeling lousy about them. If anything I needed a longer set. Twice as long if not three times as long. I was thinking that maybe we should get some other comedy acts around. Travelers like me. People on The Circuit. There were a million of us and it would be easy to pad the stage. A few lousy hacks that made me look good. Reliable hacks that would actually show up. Hacks that don't drink too much. You know, people like me, that weren't me? Non-clones. This gave me a quick double chuckle with a yuck chaser. I went into the bathroom. Looked myself over. Not my best looking, but passable. I was in no mood to brush my teeth, so I rubbed my finger on my yellow tombstones. Combed my hair. Smiled my greasy Laffy Taffys at my Hitler good looks. Made sure I had all my things and walked out the door.

⬤

When I walked into the Comedy Smithereens I was amazed at the attendance. The bar was hopping. I didn't see Shandy and JayJay or the government goons, but there must have been 20 people there. All drinking. Having a good time. The crinkly music playing. Candles on every table. Tricky Houdini slinging drinks. I sat down at my usual stool. Tricky Houdini came over to me and said:

"Damn! You see this? It's like a resurrection all over again! Whatool you haves?"

"Yeah, bud, I tell ya. Rum and Sprite, easy on the ice."

"Comin' right up!"

He put the drink in front of me. On top of a paper napkin. I drank it pretty quick. He got me another without asking. People kept coming up and ordering more drinks. Sitting back down with the drinks they ordered. The place was undulating. It seemed like people were waiting for something. But it was hard to process, because the only thing they could be waiting for was me, and my comic stylings. Things slowed down a little and Tricky Houdini came over to me.

"Bouillon, you have to do a longer set. Not only that, but we need to get some other jerks to come fill in during the other times. What do you think? You think you can do that? And maybe I will put an ad in the paper tomorrow?" I was about to answer when he had to go sling some more drinks. I sat there thinking. Watching people. Getting nervous. I agreed with him. In fact I thought the same thing. Exactly. After a while he came back.

"Well, what do you think?!"

"I agree! I had the same thought!" I had to yell because all the people talking were making it hard to hear things.

"You what?!"

"Agree! I had the same thought!"

"Oh, great!"

"Yeah, great!"

"What?!"

"Where's, Randy?"

"You ready to go on?

"If not now, then when?"

"Okay! Hold tight! Let me get you a drink and I'll find him!" Tricky Houdini made me a drink. He went to find Pink Eye Randy. A few moments went by. People lined up at the bar. Tricky Houdini came back. He yelled at me, "Okay, soon! Be ready!" I held up my drink. Both to say that I heard him, but also to show him I needed a replacement. Some moments went by. Tricky Houdini brought me another drink. Pink Eye Randy came out from behind the curtains. Knocked on the microphone.

"This thing on?" The sound of crinkly music faded. The audience clapped. Somebody shouted, "Show us your tits!" Pink Eye Randy pulled up his shirt and showed his nipples. The crowd went wild. "There, satisfied?" He was dead serious. I almost fell off of my stool, it was so funny. The guy was a comic genius. He went on, "Okay, for all you wimpy worms out there, we got you a real treat tonight, the real thing, not the fax, my good buddy from room number four, Mister Boulllliiiooooon!" The crowd erupted. Pink Eye Randy did his normal think of going to puke behind the curtains. I walked onto the stage. Chugged my drink down. Threw it at his ass. He farted. I shrugged my shoulders. The crowd drank it up. I walked up to the microphone.

"You gotta hand it to Randy guys! The guy is a real gem." The crowd started chanting, "Randy! Randy! Randy!" Pink Eye Randy did a thumbs up while he was puking. This made them even more excited. I waited for the crowd to calm down. This took a while. Someone yelled, "Tell us a joke, mister funny man." I said:

"If it's jokes you want, well, you have come to the right place, I got nothing but jokes. Where to begin? You ever eat a piece of spaghetti that was stuck in a wall outlet? I mean, that is the kind of meal that I would find very shocking..."

I delivered about 70 of my best jokes. One after the other. The bad ones and the even worse ones. For some reason the crowd just ate them up. Halfway through my set I was once again worried that I had fallen into a coma and all of this was just some dumb version of my best reality, my jokes were hit or miss at best, but now they were hitting hard every time. Like some dumb sledgehammer to the skull of all these people. But whatever, you should take it where you can get it. As I got to the end I was sweating like crazy. I would have loved another drink, but I could see that Tricky Houdini was busy, and Pink Eye Randy was nowhere to be found.

"Alright, alright. I need another drink, does anyone have one to share?" Instead of someone bringing me a drink up to the stage, the crowd just started throwing drinks at me. At first I was stunned. Thinking it was just a joke, until a glass hit me on the head and blood started running down my face and  into my mouth. I dodged off the stage and ran out the back door. This sent the crowd into a frenzy. They started clapping and yelling like baboons. Yelling, "More! More! More!" I slinked back in. Tricky Houdini handed me a drink as I walked by the bar. I got back on stage. Held the drink up. The crowd erupted.

"What are you fucking maniacs? Who does that bullshit? You can't just throw drinks at people. That aint right. Am I wrong?" The crowd was silent. They must have thought it was part of the act. I looked out. There was nothing but smiling faces waiting for me to speak. So I went with it. Not sure what else I should do. I said the first thing that came to my mind.

"Why did the dishwasher walk out of the movie? Because he found the plot dish-believable."

The crowd erupted again. I drank my drink. Dropped it to the ground. Waited for a second, braced for more drinks to be thrown at me. Instead they all got up and clapped. Hooting and hollering. I looked around. Took a bow. Then ran out the back door. Through the crowd. I could hear them clapping all the way to my room. I was confused as hell. I didn't know what to do so I just sat down on the bed and looked at the wall. Trying to process things. What the fuck was going on here? I couldn't even pretend that I knew. I made sure my door was locked and I got into bed. Then I felt a little better, so I got up and pulled the curtains shut. Feeling less exposed, I took my clothes off. Got back into bed. Naked. My head hurt and nothing about this was actually funny. I let the day wash over me like a hot dog floating in a steam table. Neither here nor there. But all around. The plastic sheet making half my body hot, and the blanket absorbing my sweat. I was sighing like crazy. Not looking forward to the thoughts that tomorrow would bring. But there was nothing I could do about that now. Shit seemed really bonkers all the sudden. And all the sudden was all that I had. I kicked and squirmed for as long as it took me to forget about everything. And when everything was done, I was right back to where I started. Being eaten alive by self-doubt.

I didn't sleep much. If I slept at all. The events of the day just rolling around my brain. Like a metal marble inside a Styrofoam cooler. A cooler with the lid on. Loud as shit. Wimpy as hell. The same weak white wall wherever the marble bounced. No new information wherever it went. Nothing to hold it in place. Making dents. Never breaking through. The night was exhausting. The day had been exhausting. My life was exhausting. My eyes were sore. My heart was sore. My body ached with age and years of drunkenness. Every tiny success followed by abject failure. I could have had it good here. The Comedy Smithereens. The racist Motel Mumbo Jumbo. Things could have changed. Given time. The bed bugs could be dealt with, I suppose. The pink eye would eventually go away, I suppose. I was taking squirts of medicine for that. I suppose I wouldn't end up like Pink Eye Randy. Whose condition I was told was genetic. People seemed to be coming around. We could have put an ad in the paper. Get some more talent cruising around. But no. Instead I get some government goons coming around fucking with me because my ex-wife thought it was funny. I suppose I could get over that, they would go away at some point, I suppose. But what was really bugging me was the audience tonight. Throwing drinks at me like I was some trained bear in some tragic Russian circus. My integrity couldn't maintain that sort of abuse. Integrity. I say that like I am a man of wisdom or something. I don't mean it that way. I mean, I didn't think this could last. Nobody can take that kind of abuse for too long. I suppose it would end very poorly. Either those fuckers kill me, or I kill those fuckers. But I don't know. Maybe it was a fluke. Maybe I should give them another chance. I mean, if this was a book it would be like one of those choose your own adventure things. I mean, do I stay here and take more abuse, if so, keep reading. If you think I should gather my shit and get the hell out of town, turn to page 89 or something. But life doesn't work that way. I had to make a choice.

Even making a choice was the same old stupid shit. Coming from the same asshole. I mean my asshole dad. For years when I was a kid I could tell what kind of mood he was in first thing because he would come into the kitchen, I would be sitting there, eating my cereal, or whatever, minding my own business, and he would come in. Say, "Make a choice." If I made a choice or not it didn't really matter. Well, that is not true. If I said nothing he would get so pissed that I would usually end up shitting blood. But the "Choice" he wanted me to make was either my right ear or my left ear. If I said, "Right" he would usually box my left ear, call me an idiot and tell me to eat my stupid cereal because I was a piece of shit. If I said, "Left" he would sometimes box my right ear then say, "What was that?" and if I said, "Left" again, he would either box my left ear and laugh at me, or just ignore me and make himself a drink. But if I said, "Right" after he asked me, "What was that?" there was no telling what he would do. He would ignore me, make himself a drink, or just scream at me about things I couldn't control, or he would stand behind me and bounce my head back and forth until he got bored. So logically I would always say, "Right." But he must have forgotten his rules or something because eventually neither answer was met with any sort of consistency. I never could tell when the rules changed. Which was somehow more stressful than my father boxing my ears at breakfast whenever he woke up angry. I mean, most of the shit he did to me I could see coming. Normally I couldn't prevent it, but I could see it coming. This thing he did still makes me jump whenever someone tells me to make a choice. Which thankfully doesn't come up very much in daily life. I mean, you have to choose things all the time. But those things aren't really a choice. I mean, choosing from the menu at a diner isn't really a choice. It is just a list of foods that you can order. And nobody tells you, "Make a choice" when you are ordering breakfast. There is nothing on the line. Not really. Even driving to the motel wasn't really a choice. The cop on the interstate made that choice for me. The car I drove. The lack of gas. I was just going with the flow.

But that is what was going through my head all night. Bouncing around in my brain. A choice to be made. With no real options on the table. I could stay here and take the abuse. Maybe life would be kind of good? Who knows, make a name for myself? Or I could hit the road. See what is out there. But I knew what was out there. I had been there. It was nothing. But there was nothing here too. Not in the way that I would want there to be something. I don't know. Maybe last night was a fluke. Maybe tonight there would be two people again in the Comedy Smithereens. Drinking by candlelight. Listening to crappy jokes from a hack. Or maybe tonight there would be a million people in there. Getting ripped. Throwing drinks at me because they thought it was a hilarious thing to do. And maybe one of those drinks would pop my eyeball out and I would have to wear an eyepatch or something.

I don't know. I don't know what I was afraid of. I felt like a coward. I could fight back. I could take abuse. I was the product of abuse. But whose abuse? This abuse seemed like self-inflicted abuse. But maybe not. Maybe everything was just fine? Maybe I was being stupid for even doubting it. I mean, what was happening. Because maybe there was nothing happening all along. You can't tell me that anything that was happening had a one to one relationship with reality, because it didn't. It was all just a bunch of random shit. Cloaked in insecurity. I mean, on one hand I had that boner earlier. I don't remember the last boner I had. On the other hand, I launched a load into my pants just because someone brushed their hand against my arm. It is all shame. Everything is shame.

I really don't know. My gut was saying, "Get in your car and get the hell out of this shit show." Everything else was saying, "Stick around, there might be some good stuff brewing here." I mean, I really liked Pink Eye Randy. He and I were simpatico for some reason. And Tricky Houdini was nice, his jokes needed some work, but that is not his fault. He just needed some training. Shandy had some special power over me. Which I didn't mind so much. The government goons would eventually get bored and move on once the paychecks stopped coming in. I really couldn't see a good reason to hit the skids. But my body was telling me to get the hell out of here before shit really hit the fan.

Stay, go. Stay, go. Stay? Go? All night this was bouncing around in my cooler. Loud as shit. Wimpy as hell. I couldn't sleep. The plastic sheet making me sweaty. The blanket making me itchy. I almost took the plastic sheet off and took my chances with the bed bugs, but my logic wouldn't allow me to. Itchy and sweaty seemed better than itchy and double itchy. I didn't know what to do. I was so tired. So exhausted. I just wanted to not think about anything. But the thoughts just kept bouncing around. Around dawn there were some bird noises that seemed nice to listen to. I got up and opened the curtains letting in the last of the night. I was still on the fence, but maybe all the Rum and Sprites were wearing off because I didn't feel like I needed to make a choice at that very second anymore. Which added a third element to my self-doubt, that maybe I was just drunk all night and was being dramatic. The third element tipped me over. That was too many variables. I couldn't take it. I closed my crusty eyes and listened to the birds. Before long reality melded with something else and I finally got a little bit of rest. There were birds bouncing on my body as I drifted off to sleep. I smiled at them in my mind. Thinking of ribbons and little people. Pink Eye Randy being one of them.

I must have been sleep walking because I woke up naked, standing by the door. Someone was knocking on it. I assumed it was Pink Eye Randy so I opened it. It took quite a bit of time for me to process what was happening. I wasn't awake, yet I wasn't asleep. I could see the two government goons staring at my naked body with their mouths agape. I felt like I was a painting that had come to life. Like them looking at me was pulling me into existence. Slowly my brain understood that what I was looking at was these two goons. Like they were a painting themselves that had come to life, and I was pulling them into existence. We ended up meeting somewhere in the middle. I don't know, I suppose I felt really heavy, like waking up from an afternoon nap where you really never fell asleep, but felt refreshed at the same time. Albeit groggy. I just stood there. They just stood there. All three of us looking stupid. I guess I looked stupider than they did because I was naked. But they did look pretty stupid. With their mouths open, and their cheap suits and haircuts. A moment went by. Then the shorter goon broke the hypnosis by saying:

"Mr. B, you got a second?" I don't know why he didn't call me by my birth name, maybe out of respect, or maybe I just heard him wrong, but that doesn't really matter. I frowned. Looked down at my dingaling. Hairy and wimpy. I shrugged. Turned around and walked over to my clothes. Bending over to pick up my pants. Giving them what I could only assume was a direct shot of my dirty butthole. This thought perked me up. I did a little giggle. Taking my time, and really giving them a show. Really letting my cheeks spread. I could feel a soft breeze caress my hairy starfish. When I pulled my pants up and turned around, they were both trying to look at anything else than what I was showing them. I smiled a big banana Laffy Taffy at them. Did my zipper and my button. Put the rest of my clothes on. Sat down on the bed to put my socks on. Then my shoes. At last I spoke:

"Make yourselves comfy." This was a joke. There was no way for them to get comfy aside from sitting on the bed with me, or leaning against the drawers that held the television up, or going into the bathroom and sitting on the toilet. They stood where they had been standing. I had some things I wanted to ask, or say, but I kept them to myself. I wasn't really in the mood for this bullshit. I waited for them to talk. I could tell they were hoping I would talk. To make this exchange less awkward. I didn't give them the luxury. They would have to work for it. They kind of looked back and forth between themselves. Then at me. Then again at each other. Then finally the shorter goon cleared his throat. Thought about his wording.

"Um, I guess we kind of thought you might have some questions for us." I twisted my lips a little. Shrugged my shoulders. I realized I was laying it on a little thick. Even for me. So I went neutral again. "No questions at all?"

"Oh, I have a few questions for sure." I didn't elaborate. They stood there waiting. Waiting. Then they looked at each other. The tall one spoke.

"Such as?"

"Such as, how much is she paying you? How did you find me? What will it take to get you goons to leave me the fuck alone?"

"We're not, what do you mean, I mean, who is, I mean, what do you mean? Nobody is paying us, not like you think at least. We are here to help, Mr. B."

"You don't know shit about what I think, let's be clear about that."

"I didn't mean to suggest," the taller one stepped back a little bit.

"Well, then don't suggest, just tell me what the fuck you want from me so we can be done with this charrod."

"Charrod?"

"Charade, do you need me to spell it out, S-H-A, oh, you know how to spell college boy, I can tell by your suit."

"Oh, I see."

"You see what?" I stood up. They both backed up. I must have looked like I was about to take a swing.

"Hey, man, we just want to have a little pow-wow, help you out, ya know."

"Pow-wow? What is wrong with people around here? Why can't anyone get with the fucking times? I mean, what? You wanna tell me I'm native now? Like you cloned Sitting Bull or some shit?"

"I didn't mean it like that, I swear! That is just something people say, I think."

"Yeah, people say lots of shit, makes it easy to tell who they are."

"We are from the government."

"Yeah, I can tell."

"Now hold on, Mr. B, let's start over. We aren't here to offend you, we just want to help." The shorter goon seemed sincere. I dropped my act for the moment. Wishing I had a drink. Thinking I should start smoking again. Anything to keep these goons at bay. I was trying really hard not to let them in. I really wasn't in the mood for new information.

"Oh, okay, say what you have to say and get the fuck

out. I need some breakfast, and I need to prepare for tonight."

"You're not the least bit curious about what we said before?"

"Which part? The lies, or the other lies?"

"Nobody is lying to you, Mr. B."

"Okay, if you say so. If that is so true, then why do you keep calling me Mr. B when you know my real name?"

"We know your name, but that is not what you go by, right? No reason to be disrespectful, right?"

"Yeah, okay, fair enough, I suppose."

"You really don't trust us."

"Why the fuck should I? My ex pays you money to hunt me down just to fuck with me, and now you want me to be all, Can't we all just get along bullshit?" I said too much. I regretted it the second I said it.

"With all due respect, Mr. B, your ex wife has nothing to do with this."

"Yeah, but you know who she is."

"We know a lot about you. She doesn't really factor in."

"So then, what? You expect me to really believe that I am some lousy lab rat out of a shitty episode of that one television show or some dumb shit?"

"Well, no. I mean, not in that way. Not in the way you put it."

"Then in what way? You just got some tubes somewhere where you make babies and give them the shittiest lives you can imagine, and hope that teaches you something? That is both repugnant and bullshit at the same time. If even half of that is true, I should shove a dirty pool-stick up both of your asses until you spit chalk."

"We are sorry, Mr. B, it wasn't supposed to be this way."

"Oh yeah! What way was it supposed to be? I grow up on a mansion and win the Nobel fucking prize? I really don't think there is anything you could say to me to make me think anything you are telling me is worth shit. No offense, but fuck you."

"You have to believe us. Things got out of hand. We swear. You have been hard to track down. They cut our budget ten years ago, and it wasn't until you got pulled over by that highway patrol a few days ago that we even knew you were still alive."

"Wait, what? What does that mean?"

"Your license plate got put into our search engine."

"Bullshit, I register my car every year. It is the one thing I keep up to date."

"Yeah, sorry, but we don't have access to those files. It is only because you got pulled over. We just got lucky that you didn't make it very far from there. That you still have the same car. And you ended up staying here."

"Fucking hell."

"We have been looking for you for over a decade."

"Oh, okay, but that doesn't change shit. If what you say is true, then what the fuck does it matter how long you have been looking for me?"

"Um, I don't know, we would have told you sooner."

"How the hell does that help?"

"I don't know, Mr. B, but we are here now."

"Yeah, okay. A lot of good it does."

"Yeah."

"Yeah."

"Yeah."

"Listen, I am starving. Can we take this sham on the road? You guys are giving me a headache."

"Anything you want."

"Yeah, right,  anything I want. I should write that down and put it in my set. Let me grab my shit." I made sure I had all my stuff. Keys, and wallet. I went into the bathroom. I really don't know why. I had to shit, but that could wait. I looked in the mirror. My face looked long and flaccid. My eyes were red. I took the pink eye medicine out of my pocket and squirted a couple drops in each eye. I came back out. Said I was ready to go. The shorter Goon said:

"Shouldn't you brush your teeth?"

"Nah, I'm good, thanks." I should have punched him in his smug face for telling me my breath smelled, but whatever, I would let the smells do it for me.

⚊⚬⚊

Instead of taking the yellow Rabbit, we took their cruiser. I got in the back. I made sure I could open the door once I shut it. Which was pretty dumb, I mean, what did that do? Had I gotten inside and the door wouldn't open I would have been fucked either way. But it did open right back up, so that made me feel better. But there was nothing that was stopping them from locking me inside now. Taking me to their rape cave and making sweet murder to me. But whatever. I dug the grave I was lying in. It was up to me to eat the dirt.

The government goons knew exactly where Shandy's was. I assumed they must be staying at a hotel nearby. Otherwise they were commuting every day to come harass me. The hotel must be close enough that they ate a few meals at Shandy's. We parked in the parking lot. The place had people this time. Lots of people. We had to wait for a table. Shandy was sweating. She was the only waitress. I could smell her vagina when she came up to us. She said hello in a forced way. Like she knew who we were, but was not happy to see us. She told us it would be a little wait. They were short on help. I knew, and she knew, and the government goons knew that that was not true. She had no help. Just JayJay in the back. Right after she said this, JayJay came out from the kitchen carrying three plates of food. Looked at Shandy. He was sweating. His sideburns glistening. She yelled, "Table four!" She didn't need to yell, but she was overwhelmed. We stood there for ten minutes. Waiting. Some people left. Then a few more people paid and left. Then some people came in behind us and started waiting. I had no idea what time it was. It was afternoon by the light. I supposed. Not much after noon. Maybe this was the lunch rush? I mean, maybe I was wrong to assume that she was not understaffed, that there was no staff to be under-ed, like maybe this is what lunch was like every day. I felt bad for her. I almost wanted to start bussing tables if that would help. But I didn't. I was stuck with these government goons. Who wanted to tell me something that was so important that they seemed like they were willing to ruin my life because of it.

Part of me was hoping Shandy would come over and tell us to get lost because she was too busy and we would never get any tasty food, which appeared to be lunch at this point. She didn't. She bussed the empty tables. Sat us at a booth. Handed us menus. Ran off. I don't know if I was the only one that could smell her vagina. I was hoping I was. Because these government goons didn't deserve the aroma. But my loins were on fire. I sat on one side of the booth. The two goons on the other. We sat there in silence. The mayhem of the diner making noises all around us. We had menus but nothing else. Just an empty table. I read the lunch menu. I hadn't seen it before. It was interesting. Mostly hamburgers and fries. Plus a Club sandwich. And a Reuben. I got very excited about the Rueben. I bet JayJay made a great Rueben. He seemed like that kind of guy. I bet it came with thick fries and slaw and a pickle. I read the fine print. It did. I looked around wondering who these people were. If they were locals or what. I looked out the window into the parking lot. There was all sorts of different plates. New Hampshire. Mass-holes, New York. I even saw a North Dakota plate. There was Ohio plates intermingled, but most of the plates were out of state. I could see that some of them were looking at me. Smiling. Like they knew who I was. This made me nervous. Paranoid. I tried to ignore it. I looked over at the government goons. They had decided what they wanted and had put their menus down on the table. I pretended to read my menu still. I wasn't in the mood to talk to them. Luckily Shandy showed up with silverware and place mats. Smiled at me. Told us about the specials. Then went back to being overwhelmed. I put my menu down. Looked at the government goons and said:

"What you thinking? The Rueben? I bet it is fantastic here." For some reason this made both the goons pick up their menus again. They must have decided they would order the cheeseburger, but were now having second thoughts. I put my hands down next to my legs. Trying to avoid another blown load in my jeans when Shandy would surely come back. I didn't think I could take it this time. Not with these goons doing an eagle eye on me. I don't think it would turn out so good. They would surely have thoughts.

Shandy was taking forever. For good reason. The place was hopping. I was starting to get nervous. Not because of the government goons, or the people looking at me like they knew who I was, but because I was thinking about the future. About what happens every time I eat at this place. I suppose what happens after I eat at this place. I had dug myself into a hole. Without autonomy, I may just shit my pants when lunch was done. I could already feel it boiling up. Just thinking about the idea that I would be stuck in the back of the government goon's car during an emergency was making the emergency come true. I got up from the table. Said, "Do me a favor, order me the Rueben with fries when Shandy comes back. And some coffee if you don't mind." The government goons looked at me like they understood. I walked to the back where the bathrooms were. As busy as it was there was nobody in the bathroom. I knocked first before I went in. Someone had just been there. I could tell by the stink. I locked the door and held my breath. I sat down on the toilet and emptied my insides. I forgot to check if there was toilet paper. I looked over in the middle of my actions. I got lucky this time. It took quite a few swipes to polish the cheeks. Eventually the shit tickets came back clean. Kind of. Clean enough I suppose. I got sick of wiping. Made sure my lemonade was done dribbling. Stood up. Flushed. Pulled my pants back up. Did the zipper and button. Rinsed my hands in the sink. I tried to wash them, but the soap squirter wasn't working as it should. There was a mound of missed soaps on top of the sink. Just under the squirter. I went to use some of that soap, but decided it was just as gross if not grosser than dirty hands. I wiped my hands on my pants. Unlocked the door. There was somebody standing outside. A middle aged woman who was wearing a cotton dress. I felt bad for her. I shrugged. Not my problem any more. I suppose. I let myself breathe again naturally. I felt like the smells of the bathroom were stuck to the insides of my nostrils. It took the smell of the diner itself to take this feeling away. I walked back to the booth. There was a coffee waiting for me. Steaming. The menus were gone. The two government goons had pops. With straws. I don't know why, but the straws seemed weird to me. I kind of expected them to be people that drank pops with ice, and as they drank the pops, they would chew the ice.

I suppose that was something my dad would do. When he thought he was being nice. Take me and my mom out to the A&W or something. He would say something like, "Order anything you want, it's on me." Like it could be on anyone else. But he didn't mean it. If you tried to order what you wanted he would correct the cashier and order for you. Meaning, a hamburger and regular fries and a small pop. The same order for both me and my mom. Then he would get the same thing he always got. The chicken sandwich with curly fries and a medium pop. Then we would stand there waiting for our order. He would never let us sit down beforehand. And he would never go find a seat himself. We all just stood there awkwardly waiting. Not talking to each other. Then the order would come. My mom would have to get the tray and follow him wherever he decided to sit. We would sit down. He would hand us each our meal. Counting how many napkins there were. Making sure we only got one. Me and my mom. Then he would take one for himself. Fold the rest. Put them in a pocket. Take the lid off of his pop. Take a drink. Get a piece of ice in his mouth. Crunch it. Unwrap his sandwich. Which was the clue that me and my mom were waiting for because it meant that we could start eating too. At this point I would usually eat a fry. My dad would scowl at me. For reasons that were never clear. I don't know if he was hoping I would say grace or something. There was no real telling. My mom would usually just poke at her food, eating slowly. Praying that I didn't say something stupid that would piss my dad off and create a scene in public. And all the while, my dad taking sips of his pop, getting a piece of ice in his mouth, then crunching down on it. Me and my mom always used the straws. Half the time neither of us even finished our drinks because the way my dad drank his pop was so upsetting. He managed to take any enjoyment out of everything. I mean, the hamburgers tasted like rubber and the fries were always cold. I don't know who he thought he was fooling, but it wasn't us. But there was nothing we could do about it. After the meal he would examine what we ate and didn't eat. Then say something like, "You think money grows on trees?" Which forced me and my mom to finish our meals even when we didn't want to. Then he would fold the papers into little squares. All the papers. If you accidentally crumpled your papers up he would make you unfold them and flatten them out. Then he would fold them. Looking at you like you just killed a puppy. Then he would get up. Dump the trash in the garbage. Put the tray on top of the other used trays. Come back to the table. Say, "Well that was a tasty treat." And if we didn't answer fast enough he would say, "What was that?" Which would force us to say, "Yes it was. Thank you!" Then he would smile. Thinking he did a good thing. And me and my mom were allowed to get up, follow him back to the car. Where he would pull a bottle of Vodka from under the driver's seat. Take a swig. Put it back. Adjust the rearview mirror so he could see me in the back of the car. Then say, "What now? The world is our oyster!" Which was totally meaningless because all it meant was that we would drive right back home. My dad making sure he wasn't driving foolishly so he wouldn't get pulled over. Narrating the whole time. "Shit, that look like a cop? Close call." And also keeping an eye on me in the back seat. Getting home. He would go to the kitchen to drink. I would go into my room to draw or be alone. My mom would either sit down on the couch and watch the television, or go and take a nap.

I thought about this while I sat down. The two government goons drinking their pops with straws. The tall one immediately went right back into it. "We just want to help." I poured some room temperature milk into my coffee and took a sip. Feeling tired all of the sudden. Wondering what the fuck my life had come to. My eyes felt hot. Red. My body was itchy. The diner was very busy. I was about to go back out to the cruiser and lay down in the back seat. Take a nap or something. Wait for the government goons to finish lunch. But just then Shandy showed up with three plates of food.

I didn't expect this. My arms were resting on the table. Suddenly I could smell her vagina, and her perfume. The tip of my dick smacked the underside of the table. I could have sworn I heard a ricochet sound. I tried to pull my arms back, but I couldn't get there in time. Shandy put the plates on the table, her hand grazed my arm. I had to hold onto the edge of the table like I might get launched out of the booth. The orgasm went all the way from my toes to the tip of my hair. I tried to hide it. But I didn't do the best job. I let out a weird noise. Both the goons and Shandy looked at me like I had just screamed out something racist. Then Shandy said, "Are you okay?" I adjusted myself in the booth. Pushing my ass towards the back. Cum running down my thigh. I looked out of the side of my eye and said, "No, yeah, I think I just got bit by a spider!" I bounced around a little. Nobody thought to look for the spider. Even me. They knew something was up, but ignored it. There was a brief moment of awkwardness. Then Shandy said, "Okay, you guys okay?" The Science Goons nodded. I nodded too, but I must have looked insane. Shandy said, "I'll bring you some more coffee." Turned around. I could see she was shaking her head. The government goons poked at their food. They got the Ruebens too. With fries. There was a little cup of coleslaw on the plates. Nobody looked me in the eyes. I don't know if they knew I had just shot a load or what, but everything was awkward. I wasn't too sad about this because it meant that we didn't talk to each other. I squirted some ketchup on my plate. Dipped a fry into it. Took a bite. It was good. Really good. I took a bite of my Rueben. Just as I had expected. JayJay made a fantastic Rueben. Crispy and juicy. A perfect combination of meat and cheese and sauerkraut and sauce. I ate the sandwich slowly. Cum dripping down my thigh. The rye bread was top notch. I thought about getting up to go ask JayJay what his recipe was halfway through the sandwich. But then I decided I could wait to see him when he came back to the Comedy Smithereens. I supposed he was pretty busy at the moment. There was still people waiting in line to get in.

Shandy never came back with more coffee. The government goons gobbled up all their lunch. I did too. Including the slaw. There was a pickle on my plate that I didn't eat. The taller goon took it off my plate without asking me first. I found it odd, but didn't say anything. We waited for the check. When it never came, the shorter goon went up to the counter to pay. Me and the taller goon walked out to the Cruiser. I could feel cum running down my leg. Birds were chirping and I could still smell a couple molecules of Shandy's perfume and vagina stuck to my nose hairs. It was a nice day. The taller goon said,

"Nice day, right?" I nodded. The shorter goon came out. Handed the taller goon a toothpick. Didn't offer me one. I assumed he had his reasons. Or maybe he was just being a dick. Which was equally possible. His fellow goon had just taken food off of my plate without asking. If anything, these goons were impolite. It was possible, also, that they were just dicks. We got into the car. I got in the back seat. My guts were feeling wavy. But because I took that shit before there wasn't any real rush. I had some time. We drove out of the parking lot. I assumed they would just head back to the racist Motel Mumbo Jumbo, but instead they took a right. I sighed. I said, under my breath "A car ride, great." The taller goon who was sitting in the passenger side turned around and said:

"What was that?"

"A car ride, great!" I yelled at them. They both recoiled, because I was so loud.

"Relax, man, we just need to talk."

"Yeah, okay, you taking me to the river to put a tiny bullet in my head so I don't spill your dirty little secrets?"

"No, we are not doing that, c'mon man, you are making this way harder than it needs to be."

"What the fuck are you talking about? How hard should this be? You guys are shady as shit. You know that right? Take me back to the motel."

"Well, what do you want from us? You won't talk in your motel room, you won't talk in the diner, I mean, where in the hell will you talk to us at?"

"Oh, I don't know? This place seems pretty good. There's some shade and like a grassy knoll." The shorter goon slammed on the breaks. Pulled the car over. Got out. Opened the back door. Yanked me out of the back seat onto the pavement. I wasn't wearing my seat belt. He pulled me to his face. I could smell the Reuben on his breath. "You don't know shit about what is good for you jokester!" The taller goon got out of the cruiser. He yelled over the car:

"Maurice, relax!" Maurice, let me go. Started pacing next to the car. The taller goon came around to our side of the car. I stood there, pretending to be unfazed. As upset as he was, as violent as he was trying to be, I could tell Maurice was out of breath from yanking me out of the car. He apparently was not used to dealing with guys like me. And by guys like me, I mean guys that don't do exactly what he tells them to do. These goons were very odd. Before, when I had been joking about being worried whether they were about to shoot me to death because they seemed as wimpy as me, now I wasn't so sure. My reuben began vacillating between my bowels and my mouth. "Mr. B, man, don't do this."

"Do what? What am I doing? You guys just showed up here giving me shit  and now it's all my fault?"

"Fuck him, Cor, he in't worth it. Let's just get done with it'n get back." Suddenly Maurice had an accent. Instead of just observing that he had an accent I had to say something.

"Where you from, Maurice, the Bronx or something? No, I know it, hold on, don't tell me, let me guess, it starts with a B, am I right?"

"Cor, I might kill the fucker, let's go!" Cor got involved.

"Maurice, give me a sec. Mr. B, knock it off, please." Maurice walked off towards the grassy knoll I had been championing. He lit a cigarette and kicked a flower that burst into a white cloud. He was kind of beautiful from the back. His anger palpitating. Like a rutting moose. I felt better once he left, but when I turned back to Cor he suddenly had an accent too, it wasn't in his words, but on his face. His face looked like how Maurice looked kicking the flower. Too handsome to take seriously, but too violent to ignore. "Man, just please, I'm begging you, it'll only take a sec."

"What's stopping you, Cor? I got a sec. Maurice gots a sec. We all got a sec. Unload it, man."

"Well, I don't. I can't, let's get back in the car and find

somewhere nice to talk." As he was trying to lure me back into the car a truck came up behind me. I could hear it first, so I moved behind the cruiser to get out of the way. Cor was caught in the middle of the car, so he shut the driver's side door and the door that Maurice had just yanked me out of in order to give the truck room. He pressed his body up against the cruiser. The truck slowed down and honked. The guy had plenty of room. He yelled, "Get out of the road, you dipshits!" It was the same guy that had chastised me for not having any gas instead of helping me with my car. Without thinking I yelled, "Tell it to your mom!" I guess the idea was that his mom was a cow and it was she that was in the road and therefore he should be upset with her instead of us. I wasn't sure if the joke made any sense. It didn't matter, the guy slammed on his brakes and put the truck in park. Soon he was coming around the back of his truck. His own door blocking the way. For some reason I focused on how ironic it was. The guy must have thought Cor had yelled the joke about his mom because he was pointing his finger and yelling, "What the fuck did you say?!" at Cor as he rushed around the back of his truck. Cor met him at the back of his truck and got in his face. "I said your mom was a cow, you redneck prick!" I couldn't believe it. I backed around the other side of the cruiser just as Maurice came barreling over from the grassy knoll. The cigarette between his teeth, smiling. His eyes looked like the black empty sockets of a skinless skull. I couldn't believe it. The redneck turned his head just in time to get socked by Maurice. Cor yelled, "It's on!" The three of them disappeared behind the truck. I still couldn't believe it as I opened the passenger side door of the cruiser and slid into the driver's seat. The car was still running. I put it in drive and gunned it while turning around. Maurice and Cor were stomping on the redneck when I screeched past them. I looked in the rearview mirror. They both stopped kicking the guy and watched me drive away. I stuck my arm out the window and flipped them off. They ran and jumped into the redneck's truck. The redneck stood up and climbed into the bed of the truck as it started moving. I slowed down to watch. I saw the redneck reach in through the open truck slider and grab Cor who was driving, by the neck. I saw Maurice punch at the guy and then I saw the truck go down into the ditch and crash into a tree. I stopped driving. I got out of the cruiser and watched Maurice and Cor spill out of the truck. I saw the redneck dive out of the truck and tackle Maurice. I couldn't believe it. I got back into the cruiser and put it in drive. I did not want to be a witness to whatever it was that was going to happen next. I felt a little bit guilty about it, but fuck them. Fuck all three of them. The redneck was an asshole that deserved to get his ass kicked and Maurice and Cor were obviously lying to me about something that was not good for me. They were not who they said they were, and as my suspicions just became verified, they were very impolite.

I cruised down the road leaving the window open. Catching some nice breezes. Smelling some good smells. Looking at nice looks. I was taking it slow at first, but then the reuben kicked in so I sped it up a little. It was a race against time. I won't lie, the car was a beast. I had to slow down because I wasn't used to driving so fast. The car was a real zesty vroomer. I almost chose to shit my pants in order to keep driving. Thinking I should take her out on the road and open her up. Too many decades of flopping around in a crusty jalopy made the car feel like it was made of thrust-muscle. Not only that, but suddenly I was popping boners again, shooting loads, bringing in crowds, I was having a second puberty all over again. By the time I reached the racist Motel Mumbo Jumbo I changed my mind though. My butthole was grinding its teeth at this point and couldn't be ignored. I was in no position to ignore it.

I pulled the cruiser into the parking lot of the racist Mumbo Jumbo motel. Parked next to the yellow Rabbit. Left the keys in the ignition. Got out. Ran into room number 4. Shut the door behind me. I jumped onto the toilet like a cartoon. Just in time for some hot lava to spray out. Hot lava and a few red hot chunks of burning coal. I grabbed the counter on one side and the bathtub on the other side to steady myself. The lava and coals turned into cheek flaps, which turned into drips. There was a moment of reprieve followed by another attack of lava and coal. After that I felt much better. I was starting to think I should reconsider eating at Shandy's. I did think of a funny joke as I was sitting there. I spent a few minutes letting the lava dribble out while I adjusted the wording of the joke in my head. I wiped until I was sick of wiping. Stood up. Frowned at the toilet bowl. Flushed. Pulled up my pants. Did the zipper and the button on top. Went over to the sink. Rinsed my hands. Looked at my face. My Hitler eyes were quite red. I pulled the bottle of pink eye medicine out of my pocket. Squirted a couple drops in each eye. Smiled my banana Laffy Taffys at the mirror. Put the medicine back in my pocket. Walked out into the room. Stood there staring at the bed. The greasy room. The greasy carpet. What a dump. I opened the curtains to let some light in. The dump doubled down, said I'll raise you and call. I was holding ace high, the dump was holding a royal flush.

I wasn't sure what to do. Should I wait for Maurice and Cor to make their way back? Should I go pick them up? Call the cops? An ambulance? Did they have ambulances around here? Surely the goons beat the redneck pretty good. I felt horrible not caring about it. I should have cared about it. I just didn't care about it. It was like leaving a couple rattlesnakes and a skunk in a box by the side of the road. They didn't have to do what they did, but they did what they did because that was what they did. Their nature. The three of them. Really. It's true that I called the redneck's mom a cow with my stupid joke, but he started it. What kind of a prick doesn't help another human when they are pushing a car because they run out of gas? What kind of jerk slows down and yells, 'Get some gas, you idiot!'? He was just as impolite as Maurice and Cor were. I was a little worried that they were going to kill him though, but that seemed a little outrageous. You can't just kill a guy on the side of the road, right? I sighed and realized I had to go back. There was no world where I could leave any of them where they were. Even if I would have preferred they suffer. My dad was that kind of dick, not me. I reminded myself of that when I walked back outside and got in the cruiser.

I came upon the two goons not far from where I had left them. Walking. They looked miserable and angry and annoyed. Maurice had a black eye and Cor had a bloody nose. I honked and waved and drove past them until I came to the grassy knoll. The redneck's truck was gone, thank god. I pulled over and turned around. I pulled up next to Maurice and Cor on my way back to the racist Motel Mumbo Jumbo. "Where ya heading, boys? Need a lift?" They looked at me like they might kill me. Both of them. I thought about leaving the car in park and running into the field. Thinking they would never chase me. That they were too annoyed to chase me. But then I thought that if they were too annoyed to chase me into the field, they would be too annoyed to do anything else to begin with. Like murder me in the cruiser. Cor got in the front seat and Maurice got in the back seat. As I drove back to the motel I could hear Maurice complaining about things, complaining about me. Talking about just being done with me and getting the hell out of here. Cor kept saying, "Shut up, Mo, shut the fuck up, Mo." Maurice didn't shut up. He kept saying, "Fuck you, Cory, I aint gunna shut up, Cory." I didn't like what Maurice was saying either. I kept an eye on him as I drove. I chimed in, hoping to diffuse the situation.

"Where you from, Maurice? Boston? Baton Rouge? Burlington? Nah, that can't be right? What's that one, Bismarck? I went to Bismark once, what is it? Yuckle's Tavern? You ever been there, Yuckle's Tavern? Who has a name like Yuckle? Am I right? And then he has a tavern? Pretty odd."

"Make him shut up, Cor."

"Please shut up, man."

After that we drove in silence all the way back to the racist Motel Mumbo Jumbo. I parked next to the yellow Rabbit. Put the Cruiser in park. Turned the car off. Left the keys in the ignition. Got out. Maurice got out. Got into the driver's seat. Started the car again. He put the car in reverse. Glared at me. Then gunned it. He turned the car as he did this. Screeched to a halt. Put the car in drive. Then peeled out. Shooting rocks at me and the yellow Rabbit. I waved. Then they were gone.

I went back into room number 4. It smelled like my bathroom adventures. I stood there looking for a second. Maybe a moment. I felt like all the fun times of the day were over, and I was now just waiting for night to come so I could start drinking and do another round on the stage. Maybe two. I needed to get my act in order. There were some new developments that I could incorporate into my routine. The joke from the toilet from before. Whatever it was with the government goons. Maybe even Shandy's sexy arm rubs. I didn't know. The world was my pearl. I stood around looking. Thinking. Adjusting. It all got pretty good. I did enough work that I found myself worn out. It was early afternoon. The perfect time for a nap. I suppose I would have rather had a rum and Sprite, a line of cocaine and ten cigarettes, but a nap would do. No reason to get greedy. I took my shoes off. Pulled the covers back. Got onto the bed, on top of the plastic sheet. Pulled the covers over my clothed body. Thought about how annoyed the government goons looked as they were walking on the side of the road. I suppose I was a sociopath, because this made me laugh a little. I drifted off to sleep.

⸺•⸺

It was dark when I woke up. I sat up. Stared off into the distance. Rubbed my crusty eyes. I had to fish some nuggets out from the corners. The nuggets came back slimy. I blinked. My eyes felt worse. I put my shoes on. Took the medicine from my pocket and squirted a couple drops into each eye. I put the medicine back. Shook off the groggy feeling. Stretched a little. Went into the bathroom. Turned on the light. Splashed some water on my face. Ran my comb under the faucet. Combed my hair straight back. Turned the faucet off. Frowned into the mirror. Turned the light back off. Made sure I was not naked. Which was always a fear of mine. That I would just walk out into the world totally naked. I don't know, but I guess that had something to do with my identity or something. That I would be totally exposed at any moment. That people would find me at my most vulnerable and just laugh at me. And there was nothing I could do about it. That if I didn't keep complete control of my surroundings I would die of embarrassment. It didn't make sense though. Not really. Half the time I was naked and didn't care. And even if I wasn't naked, people would laugh at me anyway. I was a joke. I knew I was a joke. Everyone knew I was a joke, so what was I worried about? But I was worried about it nonetheless.

I left the room. Fully clothed. I checked. I walked over to the back door of the Comedy Smithereens. I went in. The place was on fire. Packed. Both Pink Eye Randy and Tricky Houdini were behind the bar, slinging drinks. My stool was open. I don't know if this was on purpose or an accident, either way I sat down. Took a look at the scene. All the tables were filled. The tinkly music making vibes in the background. People talking loudly. Some of them pointing at me when I showed up. "There he is!" "That's him!" "Bouillon!" Pink Eye Randy put a rum and Sprite down in front of me. I sucked it down pretty fast. Then Tricky Houdini did the same. I drank that one even faster. Then they both put one in front of me. They laughed about it. Because they were both doing the same thing. I drank one of those drinks quickly, then I slowed down. Nursing the other drink.

Things calmed down enough for me to talk to Tricky Houdini for a second. I said:

"Damn! We got some fish tonight, right?"

"Sure do, buddy, we need an opening act STAT!"

"I been meaning to talk to you about that. Put an ad in the paper."

"Yeah, what?"

"An ad! In the paper!" The din was too loud to talk.

"Oh, yeah! Let's talk tomorrow!"

"Come by my room!"

The Comedy Smithereens not only needed more comics, it also needed more help, like the diner. I almost felt bad enough for Tricky Houdini and Pink Eye Randy to get behind the bar, or at the very least, to buss some tables for them, but I had other things on my mind at the moment. I was thinking it was going to be a three set night, if I could read the room right. I took a look around. Searching for Shandy and JayJay. The government goons.

The people I saw at Shandy"s today. Because part of my set depended on context. I noticed a few of the people. The woman that had gone into the bathroom after me. I didn't see Shandy or JayJay. They were probably whooped from such a busy day. The government goons weren't there either. They were probably in their hotel rooms feeling like the jerks that they were. Or in the hotel bar eating jalapeño poppers saying mean things about me.

I motioned for Pink Eye Randy to come over. He said:

"What's up, Mr. B?" He was soberish. I made the mistake of looking him in the eyes. His gummy eyes slowly blinked at me. Snot stretching between his eyelids. I had to look away. Fast.

"Randy, my god! You need to see a doctor."

"I am doing okay, Mr. B, I swear."

"I just. I just worry about you."

"Well, thank you, I am glad to hear that."

"Yeah, okay. Hey listen, I am ready to go on. Get me a drink, easy on the ice, then introduce me, if you don't mind."

"You got it, Mr. B!" He made me a drink. Put it in front of me. Wiped his hands on a slimy towel. Walked around the bar. Went to the stage. Tapped on the microphone. "Lords and peasants, we got a special treat for you tonight, straight from the Rocky Top Mountains, the one and only, Bouillllllllon!"

The crowd cheered. The crinkly music went away. Instead of Pink Eye Randy doing his normal thing of going behind the curtains and throwing up, he went back to tending bar. This threw me off a little. That was the usual schtick. I drink my drink, then throw it at his ass, he farts, and I start my set. Instead I walked onto the stage naked. My biggest fear coming true. I waited for the crowd to calm down. Then I tapped on the microphone:

"Hello," the crowd went wild. Idiots. I took a drink from my drink. I didn't have any place to put it. I looked around. I was about to just bend over and put it on the stage, instead I chugged it. Threw it at the bar. Said, "Here's your glass back, Randy!" The crowd loved it. They threw their drinks too. Pink Eye Randy and Tricky Houdini had to duck down. Otherwise they would have been smacked in their faces with beer bottles and tumblers.

"Give it up for Randy everybody! Normally he gets sick behind the curtains, I throw a drink at him and he farts and that is how my set starts, but I guess he is too good for me now. Thanks for nothing, man." The crowd booed. Someone yelled, "Randy, you think you are sooo cool!" A bottle came out of nowhere and smacked Randy on the head just as he poked it up from behind the bar. "Damn! Don't do that! Randy is good, I swear it! Sorry, Randy!" I could see Tricky Houdini wiping blood from Pink Eye Randy's forehead with a slimy rag. This crowd was awful. I did my best to redirect them.

"Listen, don't throw things at Randy, guys, he is good, throw them at me if you have to." This was a mistake. I had to dive behind the curtains. A bottle hit me on the ass. I farted. The crowd went wild. I waited for a second. Got back up. Annoyed. I didn't understand why the crowd was so rowdy. It was like some sort of abuse release for them or something. We really needed to get some opening acts in here STAT. Because this was untenable. I started my set.

"You guys ever go to Shandy's down the road? The diner. I mean, the food is pretty tasty, but have you ever noticed what happens afterwards? It shouldn't be called Shandy's, it should be called Shandy's Two, Shandy's Revenge." This was the joke I had been thinking about when I was shooting hot lava out my ass after stealing the government goon's cruiser. The crowd ate it up.

"You ever meet Shandy? She owns the place. Don't let her touch your arm though, I mean, unless you want extra mayo on your Turkey-Neck sandwich. I mean, am I right? She serves a juicy plate of creamed jeans. A hot sausage smothered in loin gravy, that is what I mean. I mean, I can barely get out of the diner afterwards because my legs are so shaky.

"And don't get me started about these government goons coming around telling me I come from a petri-dish. What is that all about? I'm science? Look at me, I look like an Orangutan Hitler. Nothing but arms. I should be going out for the swim team. I mean, if I saluted the Swastika I would knock down half of Europe with my long ass arms. I mean, my legs are so short that if I invaded Russia now, I wouldn't get there until the Allies invaded Berlin, and then I would have to turn around and come back. Which would take forever! And I couldn't even blow my brains out because there wouldn't be any guns anymore. That would be embarrassing.

"I don't know, why don't You tell me a joke? Let's do a little improv, what do you say? You, the guy with the hat, set me up." I pointed to the guy with the hat.

"What's up with gas prices!" he yelled.

"I don't know, I heard that they tanked. Anyone else?"

"What about the sun?" Someone else yelled.

"It has its ups and downs."

"What about jerky?" Someone else yelled.

"Let me chew on it for a bit."

This went on for nearly an hour. The crowd was drooling by the end. I was shooting out my best material. They would set me up, I would knock them down. Pink Eye Randy brought me drinks every now and again. In the end I was drunk. He was drunk too. The set ended with both of us singing Auld Lang Syne. Hugging on stage. While the crowd crooned along with us. "Let auld acquaintance be forgot and never brought to mind!"

I said, "Good night!" Pink Eye Randy did a puke. I stumbled out the back door. Tricky Houdini had a tear in his eye as I ran past him at the bar. I puked when I got out into the parking lot. I could hear the crowd cheering. I forced my way to my room. Weaving and stumbling. I got inside and fell down onto the greasy carpet. It took everything I had to pull myself up and get into bed. What a night. I knew I would piss myself, but there was nothing I could do about it now. I wanted to drink some water, but I fell asleep instead.

I woke up on the bed. My pants soaked. My shoes still on. I had a headache. I was thirsty as hell. It was still dark outside. I got out of bed. Kicked my shoes off. Went into the bathroom. Took a drink of water from the faucet with my hands. I took my pants off and left them wadded up on the bathroom floor. I got back into bed. It was slightly damp. The pants had soaked up most of the piss. I was still wearing my socks and my shirt. I tried to get comfortable. The shirt kept riding up my torso. I managed to get it off. Then I felt weird that my feet were covered. I reached down and wriggled out of my socks. The blanket was scratchy on my naked body. The plastic sheet was sticky at some places. I rolled myself into a sleepy burrito. Trying to remember any dreams I was having hoping to trick my brain to shut off. I couldn't think of anything concrete, but the vague memories of feelings within my dreams worked. I fell asleep again.

The next time I woke up it was light out. Mid-morning if I could read the light right. My headache was a dull thrum now. I was thirsty again. I got out of bed. Still wrapped in the blanket. I did a mummy maneuver to the bathroom. Took a drink of water from the faucet. With one hand out, the other hand holding my mummy wrap on my body. I walked back to the bed. Just as I was about to get in there was a knock on the door. I was hoping it was Pink Eye Randy. Maybe I could get him to wash my clothes for me. All my clothes were dirty at this point. And since I only had one pair of pants, having piss in them was not the best thing to have. I opened the door. It wasn't Pink Eye Randy, it was Tricky Houdini. He had a cup of coffee in his hand. Or it looked like a cup of coffee. It was a steaming coffee mug, but because it was dark brown there was no telling what was inside it. Then I smelled coffee. It was indeed a cup of coffee. He handed it to me, walked in the room. I stood there like King Tut blowing on the coffee steam. He sat down on the edge of the bed. I could see that he was smelling something. He was acting like he wasn't, but I could tell he was. I assumed it was piss he was smelling, but it could have been anything really. The room was a greasy dump. Filled with bed bugs and pink eye. I am sure there were spots on the carpet where some drunk tenant had dropped a log and didn't do the best cleaning it up. I suppose I was used to the smells at this point. In fact I am sure I created quite a few of them, but Tricky Houdini seemed a little taken aback by them. There was nothing I could do about it aside from letting some fresh air in. I didn't close the door. I just stood there looking at him. Watching him smell things. After he realized there was no winning the smell war, he spoke:

"Man!"

"What's up?"

"Oh, I don't know, doesn't Randy ever clean these rooms?"

"You got me. Not since I been here."

"Hmmm, well he should."

"Yeah, I suppose."

"Yeah, really."

"Yeah. Uh, I doubt you came here to win the Understatement of the Year Award, what's up?"

"Oh, right! Man, last night was whiz-bang fantastic!

That number you did at the end with Randy, my god, it gave me chills." I smiled. I must have blacked out at the end of the set because I had no idea what he was talking about. "I said to myself, I said, Duncan, don't cry you old softy, Duncan I am begging you." Tricky Houdini's name was Duncan. I wasn't sure if this is how he talked, or if he was just letting me know what his name was. This sort of thing happened to me sometimes. When I would meet someone and never could remember their name, and they tell me a story about themselves and interject their name so as to save me the embarrassment or something. I found it quite annoying. Because people don't really talk like that, and if they thought it was so important that I knew their name, I would think they would have the balls to just tell me outright, but whatever, maybe he actually talked like this. I mean, we never really talked ,Tricky Houdini and me, so it was a possibility. "But nothing doing, man. Here comes the old water works for Duncan-boy. Whatever. The past is the past." His mustache was the same as always. I mean, it must be a trick of the light or something, because I still couldn't tell if he had one or not. I moved towards the windows to try and get him to move his head. See if I could get some sun to shine on his lip for me. He didn't turn his head. He kept talking to me like I was standing by the door. It was very odd.

"Last night was good. Nice crowd. Sorry they threw drinks at you and Randy."

"Oh, whatever, man! A thrown drink is a new drink as far as I am concerned. Just as long as they don't break the booze, ya know?"

"Well, that is a very optimistic way of looking at things. I like the cut of your jib, man."

"Yours too. But hey listen, I'm here for a reason." It was too weird for me to have him talk to me like I was standing by the door when in fact I was standing by the window. I did a mummy maneuver back to where I was standing before. I had finished my coffee. I put the cup on the drawers that held the television in place. Next to the box of toilet paper. He looked at me again. "So what were you saying about maybe putting an ad in the paper? Did you say the weekly, or am I making that up?"

"Oh, I don't know, I say a lot of things. But, yeah. We need other acts. I don't think I can handle the whole night myself anymore. If I could ever handle it. We need openers, and maybe a door guy or something. Some waitstaff. You and Randy can't handle the crowd and run the club at the same time. In my opinion."

"Yeah, okay. I agree. Can you write something up? I can get it to the Eagle later today, I mean, or whenever you get it down."

"You got it, boss."

"You think we should charge at the door, is that what you mean?"

"Well, that and crowd control is what I mean. A crowd of freeloaders like last night? Fuck that. They nearly killed us. And they nearly killed me personally the night before. We need to weed out the riff-raff if this is going to go on."

"Yeah, I agree. How much should we charge?"

"Oh, I don't know, what did you used to do, before the interstate took your crowds away?"

"Um, that was a long time ago. The last I remember it was like two bones to get in. But that was like a long time ago."

"Okay, how about seven doll-hairs?" Tricky Houdini was doing math in his head. He grinned.

"Damn! That woulda pulled a cool 300 just last night alone. You go to business school or something?" He was serious.

"No, I just. I mean, it's just how things work, bud."

"Well, okay. Hey listen, here is your cut from last night." He reached into the back of his pants and pulled out a navy blue Velcro wallet. Pulled the Velcro apart.

I must have been hungover because the sound of the Velcro ripping apart made my ears hurt. He handed me a $100 in 20's. They were wet and smelled like mold. I placed them on top of the television. To dry out. He put the wallet back. "I had to give Randy your room rent. 20 bucks a night. Otherwise it would be more."

"This room costs $20 dollars a night?"

"Well, you got the suite."

"This is the suite?"

"Only the best for my guys."

"Well, since you put it that way." Tricky Houdini looked confused. I don't know what exactly confused him, but I wasn't going to push him to find out. He stood up. Brushed the back of his pants. Smelled his fingers. Frowned. Turned around and looked at the bed.

"You sleep on a plastic sheet?"

"Bed bugs."

"Oh, right. Okay! See you later. Write that thing up! I will get it to the Eagle asap." Then he left. I shut the door behind him. Looked at the money on top of the television. Spread it out to get more sunlight on it. Things were looking up. I stood there like King Tut trying to figure out my pants situation. I thought about taking a couple of the 20's over to Pink Eye Randy and getting him to go into town to buy me some new pants. But I wasn't sure he could drive. Or would be sober enough to drive. And I wore very specific pants. 36 waist and 24 leg. Which were hard to find. Not only that, but I couldn't imagine explaining this to him. It was just too complicated.

I went into the bathroom. I picked up the pants. Smelled them. They smelled like piss. I was hoping they didn't. Because I was so drunk last night there was a chance that I just pissed water, but apparently not. I had no choice but to run a bath. I ran only hot water into the bath. Made sure I took my wallet and the pink eye medicine out. Dropped the pants into the water. Let it run for a few moments. Until the pants were covered in steaming water. I turned the thing off. Let the pants soak. Since I was there, I squirted a couple drops of medicine in both my eyes. Put the lid back on. Took a drink of water. This made my guts jiggle. I sat down on the toilet. Made some noises and smells. Wiped until I was bored with it. Stood up. Looked at the results. Frowned. Flushed. I bent over and swished the pants around a little. Went back into the room to let them finish soaking. I wished that Tricky Houdini had brought me two coffees. I wondered where he got it. I supposed the bar. Now I was thirsty for more coffee, and some food. I went back into the bathroom. Scrubbed the pants with the bar of soap. Rinsed them with some new water. They were large and heavy. My plan was backfiring. What the hell could I do with them now? I tried to wring them out. This didn't work so well. I draped them over the toilet. Let my mummy wraps of a blanket drop to the floor. I thought about this. Picked the blanket up and threw it out of the bathroom. I couldn't think of anything worse than a wet blanket. Well, not at the moment. I got into the tub. Turned the faucet on. I pulled the spout's parasol up. The shower head sprayed me with hot water. I screamed. Nearly fell out of the shower. I was able to adjust the water. But now half of my body was bright red. I closed the shower curtain. Took a shower. Brown water flowed at my feet when I washed my butt. I needed a better diet. That, or I needed to spend more time wiping, because this was too much. I shouldn't be this dirty all the time. I got out of the shower. Leaving the water running. I grabbed my toothbrush. Put some toothpaste on it. Got back in the shower. I brushed my teeth. It hurt. Like biting live wires. I really needed to take better care of my teeth. Or go see the dentist or something. Because this was too much. I spit. The toothpaste was pink with blood. I was falling apart. I rinsed my face. Shut the water off. Got out of the shower. Threw the toothbrush on the counter. Grabbed a towel. I couldn't remember if I put them there, or if maybe Pink Eye Randy had done this. I was losing my mind. My memory was crap. I dried off. Looked down at my pants. Flaccid, heavy and wet on top of the toilet. I frowned and sighed. I had no choice. I put them on, as wet as they were. I zipped the zipper. Buttoned the button on top. Sloshed my way out of the bathroom. Bent down. Picked up the blanket. Threw it on the bed. Found my shirt. Put it on. Found my dirty socks. Put them on. This was hard because my feet were wet from the dripping pants. I put my shoes on. Went back into the bathroom. Put the medicine in my pocket. I held onto my wallet. I went back into the room. I found my car keys. The door key was missing. Whatever. I wasn't sure why I even locked the door. I looked at the money on top of the television. I wanted to leave it. To let it dry out, but I didn't want anyone to take it. So I folded it and put it in my wallet.

It was sunny outside. I stood there hoping the sun would dry my pants off. It was warm outside, but it wasn't hot. I gave up pretty quick on this idea. I got into the yellow Rabbit. Put the keys in the ignition. It started right up. I let out a breath. I backed up. Turned around and headed to Shandy's.

The road was empty. The sights were good looking. My window was down. I smelled good smells. A truck appeared out of nowhere, behind me. The guy revved his engine. Rode my ass for a while. Then peeled off. Passing me. The passenger threw an empty beer can at my car. I could see him laughing. I was about to flip him the bird, but I thought twice about it. There was no reason for trouble. Not since yesterday with the redneck. Not since things were looking up. My legs got cold. I rolled the window up. I turned the heater on. I thought about breakfast. About Shandy. Maybe it was a good thing to have wet pants. I mean, when I blew a load this time nobody could see it. This thought gave me a boner. I was starting to get a fetish brewing. It felt dirty. Like a secret. I didn't know how to stop my mind though. I was caught in some horny loop. On accident. She had awakened something in me I didn't even know was there. I started thinking about what kind of pants she would be wearing. Or dress even. What she would be saying to me when she inevitably touched my arm and sent my loins into overdrive. I was a pervert. I forced myself to stop thinking about it. My dick didn't get the memo though. I could feel the wet fabric rubbing on its head. I nearly pulled over to rub one out. But then, because I was in such a state of perversion, I didn't want to ruin the thing that me and Shandy had. Like it would be a violation of our arrangement. I felt so dirty that I nearly turned around. But I really wanted some eggs and coffee.

The parking lot to Shandy's was empty. I suppose my thinking from yesterday was correct. That they did most of their business during the lunch rush. I parked. Got out of the yellow Rabbit. My pants still soaking wet. I sloshed in. Shandy was behind the counter. I said hello. She smiled at me. I didn't wait for her to seat me. I sat down in the corner booth that I liked. The one that I could keep an eye on my car. I flipped over a coffee cup. I was about to gather all the extra paper place settings and silverware for Shandy, but then, because I was feeling so perverted, I wanted her to have to reach for them. Maybe I could see one of her boobs bend. Or catch a glimpse of her ass while she was bending over. I was really in a state. It needed to stop. But I couldn't stop it. I was in love. Or something close to it.

Shandy came over. Handed me a menu. Poured some coffee in my cup. She reached down and took the paper place mats. One of her boobs did, in fact, bend. I also looked at her ass as she bent over. This was insane. I mean, I had to pretend to be reading the menu to get a glimpse. I shot a nervous glance to the kitchen, thinking I would see JayJay standing there staring at me with a knife in his hand. He wasn't. Shandy stood up and smiled. She said:

"Sorry to miss your set last night, JayJay was under the weather." I thought about JayJay dropping dead. This made me happy. I suppose JayJay was nice enough, but he was with Shandy. Which was turning him into a jerk.

"Well, we missed you too. It was a good one."

"Maybe tonight." This gave me a fluttering feeling. "Whatool you haves?" I want you, Shandy, right now, bent over this table.

"Um, the Juicy Lucy, I guess. Over easy. Bacon. White toast."

"Coming right up!" I watched her walk away. Her ass swinging back and forth. She was wearing a flower dress. Cotton. I didn't even know what to do. I couldn't take it anymore. I poured some milk into my coffee. Forcing myself to look outside. My red rocket was on a countdown mission to be sent to the moon. It hurt. I just wanted it to be over. I drank my coffee. Distracted. I mean, I really sucked it down. I looked up. Shandy looked over at me. From behind the counter. She noticed me finishing my coffee. She came over. Poured me another cup. I don't know what happened next. I mean, I know she said, "That was quick." But she also brushed against my hand as she was pouring the coffee. I must have gone into a seizure because I was suddenly stiff as a board. My body was. I don't remember feeling such an intense amount of pleasure. When it was over she was looking at me, her mouth wide open. About to drop the coffee pot. I reached up as it fell. The glass was hot, but not burning. I put it on the table. She shook herself out of her panic. Said, "Are you okay?"

"Uh, um, I'm sorry, yeah that happens sometimes." I tried to pass it off like I had a condition.

"That is the third time now that you had a, uh, I don't know, a fit. Are you sure you are okay?"

"I'm fine. I swear! I just get overwhelmed is all."

"Well nice job catching the coffee pot, Conseco. That

could have been a disaster."

"Conseco?"

"Yeah, the guy with the baseball."

"Is that something you say around here?

"Oh, I don't know, what do you mean?"

"Well, Shandy?"

"Yes?"

"Oh, nothing, I think I need some extra napkins."

"You're too weird for words, Mr. Bouillon."

A while later Shandy came back with the Juicy Lucy and some extra napkins. She said:

"Everything look alright?"

"Looks great! Hey, you got a pen and some paper I can borrow?"

"Just to borrow? Haha! Here, take this." She handed me her pen and notepad she wrote orders on. She smiled. "I got tons of 'em." She paused for effect, "To loan only."

"Well, I would appreciate it if you added the appreciation to my check." She looked at me confused. My horrible finance joke landing as flat as 0.00% APR. She turned around. I watched her walk away. Her buns swinging in her cotton dress. I would have given anything for a nice breeze to come blowing by at that moment. Just get a little peak.

I put pepper and salt on my eggs. Took a bite. My hangover dipped a notch. I scooped some of the yolk onto a slice of toast. The yolk dripping onto the plate. The sound of the toast crunching drove my hangover right back up a notch. I started writing on the light green Guest Check number 1029:

Needed: Bouncer, Comedians, Bar Back, Bartender, Door Person. Comedy Smithereens. Pay, Normal. Inquire within. Needed ASAP.

Then underneath I wrote:

Duncan, we need to include the Comedy Smithereens phone number and address.

I ripped the paper from the notepad. Folded it. Put it

in my shirt pocket. Which I now realized is where I had put my wallet. I was having a weird day. The vacillating hangover. The wet pants. The hundred bucks. The rocket ship to the moon with Shandy. I suddenly felt very sleepy. I finished my breakfast. Put a few napkins down my pants to soak up the mess. Got up to pay. Taking the pen and notepad with me. I tipped Shandy five dollars after I paid with one of the moldy 20's that Tricky Houdini had given me. I kind of felt bad about passing this 20 off to her. But I assumed she was used to it. I wanted to tell her I loved her, but I didn't. Instead I said:

"Hope to see you tonight!"

"You too, Mr. Bouillon."

I drove back to the racist Motel Mumbo Jumbo. Parked in front of room 4. Got out of the car. Walked over to the Comedy Smithereens back door. It was locked. I walked to the front door. It was locked. I went to the office of the racist Motel Mumbo Jumbo. No sign of Pink Eye Randy. I walked back to the back door of the Comedy Smithereens. Took my notes about the newspaper ad for the Eagle. Slid it under the door. Hopefully Tricky Houdini would see it. If not, I could tell him in person. Later. Maybe write it down on a napkin or something.

I went back to my room. Took my pants off. My legs were suddenly very cold. Because they were damp. I draped the pants over the television. Hoping they would dry out. The come soaked napkins dropped to the floor. Landed on the greasy carpet. What the hell was I doing here? Everything seemed insane. Everything was either really great, or everything was really fucked up. There was no telling. I was tired. I needed a nap. I didn't need to shit my pants like normal from Shandy's. I suppose I was normalizing. Or maybe I had just cleaned myself out at this point.

I got into bed. The afternoon light was warm in the room. I suppose it was just barely after noon. Which counts. I only knew this because I had seen the clock in the yellow Rabbit. And since I had never had the toothpick you need to change that clock, it could easily be nine in the morning or three in the afternoon. Either way I needed to get rid of this hangover. I had a show to do later. I can't just wait around reading clocks. The world doesn't work that way.

The nap worked wonders. My hangover was mostly gone. My pants were dry. The late afternoon light was nice coming in through the window. I put my pants on. Picked up the cum soaked napkins and threw them into the trash in the bathroom. I squirted a couple drops of medicine in both my eyes. They looked like they were doing better. I shook the bottle of pink eye medicine. It was nearly empty. I was hoping that when I ran out my pink eye would be gone. Either that or I would need to go see Pink Eye Randy about a refill. I kind of wanted to go see him. I wondered what he was up to. How he spent his day. If he really got drunk all day, or if it was in his genes as Tricky Houdini had said. I was starting to consider him a buddy. I suppose a buddy that I couldn't look in the eye, but a buddy nonetheless. He seemed very sincere and nice. I felt a pang of nostalgia thinking about him putting me in a headlock that time when I first got the pink eye. Who does that? I suppose people like Pink Eye Randy, but that is what I mean. Aggressively nice. Tough love? Is that what tough love is?

I took a drink of water from the faucet, with my hands. Splashed water on my face. Combed my hair straight back. It was looking as greasy as the carpet in my room. I should wash it at some point. I stared into the mirror.

My Hitler good looks staring back at me. I thought about the government goons. What were they up to? Were they still pissed at me for leaving them stranded on the road fighting the redneck? Why didn't they come to the club last night? Maybe they realized the lousy money my ex was paying them wasn't worth the hassle. Good riddance. I hoped to never see them again. I smiled my banana Laffy Taffys at the mirror. This reminded me to brush my teeth. All those years of smoking and booze really did a number on my teeth. I would go sometimes weeks when it was really bad, when I wouldn't brush my teeth. I would find myself absentmindedly scraping scum off my teeth as I sat in bar after bar getting drunk, chain smoking cigarettes. As gross as this memory was it made me want to smoke a cigarette or ten, to drink a gallon of whiskey, hunt down a guy that has the goods, spend the night doing blow off of some random barfly's dirty ass in a cheap motel room in Florida or something. I looked down at my fingernails. They were looking long. I walked out of the bathroom absentminded. Chewing on my fingernails. Chunks of grit and old food flavors kept showing up. I drifted back into the bathroom. Saw myself in the mirror. Chewing on my fingernails. I frowned. I turned off the light and left the bathroom. I never did brush my teeth.

I paced around the motel room for a while. Leaving tracks in the grease wherever I stepped. Pink Eye Randy really needed to clean this room. It was disgusting. Was this really the best room he had? I was about to go peek into the windows of the other rooms to find out before I thought twice about it. I didn't want to know. I really don't think I could take it. I don't know what I would find out, but the risk was too great. I mean, if I was Siddhartha, I really didn't want to know what was over that wall, if you know what I mean. I was afraid I might just get a Buddha-head the second I peered in. That, or there would be a dead body or something. Or a bird sanctuary. Or a counterfeit prescription drug operation.

Or anything, really. Or most likely, shitty rooms like mine, just worse. Or better.

I thought about Shandy. Her buns swaying in her cotton dress. The .05 seconds of absolute bliss she had brought to my life recently. I couldn't figure out how she had so much power over me. What was her secret? Who was she? Did she feel it too? Was it love at first sight? I suppose it was not love at first sight. In fact I couldn't have cared one way or the other about her when I first met her, but time changes things. I mean, it was three times now that she sent my rocket ship to the moon. Was my body making up for lost time? Did I have a tumor on my brain? This last thought made me nervous. It distracted me. Because things were so good all of the sudden, maybe I was just some vegetable case lying brain dead in a hospital room and this was my version of heaven. It would explain a lot. I couldn't handle this line of reasoning. I could feel a full on panic attack coming. I made sure I had my car keys and wallet and left the motel room. I got into the yellow Rabbit. Started it. Let out a sigh. Put it in reverse. Did a U-turn. Drove out of the parking lot. Not sure where I was going. I suppose I was heading towards Shandy's, but I wasn't going to Shandy's. I just needed some fresh air. Some time to think, or not think. I really just needed to not be in the motel room. It was getting depressing. And I was afraid I would start drinking if I stayed there any longer. I didn't want to get drunk before my set. Well, not drunk yet, if I started drinking now I would bomb. I didn't want to bomb. I cruised down the road. Looking at the sights. Smelling the smells. It was nice. I felt relaxed. I let out a fart. It smelled. This made me think of my dad.

My dad used to always do this thing when we were driving together. If it was just me and him in the car. Me sitting next to him in the front seat. Rain or snow. Winter, Summer, whenever. He would fart. Then instead of letting the fart go out his window, he would roll his window up, then roll my window down, just a crack, so the fart had nowhere else to go but into my nose as it left the car though the cracked window on my side. He thought this was hilarious. If I tried to plug my nose he would punch me in the shoulder so hard that tears would come to my eyes. So every time this happened I would just have to sit there and take it. And his farts were quite nasty. Rotten guts from all those years of drinking. His horrible diet. The smell would get stuck in my nose hairs. I would try and hold my breath. If he could tell he would punch me. Even if he couldn't tell there was nothing I could do about it. The farts would last for minutes at a time. Sometimes the smell would go away, and then, just like that, he would lay another one on me. He would say things like, "Take a whiff, son, of god's green earth, isn't it glorious.?" And if I didn't take a whiff, he would punch me.

This all came to a head when I was 14. He had been on a bender because he had lost another job because of his drinking. He insisted on driving me to this art symposium thing I had to go to after school. My mom tried to stop him from taking me because he was drunk and if he got pulled over he would lose his license permanently because he already had too many DUI's. He wouldn't take no for an answer. We left the house with my mom crying at the kitchen table, wiping blood from her nose. He was silent. Upset. Drunk. He was driving okay. I was trying to explain where we were going. This made him more upset. He said something like, "I know where I am fucking going you retarded faggot." He got lost. Then, when he realized he was lost he tried to make up for it by doing the fart thing, hoping I wouldn't notice. I could see him raising his leg out of the corner of my eye. Braced myself for the stink. Instead what happened was a wet fwap. I looked over quickly. The look in his eyes. Surprise. The smell of shit entered the car. He had shit his pants. He pulled over. Screamed at me to get out. Turned the car around and squealed off back home, I suppose, that is if he could find it. He left me stranded. My bag of art things heavy and useless. I left them there on the side of the road and walked back home. It took me two hours. The car was parked horribly in the driveway. Askew. I looked inside the car. There was a brown stain on the driver's side seat. My dad was waiting for me at the front door. He was drunk and swaying. Wearing fresh pants. He said, "Where is your art shit you little faggot worm? That shit costs money." I didn't say anything. I pushed past him. He tried to swing at me. Then fell to the ground. I was as big as him at this point. I thought about kicking his head, just to find out. I was too tired to do that though. I walked into the house. My mom was watching television. She said, "Hi honey, how did the symposium go?" I ignored her and went straight to my room. Shut the door. Put on a record of some obscure rock band that I had just learned about. Put my headphones on. Laid down on my bed. Closed my eyes. In the morning everything was just the same as usual. Like nothing had happened. My mom made me breakfast. My dad in bed, hungover, I could only assume. I ate breakfast and left for school. He never tried to pull that fart trick on me again.

Yet he did. Every time I farted in my own car I thought about that fucker. About that exact moment in my own history. But who am I? According to the government goons, he wasn't even my real father. What the fuck does that mean? Am I just a bunch of shitty memories that didn't need to happen? I mean, I can't even fart in my own car without it causing me duress? That is pretty fucked up. And to tell me that it has all just some shitty experiment? That is too much to handle. Fuck. That is too stupid. What was I thinking? How did my ex have such a strangle hold on me that she could just fuck with me this way? I was beginning to think I was on the edge of a total meltdown. And there was no way out. I thought about driving the yellow Rabbit into a telephone pole just to end my misery, but I looked down, I was going 40 miles per hour. The best I could hope for was a paper cut. I did the best thing I could do for myself, which was to promise myself to never fart in my car again. But I did this every time I farted in my car. And it always ended the same way. I would forget, and do it again. Then I would have to process all these emotions once again. I didn't need to kill myself, I just needed a better memory so I wouldn't pull this shit on myself again.

When I got to the town, I drove by Shandy's. There were cars in the parking lot. I pulled the yellow Rabbit over. Looked inside. From a distance. I could see Shandy running around. Taking orders. Slinging hash. My heart did a little flutter. What was happening to me? Love was in the air. I laughed at the thought. She looked out of the window at one point. I waved. She couldn't see me. I was too far away. I think. That, or she ignored me. I pulled back onto the road and drove through town.

The town ended. Then it was more fields and trees and birds. I didn't feel like driving anymore so I turned back around. I got back to Shandy's. I didn't stop this time. Maybe Shandy and JayJay would come to the Comedy Smithereens tonight. I would be glad to see them. Maybe they would sit in one of the tables at the front and I could look up Shandy's dress. Maybe see some pubes poking out of her underwear. This thought made me too distracted to drive, so I forced myself to turn on the radio. I poked around until I found a station that came in clear. I was surprised at what I heard. It was Pink Eye Randy. He was talking about the Comedy Smithereens.

"Ladies and Germs! Come on down to Comedy Smithereens! We got booze, tables, yucks, and fun times. Candles even! We got this guy that looks like Hitler! Hitler! Hitler! He lives in the Motel! Motel! Motel! Room number four! Four! Four! He even tells jokes about dishwashers!" The ad cut to me telling a dishwasher joke, "Why was the flamboyant and boring gay dishwasher like a steak? Because he was a flaming yawn!" When did he record that? How? "Whoa! That's deep, Bullion, tell me more! Come on down! Comedy Smithereens! Eens! Eens! Every night, between eight and midnight! Midnight! Midnight! RIght next to Motel Mumbo Jumbo in beautiful Drei-Ecken, Ohio! Be there or be square! Seven dollars at the door. Two drink minimum! Minimum! Minimum! Paid for by the Randy Fund. I'm Randy, and I approve of this message."

I had to pull over. It was a really good ad. There was honking noises and canned claps and canned laughs throughout. The tinkly music underneath. I wasn't so sure he should have used the flaming yawn joke because I was still on the fence if it was homophobic or not. I mean, I didn't think it was, I thought it was more of a satire to the gay community that a guy could be both flamboyant and boring at the same time, and that a steak was named after him, but I could see how it could be interpreted as homophobic. But then again Pink Eye Randy mentioned that I looked like Hitler, so maybe that joke would get lost in the fray. Or who knows? Maybe the locals liked that sort of thing. But then again, I wasn't so happy with the idea of people showing up just because I looked like Hitler, but then again the last two nights the crowd was such assholes that they injured me, Pink Eye Randy, and Tricky Houdini. I mean, who the hell knows. But damn! It was a good ad!

I got excited all of the sudden. I got back on the road and gunned it. Meaning I was going about 42 miles per hour by the time I got back to the racist Motel Mumbo Jumbo. I pulled into the parking lot. Parked in front of room number four. Heard Pink Eye Randy's voice yell, "Room number four! Four! Four!" From the ad. I turned the yellow Rabbit off. Got out. Went into the room. I had some thinking to do. And I needed to do it now. I pulled the curtains shut. Paced around the room. Leaving tracks on the greasy carpet. I didn't have much time. I would need at least two new jokes by eight. Otherwise tonight would be just like last night. I could feel the hairs on my arms stand up. This was serious business. My mind felt alive as Mozart's brain must have. I could swear I could hear Fur Elise playing up there in the empty Styrofoam cooler. The metal ball bouncing on the piano strings of my yuck factory. In the distance a dog barked, I could swear though that it was laughing. "I'm so funny I make dogs laugh." I decided.

I paced and paced. Nothing was coming. I kind of thought up a joke about Dubai that I couldn't get the wording right. That counted for something. I was trying to work in something about my father and the farting incidents, but abuse jokes don't go over so well. Even the ones that are about you yourself. They get you sympathy with the audience, but it never translates into chuckles, instead it makes you look damaged. Like, my dad used to hit me so much when I was a kid I didn't know baby teeth fell out on their own until I read it in a book when I was an adult. Or something. Not so good. But him shitting his pants after being an abusive asshole might work. I would have to think about it. I was looking for something more light hearted though. A dishwasher joke perhaps. Maybe I could combine a dishwasher joke with my Dubai joke. That could count for two jokes I suppose. I don't know. Time was running out. I was starting to get nervous. I had to stop pacing and run into the bathroom and shoot out my brown anxiety. This helped a little. But then the smell drifted into the room and made things worse. I went outside for a walk. Hoping to clear my head. It was starting to get dark. I walked out into the front parking lot of the Comedy Smithereens. This was a big mistake. The place was packed. I went back to my room and paced something fierce.

"Okay, he goes to Dubai, then what? Display case? Dish-play case. Bull in a china shop? C'mon man! focus. What, is he on vacation? How is that possible with a dishwasher's earnings? C'mon man! The logic doesn't need to work in the global sense, you know that! Just focus on internal logic. He goes to Dubai on vacation, okay, nice, then what? He buys a gift for his Canadian girlfriend? Why is she Canadian? Because nobody believes a dishwasher would have a girlfriend? Okay, that is something to work with. He goes on a vacation to Dubai, goes into a china shop to buy his Canadian girlfriend a gift. Then what? He is looking at shit, he picks something up, he drops it. The guy behind the counter gets pissed. The dishwasher says he is sorry. The guy says. Well, shit. I mean, the dishwasher doesn't have money, but he is on vacation. Ugh! Maybe I should try the dad shitting his pants joke, this one is a real Sherlock Holmes."

I kept working on it. Pacing. My stomach was in a knot. I might choke tonight. I just might choke. Oh my god, stop saying that! I slapped my face. I needed a drink. Where was Pink Eye Randy? Maybe I could get him to get me a drink. He was probably bartending. But that could be good. Maybe he could bring me a Sprite and Rum. Easy on the ice. Maybe there was a number I could call? Maybe I should keep that stuff in the room from now on? Well, no, that would be a bad idea. I know how that ends. Not well. See! This is why we need openers. I can't be the only guy up there. If I tank the Comedy Smithereens tanks, and if the Comedy Smithereens tanks we all tank. There was just too much pressure. I paced around a few more times. Said fuck it. Went into the bathroom. Took a gander at my Hitler good looks. Smiled my banana Laffy Taffys at the mirror and made my way to the back door of the Comedy Smithereens.

The place was hopping like I suspected. My stool was open. I looked around the room. Looking for Shandy mostly, but also the government goons. They were nowhere to be seen, but Shandy was sitting in the front. Wearing her cotton flower dress. I felt a pang in my loins. I didn't see JayJay with her. This was both good and bad. Good because I was starting to see JayJay as a threat, but bad because I would probably have to talk to her at some point. I was too nervous for that. I suppose I should have brushed my teeth. I almost went back to my room, but it was too late for that nonsense. I sat down on my stool. Pink Eye Randy came up to me. I tried to avoid his eyes, but accidentally got an eyeful of his snotty eyes. I looked down and blinked really fast. Nothing doing. What I saw was burned into my eyes.

"Whatool you haves, Mr. B?"

"Hi Randy, a rum and Sprite, easy on the ice."

"Coming right up."

I chugged it down. Then I chugged another down. Then I got a third one. I nursed it, kind of. By the fifth one I was feeling better. Giddy almost. I listened to the din. The tinkly music underneath it all. People seemed to be enjoying themselves. None of them seemed to be looking at me like I was some novelty. I suppose a few of them pointed, but it didn't seem hostile. I was starting to think we had broken the abuse spell from these animals. After a while I looked at the door. There was a new guy standing there. Well, not a guy in the dude sort of meaning, but a person that looked like a bouncer that was also taking money and checking ID's. I felt like I had seen her before but I couldn't place it. Most probably I had seen her at Shandy's during the lunch rush or something. This explained the change in the crowd. I mean, give something to someone for free, they will hate you for it. Charge them for it and make them show ID to prove it and they will think they are in love. A tale as old as the hills.

By the time I was ready for my next drink I was also ready to go on stage. I summoned Pink Eye Randy over.

He leaned in a little. I could smell something on him. Not really booze, but more chemical like. Maybe he didn't drink? Maybe he drank window cleaner or something. Something industrial. I said:

"Randy! That ad was spot on! When did you do that? I mean, how did you get the audio?"

"I have skills Mr. B, don't you worry about me."

"Okay, well, you did a great job. Hey, listen. I am ready to go on. Introduce me, then bring me a new drink in about 20 minutes, okay?"

"You got it, Mr. B." Tricky Houdini came over.

"You ready Mr. B?" He yelled so loud that both me and Pink Eye Randy instinctively covered our ears.

"We were just talking about that."

"And?"

"Yes."

"Okay, Randy go introduce him, and then in about 20 minutes bring him another drink." Me and Pink Eye Randy would have looked at each other, to express how annoying it was that he just said what we just said, but I couldn't look at Pink Eye Randy, and Pink Eye Randy didn't seem to be the kind of person that found irony confounding.

"You got it, boss!" Pink Eye Randy said.

He went out and around the back of the bar. Walked on to the stage. Tapped on the microphone. Said:

"Is this thing on?" The crowd cheered. The tinkly music faded. "Hot dogs and Mustards, straight from the bowels of the French Riviera, Boouuuullllionnnnnnn!" The crowd went wild. Pink Eye Randy got down from the stage. I walked up onto the stage. Holding my drink. I put it down on the stage. In a place I wouldn't kick it over. I looked up. There, just like that, I was looking up Shandy's dress. She was sitting open legged. I could see pubic hairs poking out from the sides of her panties. I thought I might pass out. I stood up fast and nearly fainted. I put my arms out. Did a body wiggle. The crowd thought this was part of the act. It wasn't. I thought I might just drop dead at that moment. What the hell? Was that on purpose? I could see Shandy laughing as stars floated around the corners of my eyes. Her knees billowing in and out, in and out. Showing her florid panties and dark black curlys each and every time. It was too much. I bent down. Picked up my drink. Didn't look up Shandy's dress. In fact I looked to the back of the stage. I stood back up. Chugged my drink. Threw it behind myself. The crown cheered again. It was all too easy. I should have just put the microphone to my butt and let one rip. Then dropped the microphone on the stage. Then walked off. They would have eaten it up. That is how stupid people are. But I didn't do that. I instead went into my normal schtick. Dishwasher jokes. Jokes about buying groceries. The joke about fast food. It was all going quite well.

20 minutes went by. I told my chuckles. Catching a glimpse at Shandy's billowing crotch every now and again. I was holding my boner in so fiercely that I thought I might grow an inny. Pink Eye Randy showed up with a new drink. Handed it to me. I said:

"Randy everyone! Give it to Randy" They cheered. He bowed. "Hold on Randy, get up here! I want to ask you something." Pink Eye Randy hesitated. The crowd started chanting, "Randy! Randy! Randy!" He got on the stage. I said, "Okay, this is a new thing, it's called, Let's Ask Randy! When I say, What do you think, you say, Let's Ask Randy! okay?" The crowd cheered. I said, "What do you think?" The crowd yelled, "Let's Ask Randy!" I said, "Okay Randy, what do you think? A watermelon or a football?" Randy thought for a while. Then I held the microphone to his mouth. He said, "A football." I said, "What I meant to ask was, what would you rather have up your butt? A watermelon or a football?" The crowd went wild. I could see up Shandy's dress. She was billowing faster. Her knees moving in and out. Like she was fanning a flame. I said, "What do you think?" The crowd yelled, "Let's ask Randy!" I said, "Okay Randy, what do you think? An ingrown hair, or a boil?" Pink Eye Randy looked confused. I held the microphone to his mouth. He said, "An ingrown hair I guess." I said, "What I meant to ask was, what would you rather chew on an ingrown hair or a boil?" The crowd went wild. I could see something wet flowing out from Shandy's panties. It was either piss, or she just squirted. Pink Eye Randy looked annoyed. I felt kind of bad. I wasn't making fun of him. It was just jokes. I said, "Randy! We just joke here! Everyone give it up for Randy!" The crowd cheered and cheered. I whispered in his ear before he got off the stage, "Thanks man! Bring me another drink in a few." He got off the stage. Still looking annoyed, but focused on the idea of getting me another drink in the future.

I did more of my set. Jokes about being late to work. Jokes about having hangovers. Jokes about angry girlfriends. I did them all. In the end I was very worn out. I was on fire tonight. I was sweating. Shandy's wetness kept me going. Her chair was literally dripping wet by the time I did my last joke. It was the joke I was working on earlier. I was nervous. It was either about to be a great success or a great failure. I sighed a little. Looked down at Shandy's billowing wet thighs. Then said:

"So the dishwasher went to Dubai for vacation. He thought it would be good to bring a nice gift to his Canadian girlfriend. Why she didn't go on the trip is unknown. I mean, Canadian girlfriends, right? Do they even exist? So he goes into a fine china shop. He is looking around. Looking at things. He goes to the dish-play case." The crowd let out a great big HAHA. "He goes to the dish-play case and sees something he likes. He says to the guy behind the case, "Hey guy, let me see that cup, it looks real good." The guy behind the case takes it out. He hands it to the dishwasher. Now the dishwasher has been eating greasy food all day and his hands are covered in oil.

He drops the cup. It falls to the ground. It breaks. The guy behind the counter gets really mad. He says, "You owe me money for that!" The dishwasher doesn't know what to do. He saw the tag before he dropped it. There was no way he could afford it. He says, "I can't afford that." The guy behind the counter says, "Du-break it, Dubai it!"

As the last words left my lips I knew how stupid the joke was. But that didn't matter. The crowd ate it up. Shandy squirted like a fire hose. They all stood up. Screamed. Hooted. I bowed. Left, right, left, right. I said, "Thank you, good night! Tip your bartender!"

I was out of breath. Sweating like crazy. I went to the bar as quickly as I could. To get a drink in before running back to my room. Tricky Houdini had a drink ready for me. He told me I did a great job. I smiled at him and dropped the drink down my throat. As I turned to run out the back door Shandy was standing in front of me. She said, "Hold out your hands." I did as she said. She slapped her wet panties into my open palms. Kissed me on the cheek. Said, "That was some funny shit, joke man." She turned around. Walked out the front door. I stood there stunned. Her wet panties dripping in my hands. I was beside myself. I ran back to my room. There wasn't even a question. I had shot out four loads before I could even understand what was happening. I mean, I knew I was on the bed, and my pants were down, and the wet panties were on my face. But aside from that, the world had disappeared from where I was lying. I suppose it was love. Or something close to it, because I had never felt like this before. I squeezed the panties. Wetness fell down my face like waters. Some of it got into my nose. Some into my mouth. It was salty. I still didn't know if it was piss or squirts, but I did know that spring was in the air.

I woke up with Shandy's panties still on my face. They were just damp now. My pants were down around my ankles. My shoes still on. Come dried all over my stomach. The late morning light driving through the window. I took the panties off of my face. Looked at them. A pang of lust sprang up in my loins. I ignored it. Kind of. Later, I thought. I folded the panties. Put them under my pillow. Stood up. Scratched the come off of my stomach. It flaked like some sort of naughty dandruff leaving a pile of dick crystals on the greasy carpet. I rubbed them in with the tip of my shoe. I pulled my pants up. Buttoned and zipped them. Went to look outside. To see if anyone had seen me in bed like I was. I looked down. There was a copy of the Eagle in front of my door. I guess someone must have seen me. Probably Pink Eye Randy or Tricky Houdini. Those two didn't count. I bent down to pick up the paper. A little fart squeaked out. I stood up. Opening the paper. My insides told me they needed to get out. I went into the bathroom and sat down. I read the cover. Nothing of interest. Then I flipped to the ads. There in big black letters: Needed: Bouncers et cetera. Comedy Smithereens et al. It looked good. I hoped it would work. Last night was good. Really good, but I couldn't keep going like this. It was just too much pressure to perform all alone. I spent the rest of the shit trying to do the Word Scramble. I got caught up on one of the words but I was able to solve the riddle; Why couldn't the student finish his math homework? Because it kept MULTIPLYING. After I solved the riddle I was able to solve that last word. PLYMOUTH. The P and Y were the circle letters. For some reason the only word I could come up with at first was MOUTHPLY. There isn't a word Mouthply. I mean, I did think Ply Mouth at first, but Ply Mouth isn't a word either. Ply is. And Mouth is. I mean, I guess the spelling of Plymouth is what threw me off. I put the Eagle next to the sink. Wiped until I got bored. Stood up. Looked down. Frowned. Flushed. Thought about taking a shower. Thought about going to Shandy's for breakfast. I didn't think I had it in me to see Shandy. I was embarrassed, but also full of feelings. In the end I realized I didn't have much choice. There was slim pickings for food around these parts. And I didn't want to show up looking like I had spent the night covered in come with her panties on my face. That seemed like poor form. I took a shower. Brushed my teeth. Combed my hair. Put on my cleanest dirty socks. My cleanest dirty shirt. My pants were what they were. Until I could solve that issue, I was a come as you are kind of guy.

I made sure I had my wallet and my car keys. Left the room. Got into the yellow Rabbit. Started it. Let out a sigh. Backed it up. Just as I was pulling out Tricky Houdini came running up. He must have been waiting for me. Peeping out behind some blinds somewhere. I cranked the window down. I had my foot on the break. I put the car into park and let off. I said:

"News from the front?" Tricky Houdini looked really confused.

"Huh?"

"You were just running up like, or never mind, give it to me straight doc, I can take it." He looked even more confused.

"Huh?"

"What's up?"

"Oh, did you read the ads?"

"Yeah, looks great. Any fish biting?"

"Huh?"

"Anyone call?"

"Oh, yeah! That's why I came out here. Tons of calls. We got a full line-up tonight. I wasn't able to do interviews so I just had the guys tell me a joke. They were pretty funny. So I guess we will see. I got a few people coming later to test out for the wait stuff. I think our problems might be solved, Mr. B!"

"That's great news, Duncan."

"Yeah it is. You heading out?"

"Nah, I was just making sure the transmission was working." He cocked his head to the side.

"Huh?"

"Yes. I am heading out. Gonna get some grub."

"Oh, good. I won't keep you then."

"Bye, Duncan."

"Bye, Mr. B." He walked away. That was an odd fatuous waste of time. Whatever. It takes all kinds to make a society I guess. I put the yellow Rabbit in drive again and drove off down the road.

The drive into town was nice. The things I saw looked good. The smells smelled good. Until they didn't. They were doing a lot of manure work on the fields. Every now and again I would drive through a cloud of cow shit dust. Which wasn't too unpleasant. I suppose. With regard to certain manures. I mean, in the hierarchy of manure smells, cow shit is on the top. Goat shit and pig shit is at the bottom. Horse and sheep somewhere in between. I suppose.

When I got to Shandy's the place had customers. Not as many as the lunch rush, but more than normal in the late morning. I suppose that doesn't mean too much. Considering that usually I am the only one there in the late morning. I parked the yellow Rabbit. Got out. Went inside. I waited for Shandy to seat me. She was all sorts of cheery. She gave me a nice booth that I could keep an eye on my car, but not too close to other people. Other people that were looking at me like they knew who I was. I guess this is what celebrity is? Going around having people gawk at you like you might break into some song and dance maneuver. I got into the booth. Turned a coffee cup over. Shandy poured coffee into it. Handed me a menu. Took the other place mats and silverware away. She said:

"That was fantastic last night, Bouillon. I pissed my pants from laughing, I mean, you know that. Haha! I can't tell you," Shandy's voice dropped down into a whisper. "when I got home, I was so worked up that me and JayJay went at it like teenagers! Don't tell anyone." My heart sank. I looked up. JayJay's head and sideburns were poking out from the kitchen. He was giving me a thumbs up. Typical. I do all the work and the babe goes home with the goon. I tried to seem pleasant. But I frowned. Shandy didn't notice. She said, "Juicy Lucy?"

"Same ol'."

"Coming right up!" She took my menu. I watched her ass sway back and forth. She was wearing jeans today. Jeans without back pockets. I could see panty lines. I couldn't stay mad at her with an ass like that. I wanted to tell her that I also went home and acted like a teenager. Four times. With her panties dripping into my mouth. But that sounded so very crude, even in my own perverted head. I instead put some milk into my coffee. Stared out the window. Making sure nobody was breaking into my car.

I couldn't figure Shandy out. Did she know she was fucking with me? I mean, I know she knows about giving me her panties. She alluded to it just now. Did she think I would just take her panties and what? Do what with them? Hang them on the wall? Frame them? With a caption like, "Squirts for Yucks." Who knows. Maybe she and JayJay were into some weird swinging thing. That is the kind of thing that happens in small towns like this. Maybe she would invite me to a key party or something? I mean, things get freaky sometimes. But I didn't want that. I didn't care about that shit. I just wanted Shandy. All to myself. And this was just dashing my hopes.

She brought me the Juicy Lucy. I was afraid she might touch my arm again. Send me to the moon. Or not. Maybe last night took the rocket out of me. She didn't touch me, she just put the plate down. Refilled my coffee cup. Smiled and walked away.

I tore into my breakfast. I suppose I was hungry. I was finishing when I looked out into the parking lot. The government goons cruiser was pulling in. I sighed. They parked next to the yellow Rabbit. Got out. Took some pictures. They had a third goon with them this time. Not as tall as the tall one and not as short as the short one. She was somewhere in the middle. She had a pony tail. Darker skin. She looked just as dorky as the other two, but female. I waited for them to come in. They took forever. Talking in the parking lot. Making gestures. Pointing to the yellow Rabbit. They were all carrying clip boards. Writing things down. I was annoyed just watching them. I couldn't imagine what they would say to me. I didn't want to hear it. Shandy came back. Took my plate, refilled my coffee. She said:

"You okay, Mr. B? You look annoyed."

"Those fucking goons are back and they brought an extra."

"Yeah, they have been poking around. I keep meaning to come talk to you about it. They ask a lot of questions." I looked up at her. Kind of irritated with her now.

"What do you mean?"

"I don't know, they just come around, ask useless junk and then skid."

"What kind of useless stuff?"

"Like, what do you do? What do you eat? Do you pay

with cash? Dumb shit like that."

"Shandy! My lady, I wish you would have come to me with this information."

"Yeah, I know Mr. B, but since you started coming around this place has been a mad house. I can barely get a moment to piss, let alone give you reports on weird goons poking around. I hope you don't hate me."

"I don't hate you, baby. It's kind of the opposite. It's just a rough world out here, we need all the help we can get."

"Well, if it is any help, last night I thought about you when me and JayJay were going for round four. Well not you in the real sense of the word, but more like your jokes. It was kind of the best, um, release I had had in a very long time." She smiled down at me. Touched my arm. I went into a fissure. My bottom teeth poking out of my mouth. My left leg going stiff as a board. "Mr. B! Are you okay" I came back to my senses. Out of breath. Embarrassed.

"Whoa. Yeah, no, I am okay."

"Don't scare me like that!"

"The feeling is mutual."

"Seriously, Mr. B, that was scary. I think you should see a doctor."

"It's not a doctor I need, babe, I need a shrink and a bottle of the brown stuff."

"Maple syrup?"

"Close enough."

"You sure you're okay?"

"I am just fine, I couldn't be better." The cum was dripping down my leg. Shandy looked worried but took me at my word and walked away. I took my used napkin and shoved it into my pants. How the hell do you deal with something like that? I needed to start wearing a coat into this place. Or maybe a cardboard box. Keep my feelings to myself. Give my ding-dong a break. My ass was hurting since I had come so much in the last little while. Maybe I did need to see a doctor. Can a prostate explode from too much use? I was afraid I might just cum my heart out of my dick hole if I kept this up.

The government goons came in. All three of them. They stood next to my booth. Clipboards in hand. I motioned to them to sit down. All three of them got into the one side of the booth. The tallest by the window. The middle one in the middle. The shortest one on the edge. I could see Maurice was halfway on and halfway off of the booth. Splitting his butt. I could have easily gotten up and offered him a seat on my side, but I wasn't in the mood. These cockhorses needed to take it on the arches. Yet they just buzzed around like suspicious mosquitoes.

We didn't talk. Shandy brought them menus. They all ordered coffee. Nothing else. Shandy looked at me like maybe there was something she could do to help. I shook my head. She took their menus and walked away. None of them drank from the coffee cups they turned over. My guess was that all three of them had to pee. But for some reason they didn't go to the bathroom. They were on a mission of some sort. Like it was a point of pride or something. I just stared at them. Feeling nervous for them. I couldn't tell why they didn't just talk to me. Like they wanted me to talk first. Like I had the questions on my mind that they wanted to answer. I grew more annoyed than I already was. I said:

"Just fucking pee, you idiots!" All three of them got out of the booth and went to the bathroom. It was almost as bad as with Tricky Houdini. Are fatuous maniacs just running around these days? They left so quickly their clipboards stayed behind. I took the middle one and turned it around. It was some weird checklist of my comings and goings. My daily routine. When I woke up. What I ate. How fast I drove. With things written down in the margins. Like, Subject scratches ejaculate off stomach with fingernails. Shit like that. My full name on the top of the paper. My license plate number. My date of birth. A description of what I looked like in bold font. Long arms, short legs looks like a worn-out Hitler. Bright yellow teeth. It was all just an abuse of my privacy. They all three came back. Stood at the edge of the table. Looking sheepish.

I was feeling a little baffled. The last time I saw Maurice and Cor they seemed like they could possibly kill me. That underneath their goofy outward appearance there was something sinister underneath. Now they were right back to being complete doofs. Was the tough guy stuff an act or was this an act? I mean, they didn't kill the local, not that I know of. But I am certain they beat him up pretty good. I didn't ask the questions I had on my mind.

"Look, sit down. You obviously have something to tell me." I turned the clipboard around and put it back where I found it. The three government goons slid into the booth. The short one with half his ass hanging off. I thought about his butthole getting rubbed by the edge of the Naugahyde. The wire edge that holds the booth together rubbing the turds off. Transferring the shit to his tighty-whities which I am sure he was wearing. I bet it felt pretty good. Actually. There is nothing like a good asshole scratch after a long day of doing god knows what. I said, "Sock it to me, I am all ears."

"Mr. Bouillon, I know you don't want to hear this, but we have been watching you for a while now. It is our job. We just want you to know that." This was the taller one speaking.

"I can see that. What's the point?"

"We just need you to come with us, we need to do some lab tests, then you are free to go."

"And why do you think that is something I would want to do?"

"Well, science I guess."

"And I will get something out of this?"

"See! I told you he would say that! Didn't I?" The middle one seemed elated that she had called it.

"Rona, not now." Rona looked embarrassed. She didn't mean to speak so quickly. I suppose.

"Sorry, sir." This meant that Cor was the guy in charge. Which I found annoying. Typical. Three government goons giving me the grief, and the tall white one was in charge. Things never change.

"Look, Mr. Bouillon, what you are is important to us. We just need some time with you, and then we will leave you alone." I wasn't buying it. They would never leave me alone. I was still convinced that Lizard had sent these jerks to fuck with me. I knew they were blowing smoke up my ass.

"What do you think, Rona? You think I can only operate when there is something on the line? A tit for tat sort of thing? What do they call that, transactional?"

"Well, if you are a sociopath."

"And, am I?"

"Rona!" Cor couldn't stop her.

"Maybe. You're not not a sociopath."

"Okay, fair enough. I mean, what is it? I like runny eggs? Scratch dry ejaculate from my stomach with my fingernails? Get up around noon? What is the big wow that makes me such a horrible asshole? Because I drive a dying car? My hair is greasy? I only wear one pair of pants? I'm out on a limb here."

"Yeah, I don't know."

"Rona stop! I order you."

"Dude, let her talk." I said. Rona turned her head towards Cor. He bit his teeth. I grinned.

"Well, your jokes are pretty dumb, I watched your set last night, I didn't understand why people liked it."

"And?"

"You went back to your room with the waitress's panties and masturbated a bunch."

"And?"

"I don't know, you seem pretty self-absorbed. You left these guys stranded on the side of the road. That was kind of mean."

"And I eat my eggs runny, and I drive an old car? What else? I picked my nose one time? You guys are idiots. I don't..."

"Look at these." Maurice showed me a couple pictures of myself. When I was very young. A child. One of them I was smiling and holding up a yellow metal dump truck. The other one I was showing off a missing tooth. Which when I looked at it it just reminded me of my dad punching me.

"Okay, thanks for the memories."

"Who took those photos?" Cor asked.

"Does it matter?"

"It wasn't your parents."

"So? And how does that matter, and what makes that true? Those are just pictures of me being a kid."

"The government took those photos. When your dad was passed out and your mom was watching television. This proves it."

"Proves what? That people can take photographs?"

"Don't you remember people coming to talk to you when you were in the backyard?"

"I remember being alone a lot."

"You don't remember strangers coming to the fence and luring you over with candy?"

"Are you fucking kidding me! Your proof that I am some sort of science marvel is that there was a ragtag group of pedophiles lurking around in the backyard while my mom watched television and my dad was passed out drunk? Yeah, okay. This is bullshit. You guys have lost me. I am out of here."

I got up and gave Shandy a $20 as I walked out the door.

"Don't serve those jackasses anymore. They suck."

"Yeah, I can't do that, but I can spit in their eggs if you want."

"Oh, it doesn't matter. Fart on their pie."

"I'll try."

"Shandy, you are one of the good ones. Hope to see you tonight."

"Not tonight, I am a little sore from the romps. Plus my gut hurts from all the laughing. Maybe tomorrow."

"I understand."

"I will bring some fresh panties next time. Haha!" Shandy! What the hell was she thinking?

"Don't sneeze under water." I said.

"Why not?"

"It hurts like hell."

I left the diner. The thought of Shandy putting on fresh panties just to come to my show was a little much. Who the hell did she think she was? The napkin in my pants fell down to my socks. I shifted my leg and let it fall out onto the pavement of the parking lot. The government goons were a farce. I could see them looking at me as I walked to the yellow Rabbit. I took out my key, scratched it on their cruiser. They looked amazed. I flipped them the bird. "Write that down in your logs, fuckers." I said this out loud. Maurice moved to my side of the booth. They looked like they were going to order lunch. I got into the yellow Rabbit. Started it. Then sighed.

The ride back to the racist Motel Mumbo Jumbo was equal parts farm smells and anxiety. For all my bravado the government goons got on my nerves. I couldn't see the outcome they were looking for. I suppose if they were just fucking me, trying to get me rattled on my ex's account, it was working to some degree. I had no idea how to get rid of them. I also had no idea what their next move would be. Were they just going to lurk around until I folded? Did what they wanted? Even that wasn't clear. What they wanted. A chit-chat and a mindfuck for their own amusement? Maybe they needed me to have a break-down before they gave up. Maybe I was getting too close to the truth. And they were just running interference so I would get distracted from my main goal. But I had no main goal. I was not looking for the truth. I could care less what they were up to. What anyone was up to. All I wanted was some food every now and again. Some yucks. Some drinks. Maybe a nice place to sleep at night. A car that didn't make me sigh whenever I started it. Maybe a hand job from Shandy. I mean, I was well past the middle of life in the grand scheme of things. I ached. Had the shits all the time. Drank too much. Slept like shit. My teeth were yellow. My face looked like someone painted it on a leather mitt and used it to catch baseballs for decades. I was neither handsome, nor charming. I had a few good jokes I could spit out at any given moment, but I wasn't no Gilbert Godfrey. Nobody was going to put me on the television any time soon. I suppose I really didn't get it. What was the appeal?

I chewed on these thoughts for a while. Not getting very far. All that happened, really, is that I made myself feel like shit. Like a loser who got lucky a few times in my life. And now I was sleeping on bed bugs with pink eye, living in a racist motel, and telling second rate jokes to jerks who had no clue what was truly funny. I mean, I did make Shandy piss herself, or squirt herself, or whatever. That made me proud. But the rest of them? With their bawdy laughs and hollow claps. Throwing drinks at me and Pink Eye Randy and Tricky Houdini. Drunk riff-raff, that is all they were. But whatever. They were paying my bills, so that was something. And they did seem to be multiplying. Maybe the Word Scramble had a point. It wasn't math homework I was doing though, it was something else entirely. What is the opposite of math? Philosophy? Why didn't the student finish his philosophy homework? Because he Kant. Whatever it was, that is what I was doing, and it seemed to be working for me. At least right now.

I pulled into the parking lot of the racist Motel Mumbo Jumbo. I really needed to talk to Pink Eye Randy about changing the name. For his own sake. For his business's sake. Just as I was thinking this I looked around. The parking lot was full. Every room had a car in front of it. I pulled in front of Room four, parked and got out. I walked into the Office. Pink Eye Randy was checking someone in. He said:

"Okay Mr. Chaos, here is your room key. Room number seven. I hope you have a nice stay." Mr. Chaos said thanks and wheeled his luggage past me and out the door. I watched Pink Eye Randy write something down. I said:

"Hi Randy, busy day?"

"You know it, Mr. B! We got a full boat." I was doing my best to not look him in the eyes.

"Mr. Chaos, that sounds phony."

"Oh, no, not really, his full name is The Harbinger of Chaos. He is performing tonight. I think he does Egypt jokes."

"No shit! Well great. Hey! I need more eye stuff, you got some?"

"Of course, Mr. B, I have a whole cabinet full of them. Have as many as you want."

"Yeah, okay. Give me two, just in case." I sighed. Thought of having pink eye for two more bottles of medicine was beyond depressing. But it is better to have it and not need it, they say. When he handed me the bottles my eyes suddenly felt itchy and red. They burned. I suppose it was all in my head, which would be a good thing. But then I caught a quick corner of Pink Eye Randy's right eye, a snotty stream of gunk flapping in some breeze I hadn't noticed. I looked away fast. But the image stayed. I made sure I held the bottles in just the one hand and didn't touch anything. I said, "Thanks, Randy, I'll see you tonight."

"You got it, Mr. B!"

The walk back to my room was quick. I could see Mr. Chaos getting something from his car. I was about to go talk to him, but I could feel the bottles of medicine sinking into my skin. Pink Eye Randy's dirty mitts snaking their disease into my bloodstream. I went into my room and washed the bottles. I put them on the counter next to the sink. I washed my hands. I took the nearly empty bottle of medicine out of my pocket and squirted a few drops in both my eyes. Put the lid back on. Shook the bottle. Pretty low. I was glad that there was new meat for the stage. The pressure seemed to drop a little. Then I realized I was an idiot. I had a good thing going. Just me on the stage. No competition. No time slot. No egos to contend with. I realized that just having a bouncer at the front door had solved all of my problems. I mean, people just needed order. We gave them order by charging them money at the door and having a body ready to knock heads if any trouble started. I wished I would have thought of that. Now I had to wait for other jerks to do their two bit bullshit. Then what? I go on at nine? Ten? All this meant was more time waiting around to drink. More time thinking about how shitty my material was and how I needed new jokes. What a moron I was. God-damn-it! Why couldn't I just leave well enough shit alone sometimes. I always had to have the easy thing. The thing that everyone else wanted. Why do I do this to myself?

Of course it was my dad's fault. The way he treated my mom. The millions of times I chose to behave a certain way to get him to leave her alone. I mean, I am no hero, that man was brutal. But there were some times when I could act like enough of a jackass that he would stop beating her and come after me instead. I mean, I can't even say that I was acting on her best interest. Quite the opposite. It was easier to take a beating than to watch her take one. She was brittle and she screamed a lot. Usually after he beat her there would be hours and hours and hours of me wanting to help her and my father saying, "You help her, I will beat the brains out that stupid little head of yours." He would sit there watching her bleed. Chugging vodka by the glass. Saying shit like, "You did this to yourself. You know that, I hope you know that." And then he would wait for her to speak. If she didn't he would either throw something at her, or get up and spit on her. Then when she finally said the golden words, "Yeah, I know." He would say, "Good, so we agree." Then I would have to wait hours until he got so drunk he passed out in his chair. Then I would help her up and help her get into bed. I couldn't wash the blood off because if I did this he would notice when he woke up from his stupor. In the morning it was a different story because he wouldn't remember, but by then my mom would have washed the blood off herself. Put on heavy makeup to cover the bruises. And my dad would come into the kitchen and do his, "Left or right?" comedy routine.

When I was very young I could distract him when he was beating her because I was a smaller target. I could say something stupid that I knew would annoy him and he would give up on her and I could run away and he would chase me and beat me there. Forgetting what he was doing before. But as I got older and bigger I became as much work to beat as my mom was. And then it stopped working because I became more work to beat than my mom was. At that point there was nothing I could say or do that would distract him. Short of killing him or something. But I was way too afraid of the man to even think of doing something like that.

I mean, maybe I am wrong. Maybe my inability to do things in my own self interest comes from somewhere else. But the idea of doing the wrong thing for my own benefit was something I found impossible to factor in. Maybe I wasn't a sociopath as the government goons had said. Maybe I really did just want to help my mom out. At a certain point the beatings I received seemed like my dad was phoning them in. He was a small man. Flaccid from drink. His anger seemed to be merely his nerves hot-bright with frustration and alcohol. But my mom was aging as he was aging, I mean, as they got weaker, I got stronger. But so what? A beating still sucks. I don't know. I don't even know. Maybe I am conflating two things. Maybe my inability to make good decisions for my own benefit just comes from the cowardice of the human condition. Maybe the opposite of math really is philosophy? Maybe it was a really good thing that there was fresh meat for the stage. And maybe I could find it in my heart to relax and have a few yucks of my own before getting on stage. I mean, I was the top dog here. Nobody was going to take that from me. I guess. The Harbinger of

Chaos doing Egypt jokes, though? That might be a hard act to follow.

———

I took an afternoon nap. I could feel a fire under my pillow. I dreamed Shandy's panties came alive and grew into a monster that ate me whole. My head was sleeping in a campfire at first. Then the fire turned to her panties. Then the fire of her panties grew bigger. Grew teeth. Then they started to eat me like a python. Then when they reached my loins, they bit down and warm ooze spurted out. I woke up with pants full of cum. This was really getting out of hand. I needed new pants asap. Or at least some underwear. I thought about getting in touch with Pink Eye Randy. To get him to go find me some underwear. I mean, there was no way for him to find the pants I needed, but I wore regular underwear. I suppose though that I didn't need underwear, not really, what I needed was diapers. I was starting to think I should see a doctor. The amount of loads I was shooting. Maybe I was going through menopause? A second puberty. This was really something absurd. I couldn't chalk it up to love anymore. Shandy didn't love me, I found that out today at the diner. But she might be sexually attracted to me. And I didn't have any special feelings about Shandy, just feelings I haven't felt in forever, if ever. Maybe it was all just build-up from so many years of feeling nothing? Is that a thing? Can you feel nothing for years and years and years and then suddenly you are overwhelmed with deferred emotions? I suppose that happens all the time. Oldsters tend to get real sentimental at the end of their lives. Maybe that is what was happening? Maybe I was dying and shooting all my life-long pent-up feelings about life out the tip of my wimpy worm? Like my anguish was milking my prostate.

It was all very confusing. And annoying. My pants were ruined at this point. I had no way to get around it. I just had to own it. I was gross and uncomfortable, with pink eye and bed bugs, and a hair-trigger worm. Whatever. My only real gripe was the smell. Did I stink like cum all the time now? Or piss? Or I don't know, pink eye? Does pink eye smell? Have I noticed Pink Eye Randy stinking up the joint? I mean, he did smell like industrial cleaner last night. Is that what I smelled like? I suppose it wasn't the worst smell. It was kind of pleasant, actually, if you have to smell like something. It is better than farts or a manure truck. There was no way to assess this problem. I couldn't smell myself.

I paced around the room. Trying to think of when to go into the bar. It was late enough and I was getting curious. I couldn't take it anymore. I told myself I would just nurse a couple of drinks and watch the new talent. See what I was up against. I went into the bathroom. Combed my hair straight back. Admired my Hitler good looks. Smiled my banana Laffy Taffys into the mirror. Looked down at my crotch. There was stains that could only be interpreted one way. I sighed. What can you do? I was thankful it was going to be dark in the bar. I just hoped nobody would notice. I left my room. Walked into the back door of the Comedy Smithereens. I heard the comedian on stage say:

"And then I said, What? do you have like a cow in your pants, because I can really smell your dairy-air."

The crowd chuckled and yucked. There were a few claps. The place wasn't full up yet. It was early. I could see the bouncer at the door letting people in, taking money, checking ID's. She seemed good at the job. The government goons were sitting at a table in the back. With their clipboards. All three of them on one side of the booth they were sitting at. Drinking drinks that I could only assume didn't have booze. They waved at me. I waved back. I thought about going out to the parking lot to let the air out of all four of their cruiser's tires, but I didn't. Not because I thought it would be a shitty thing to do, but because I wanted a drink and I wanted to hear the jokes coming from the stage. I could do it later just as easy.

My stool was empty. I sat down. There was a new bartender. Some guy with long greasy hair. He had about a pound of dandruff flakes on the top of his head. A part down the middle of his greasy black hair. He had pimples and greasy wires growing out of his face making a very perverted goatee that looked like it was melting down to the tip of his chin. He looked too young to be bartending. I tried not to look at the dandruff. I don't know what is worse, an eyeful of Pink Eye Randy's snotty eyes, or the thought of a glassful of dandruff flakes? I thought I should ask Pink Eye Randy this question during the "Let's Ask Randy!" section of my set. That was a bad idea though. It would only confuse the poor guy. He was too pure for such things.

The new bartender was quick and attentive. I didn't like how the top of his head looked, or his slimy goatee, but his service was impeccable.

"Oh, you're Mr. B!"

"Oh, yeah?"

"I can tell by the, uh, I've been saving your stool for ya, I even wiped it down earlier! Clean as a whistle!" He tried to hide the first thing he said. I didn't let it go.

"Tell by what? How handsome I am?"

"Well, I mean. Seig Heil?" He looked like he was about to do a Nazi salute. I stared at him and slowly shook my head. Even in the darkness of the club I could see his face turn red. Which didn't mean anything. Whether he was embarrassed because he thought I looked like Hitler or whether he was embarrassed because he was socially awkward was beside the point. The question was whether he took the job specifically because I looked like Hitler. And if that was true, why? "Whatool haves? Oh! Hold on, Duncan told me!" The dandruff soaked Hitler Youth tried to remember the drink Tricky Houdini told him I drank. He couldn't remember.

"Rum and Sprite, easy on the ice."

"Fuck, right! I knew it was weird, I mean, uh, unique. Coming right up, sir!"

He made my drink. I watched dandruff flakes bounce around on top of his head. Some of them falling into the glass. There was no end to my troubles at the Comedy Smithereens. It really was something that someone can make Pink Eye Randy look like a clean and preferable bartender. The dandruff soaked Nazi Youth put the drink in front of me. On top of a square napkin. I took a drink. The edge of the glass tasted salty. I spit a dandruff flake off the tip of my tongue. I held the glass up, "To the Fatherland." Once again the youth was about to salute. I glared at him. He scooted off to help someone else.

The comedian on stage was finishing her set. I could tell by the way she worded her joke. It had something to do with a roommate and having a lover over. I got distracted by her moves. She kept stabbing at the audience like she was giving really aggressive hand shakes at some politics convention or something. She looked like she was funny. I managed to catch the last line, the big finisher:

"I mean, it's one thing to hang a sock on the door to let me know you are bangin', but to walk around the apartment with a sock on your dick and balls all the way to the bathroom and back? What is this, the 90's? Am I right? You know I'm right. Thank you, good night! I am Ruth Gator-Bait Ginsburg! I'll be here all week! Check it, ya'll!"

The crowd clapped. They seemed to like it. The lights on the stage went down. The tinkly music came up. People speaking. The sound of ice hitting glass. The usual din. I sat there nursing my salty rum and Sprite, easy on the ice. Lipping dandruff off the tip of my tongue. I was wondering what would come next. How to stay sober until I got on stage. Wondering where Pink Eye Randy and Tricky Houdini were. What Shandy was up to. About her exhausted vagina and JayJay's lousy sideburns. They were probably watching television and taking it easy. Sitting on a couch, snuggling. I wasn't jealous of JayJay, but if I had a sweet piece of tail like Shandy at home, I don't think I would be here either. I thought about him giving me a thumbs up today from the kitchen. Smiling. It felt like sneezing underwater. I knew better than to think of him and his personal life with Shandy, yet here I was, thinking about JayJay and his personal life with Shandy.

I nursed another drink waiting for the next act. I was wondering what time it was. When I was supposed to go on. The suspense was killing me. I was tapping the brakes, but my engine was yanking my body forward. Ruth Gator Bait Ginsburg took a stool next to me. Ordered a gin and tonic from the dandruff soaked Nazi Youth. She said, "Damn! Finally a cold one to whet my whistle." She took a drink. Then let out a long sharp whistle. "Yep, it worked." I turned. Held out my drink, "Nice one!" I left it vague. She could interpret it how she wanted. She raised her glass. "You're the Bouillon that everyone has been bragging about, yeah, yeah, I can see it."

"See it how?"

"You know the..." She put two fingers under her nose and raised her arm. I assumed she was being a dick. She was young, or looked young. Not that I could tell how old people were anymore. Everyone I met looked and seemed decades younger than I felt. But Ruth Gator Bait Ginsburg looked like she was in her twenties. She was handsome with a very odd haircut. Like she was wearing a wig. Like her bangs quit early. Like instead of starting where the edge of her face started, they started next to the edge of her eyes. Like she had cut her hair just so she could see out. Like a cartoon dog. Like her hair was almost a helmet. She looked Asian, but I wasn't sure. I didn't care that she was being a dick. I was used to abuse. And this is how things worked. Constantly trying to undermine the other acts. Especially the headliner. Get them to choke. Make yourself look better by comparison. It was part of the game and it worked sometimes. Not that I had ever been the headliner. It also meant that she was intimidated by me. Which I found pretty stupid. There was no competition. The only real threat was the threat of having a shitty slot during the night. And she already had it. The first one. A scant audience. Even if you gave the best show of your life, when no one was there to see it, you might as well be farting Mozart pianos in the woods, if you ask me.

"Southern California."

"What?"

"That's where you're from."

"Yeah? No shit, Sherlock. You read my bio or something?"

"Well, no."

"Because I am Asian, then?"

"Well, no, I mean, you sound like you come from like the Bay area or something."

"Because I am eating a burrito?"

"You're not, I mean, what?"

"I'm just joshin' ya, bro!" She looked around."What is this place? We're in the middle of nowhere. How is there a crowd like this? And that motel room, right? And that Randy guy? What the hell with those eyes? I have no idea what I got myself into."

Luckily the lights came back on the stage so I didn't have to talk about poor Pink Eye Randy and his impossible eyes. The music faded. Pink Eye Randy got on the stage. How he slipped in without me noticing was confusing.

"Lyme's diseases and germaphobes, we got a special treat for you, straight from an archaeology dig in Egypt, the Harbinger of Chaos!" The crowd cheered. There was more people now. The place was filling up fast. Pink Eye Randy left the stage and disappeared before I could see where he went.

Satirical Egyptian music played as the Harbinger of Chaos walked onto the stage. He was wearing a top hat and a dashiki. He said:

"Great to be here! Thanks for coming out! Speaking of coming out, did you hear about the gay mummy? He was trying to stay in the closet, but he couldn't keep it under wraps." The crowd laughed. A couple people clapped. So true.

"Listen, it's okay, I can tell that joke, I am gay myself. When I came out to my mom, she said, That's fine by me son, but don't tell your dad, just last night I was trying to get him to explore some things in the bedroom, I brought out a strap-on, and he looked at it, frowned, said, I am sorry honey, but I don't think anybody actually likes it in the Sphinx." The crowd really liked this joke.

"Why are the pyramids called pyramids?" The crowd yelled, "Why?" The Harbinger of Chaos said, "Because ancient polyhedrons sounds like a prog rock band. And the whole prog rock movement was an answer to a question nobody asked." This led to guffaws and claps. Cheers even. Someone yelled, "I love prog rock!" He then explained the joke to the crowd. Which was just a list of bands and a short history of music from the mid-60's to the early 70's. It was quite fantastic, but very odd and informative.

After that it was pure Egypt. The jokes went on for twenty minutes or so. I was blown away that he could milk so many jokes out of ancient Egypt. He had a Hieroglyph joke. A Thebes joke. A joke about Cleopatra. A bunch of Jokes about the Nile. He even had a joke about Imhotep that was too clever for words. I was having a lark when Pink Eye Randy tapped me on the shoulder. I looked at him without thinking. His snotty eyes blinking loogies between his butterfly eyelids. I recoiled.

"Damn, Randy! Don't scare me like that!" A bunch of people glared at me for being so loud. But I really was surprised.

"Sorry, Mr. B, but you are on next."

"No shit? But I am not ready, where the hell have you and Duncan been?"

"Backstage. Where have you been? We have been waiting for you."

"Backstage? There isn't any backstage."

"Yuh-huh, there is a green room and everything."

"Don't you think you should have told me about this?"

"We did."

"You did not."

"We did, it was in that contract I slid under your door."

"That never happened."

"I am sure of it, or at least I am kind of sure of it. Which room do you live in again?"

"Number four, Randy, I live in number four."

"Hmmmm."

"Hmmmm?!"

"Well, it doesn't matter, you are on next. Are you ready?"

"I am not! I just told you that!"

"Can I help you get ready?"

"Randy!" The same people glared at me. I lowered my voice to a hiss. "Randy, give me four rum and Sprites, easy on the ice. STAT!"

"I am not the bartender anymore, Mr. B."

"Do it!" I hissed. The dandruff soaked Hitler Youth had snuck off to the bathroom. I had seen him walk away. Pink Eye Randy pouted his way behind the bar to make the drinks. His shoulders like a windless sloop. He didn't want to do it, but he did it. It was very dramatic on his part. He slammed things around, threw his hands up, bent over like he was going to fart, shot the Sprite out of the soft drink pistol like it was the hardest thing in the world to do. I had been very annoyed with him, but his theatrics were amazing. I loved it. He was a child. Sprite went everywhere. Rum went everywhere. If it wasn't for his snotty eyes, I believed he should have taken a bus to Hollywood. That his antics alone would have started a new silent movie era. His actions were transcendent slapstick.

I drank two of the drinks as fast as I could. Pink Eye Randy just stood there looking at me. Glaring through his snotty eyes. Holding the soft drink pistol. The peanut gallery that was Ruth Gator Bait Ginsburg chimed in.

"Slow down there, Caligula, you're gonna hurt yourself." I glared at her. I turned to Pink Eye Randy:

"Thanks, Randy."

"Okay, Mr. B. You good to go on in a few?"

"Randy, you need to stop asking me if I am ready."

"Okay, Mr. B, but are you?"

"Randy, I am ready to go on. If you can get this through your slimy snail-trail eyes, communication is very important. You and me and Duncan are going to have words tomorrow."

"Words are like turds Mr. B, you can't flush them until they come out."

"Randy!" I got glared at again.

"Just sayin', Mr. B." Ruth Gator Bait Ginsburg chimed in.

"Brutal."

"You too!" I hissed.

"What'd I do?!" Ruth Gator Bait Ginsburg said. She thought she was being cute. I turned back to Pink Eye Randy.

"Words. Tomorrow."

"You're a total bummer, Mr. B." I was having a hard time being mad at either of these jerks. They were funny as hell. I was actually mad at Pink Eye Randy and Tricky Houdini, but just because they could have just told me what was up. I was in my room. They could have easily come by. It would have been really easy. But the crowd was good, and the vibes were good. The Harbinger of Chaos had one last joke. I could tell by the way he framed it:

"Alright, I got one last thing to say to you guys, you have been a good audience, you should hand it to yourselves." The crowd cheered. "Speaking of handing it to yourselves, did you hear about the teenage Pharaoh that couldn't explain to his mom why he had so many Kleenex in his waste paper basket? He told her it must just be allergies. She was skeptical. He didn't know what to do. He didn't want to tell her the real reason. So, from then on out, whenever he was masturbating he would yell, Cartouche! as he was finishing. To which she would yell back from another room, Ra bless you! This ruined it for the young Pharaoh. He had to stop. Long story short, his mom really Dashur'ed his Mastaba! Thank you! I will be here all week! Tip your bartenders! The formidable Bouillon is next!" The crowd cheered. Someone yelled, "Seth!" It was maybe an old fan or something. The Harbinger of Chaos bowed. He took off his top hat. He bent back up. Disappeared into the green room that was news to me.

The lights on stage went down. The tinkly music came back up. The crowd got loud. People started coming up for more drinks. I turned to Ruth Gator Bait Ginsburg, she was gone. I was sitting there with two full drinks. Waiting to go on. Full of nerves. Ruth Gator Bait Ginsburg had gotten to me. Fucking hell. Comedy is fickle shit.

Once again I was in limbo. Waiting to go on. Not sure what Pink Eye Randy was up to. Do I nurse my drinks? Do I chug one and just not drink the other. The sweet spot was slipping away and there was nothing I could do about it. I did the only thing I could do. I sat there stewing.

The Comedy Smithereens was in full swing. Capacity I suppose. I looked over at the door. Nobody was coming or going. The bouncer looked bored. Surveying the scene. The people seemed as antsy as I felt. The government goons were checking me out. Taking notes. Not drinking their drinks. What an irritating trio of jerks. I nursed one of the drinks. Trying to go over some of my materia in my head. It was getting really hard to focus. I needed to go on now, or I would lose any steam I had in my guts. Come on, Randy! Where are you? I could feel the crowd getting bored. They didn't seem like they were drinking so much anymore. Checking their watches. Conversations halting. Looking around. Wondering what the fuck. This was torture. Was Pink Eye Randy torturing me on purpose? For making him make me drinks even though he wasn't a bartender anymore? It wouldn't surprise me. He seemed like a really nice guy, he also seemed like the kind of guy that could hold a grudge. Maybe he was still pissed about the time I kicked him in the butt on stage and he farted? Or when I got the crowd to throw drinks at him and Tricky Houdini? Maybe he was just in the green room doing coke with Ruth Gator Bait Ginsburg and the Harbinger of Chaos? Maybe I should go back there and check it out. A little bit of a bump might do me good right about now. I mean, who the hell knows what was happening. Maybe Pink Eye Randy was building tension. On purpose. To get the crowd fired up. If that was true it was backfiring. Nobody seemed worked up. They just seemed like they might stand up and leave at any moment. Satisfied with whatever they had already seen that night. Their $7 all paid up. Their two drink minimum expired. Fucking hell! C'mon, Randy! Let's go! I almost went on stage and just introduced myself just to keep things moving. I would do the set a Capella if I had to. I suppose Pink Eye Randy's plan of creating tension was working, but not the way he wanted it too. It was only working on me, and the longer I waited, the more stressed out I was getting, the worse the show was going to be because I had a very big problem if I couldn't shut my brain off before getting on stage.

I was about to stand up and just go back to my room. Fuck it. Fuck it all. I don't need this shit. I made this place what it is today. Me alone. They wouldn't have nothing without me. I was almost crying, I was so frustrated. I felt like a teenager. Not the teenager my father would beat for no reason whatsoever, but the teenager that went to school and tried to fit in with society. The teenager I was when I wasn't at home, when I didn't have to worry about my mom, or how much vodka was still in the bottle before my dad would pass out. I felt like the teenager that nobody paid attention to, even though I thought I was a good artist. The teenager that would put everything on the line for a single drawing that I thought my teacher would love but instead was met with a Luke-warm response. A litany of criticism, and what they believed was tough love, meaning they thought I just needed to try harder when in fact it was the opposite. I needed easy love. Love that was unconditional. I wondered if my teachers ever figured out how bad my home life was. I hope not, they would have been pretty devastated about how they treated me if they knew the truth. Or not. Maybe they knew and they did this on purpose. Like how abuse breeds abuse, they got a kick out of making me feel like a loser when I was the most proud and most vulnerable. My god! Why was I thinking about this right now! Fucking Randy! Where the fuck are you?

I could feel my ears getting hot. I smelled the club for what seemed like the first time. The breath from all the loud talking. The dirty dish rags. The dirty ice, long melted in my drinks. Even the stools had waves of old butts floating just above them. I hated the smell. It was the opposite of good. It stank. And the noise. The noise was hurting my ears. Everything was too loud. The tinkly music. The din of lousy conversations. I swear I could hear the government goons writing on their clipboards. I started seeing white lights out of the corners of my eyes. Just slivers at first. Then it came in waves. The white light. There was tiny black spots that I couldn't focus on. My ears went sideways. I panicked. I stood up, thinking this would help. It didn't. I sat back down again. My mouth was full of saliva. My skin hurt. Like tiny pricks. Like I was passing kidney stones out of my pores. I didn't know if I was dying or not. It seemed like I was dying. I chugged both my drinks. This did nothing. I got up again. Started pacing back and forth behind the people sitting next to me on stools at the bar. Strangely nobody noticed. The tiny black dots got bigger. There was a lightning bolt dividing my vision into two. I tried to run away. To get away from what was happening. I got around the side of the horseshoe bar. Into the hallway leading to the exit door that led to the racist Motel Mumbo Jumbo. A few people were standing around. Waiting for the bathrooms.

I got outside and puked just in time. I was down on all fours. Some of the vomit splashed up and hit me in the face. The ground was hard dirt. And gravel. I puked again. Then that was it. My eyes went back to normal. I stood up. Breathless from the adventure. I wiped my mouth with the back of my hand. I blinked tears out of my eyes. I felt better. I stood there for a moment trying to think. I felt like I had seen this sort of thing before. I suppose I had seen a lot of people puking in my life, but there was something specific that I couldn't quite remember. Chicago? Daytona? That place in Arizona? Then I remembered. It was here. Here at the Comedy Smithereens. The first day I got here. Pink Eye Randy was doing the same thing when I showed up. Not at this door, the front door, but it was the same. I remember telling him that things would get better, and then he gave me a thumbs up and puked some more. Then I went inside.

This thought sucked. The idea that my pink eye was morphing into something else. That maybe it wasn't just pink eye as Tricky Houdini had said, that it had something to do with Pink Eye Randy's genes. God, I hope not. I hope there wasn't more coming to me. That my eyes would get worse. Start dripping snot out of them. That I too would start smelling like industrial cleaner. Start living in some interstitial space where daily activity was both confusing and hidden from view.

The door opened behind me. Some guy said, "Hey, man, I think you're on." I could hear in the background, "Bouillon! Bouillon! Bouillon!" like a chant. Coming from the crowd. They must think that this is part of the act. Fucking Randy. You had one job. I had no choice but to go back inside. The guy that told me they were looking for me held the door open for me. I walked behind the bar. Grabbed the first bottle of booze I could get. The dandruff soaked Hitler Youth looked at me with his mouth hanging down. I glared at him. Walked around the bar. Past all the assholes that ignored my dying. Or whatever you want to call it. My moment. Past the tables with people and candles. I got up on the stage. Pink Eye Randy was still there. I glared at him as well. This backfired like nothing else. You can't give the stink eye to a snot eye. You will regret it. I guess it worked though. Because he ditched fast. I was left with his eyes burned into my brain. I was angry enough though that I was able to just push through it. I knew the memory would come back to me later, but I didn't have time to process it just yet.

"Well, hello!" The crowd erupted. I guess Pink Eye Randy got what he wanted after all. "Hand it to Randy." The crowd yelled, Randy! "Now hold on, don't give it to him, hand it to him, he had one fucking job, and it wasn't to leave me in a lurch. I suppose he has two jobs now." Someone yelled, "What's his other job?" I said, "Oh, shut up." The crowd got confused. There is nothing funny about a guy just being an asshole on stage. Airing personal grievances. I started my set with the old chestnut about going to parties, and how I don't like pasta. "Then I said, I might be antipasto, but I am prosciutto!" This struck a nerve. The crowd went wild. I did a bunch of dishwasher jokes. A joke about a haircut. A joke about my ex getting her panties caught in a dress she was zipping up, "The last time I heard anyone struggling with a G-string like that Cream was playing the Fillmore, and Clapton had been on a week long cocaine bender."

My set was stupid. Predictable. Angry. It took me a while to realize I was on stage. To forget all the things that had happened in the last couple hours. About mid-set I realized that I had been standing there holding a bottle in my hand the whole time. I looked down. It was a bottle of Malibu. Of all things. It had a pour-spout. I took a drink. Sucking on the spout. The crowd loved this. Why were people so stupid. I really was angry. Very angry. The coconut liquor was gross. But it did the trick.

"Oh, man, it is like licking Fabio's balls when he vacations in Hawaii. Like I just did a cool hang ten on my boogie board, crawled up the sandy beach, and then I found myself face to face with his oiled balls. Tanning in the sun. Then I just start licking them. Nasty shit. I can taste the sweat dripping down his ass-crack. It's not funny. Let me have another taste. Yep, the same."

I could do no wrong with this crowd. I did a joke about hunting moose in Vermont that should have just tanked but gave one of the biggest laughs. I made a bunch of smooching noises. Saying that hunters in Vermont lure moose in by saying, "Hey, moose-moose-moose-moose-moose." Which was a dumb joke to begin with, but I had just thought it up on the spot. I did a joke about going to the hardware store. About how I went inside to get a hummingbird feeder and ended up getting a hummer in the stock-room, "You're a pretty good sales-person, but I don't think I needed the demonstration."

All the bad jokes went on for a while. There was really no end to them. I only quit because I ran out of Malibu. I was tired, and it had been a rough day. I wanted to end on a high note so I said:

"Let's end on a high note. I'm out of booze, and these jokes could go on for hours." The crowd went wild. I said, "No, really, I am done. See you later." The crowd chanted, "Bouillon! Bouillon! Bouillon!" I didn't get it. I dropped the bottle of Malibu on the stage and walked off. There were calls for encores as I walked out of the Comedy Smithereens. I had no intention of getting back on stage. I was done. I walked out the exit door by the bathrooms. Stepped over my pukes. Walked across the parking lot. Went into my room. Shut the door. Locked it. I was done. My nerves were broken. I needed something else.

I woke up feeling foul. The taste of coconut in my mouth. All the bad attitudes from everyone the night before. I was more hungover than normal. Because of the Malibu. I slept horribly. I knew I had slept because my tongue hurt. I must have been chewing on it all night. My mouth was dry. I must have been snoring. Mouth open. My teeth were raw from the pukes. I didn't remember brushing my teeth before getting in bed. I didn't remember anything after getting off stage. I was naked. Which meant that I took my clothes off. The plastic sheet wasn't sticky or wet. I didn't piss myself. I felt hollow. Shaky. Dry. Like a dead worm on the sidewalk. The sun was out again, I wasn't drowning anymore, instead I was baking in the sun, dead. A dead wimpy worm that had crawled out of a mud hole. I hated being hungover.

It got old, really fast, but it was my only friend. Or at least my most reliable companion. My unconditional companion. I suppose there was a condition, and that condition was that I drank, but being drunk and being hungover are two different things. Very different. Being drunk is great. It was all up and up until you plateaued. Then it is either black out, or pass out. Sometimes puke. But there is a limit to it. You can only get so drunk before your body gives out. Being hungover is a different story.

It was limitless and had endless subtleties. You never think you are going to die from drinking. And even if you do, you don't care. Bring it. The best death for a drunk would be to die while drinking. It would be justice in a way. Drinking is a coward's game for the most part. And to be drunk is to give into cowardice. And to die while being drunk is a coward's way out. But you never think about dying when you are drunk. You might think of killing yourself, or make choices that lead to your death, but the abstract idea of dying is inherently muted.

But a hangover. A hangover is torture. The opposite of being drunk. If drinking is cowardice, then having a hangover is an exercise in bravery. Living every single second of life as it comes your way. Sensitive to every sound, every particle of light, a change of breeze, an errant smell. All these things could be your last interaction with life. Because you are dying, and you know it. You just have to stand there and take it. I don't know. I am being dramatic. But as you sit there thinking things like, "A hangover can't kill you." Then you think, "Oh, shit, I have thought that before, this time is different, this one will kill me for sure." Then you space out for a second and the light changes outside and suddenly every fiber of your being wakes up to tell you there is danger coming. And your hands start shaking. You start listening to your heart. Which starts to beat faster. The headache isn't dehydration, it is a stroke. You find yourself pleading with god, or whatever, the universe, to just give you one more second to figure it out before the blackness takes over. And then you go back to normal for a few minutes and feel stupid for being dramatic. Then it all happens again.

And, I don't know. Addiction. The shame of addiction. To even call drinking itself cowardice. The stigma. To break the cycle. To never drink again. To live in a world where you can drink without consequence. To process life without immediately being forced to regret even trying. It is not fun. No drunk is having fun. No alcoholic is having a good time. It is all just maintaining, or aversion.

I don't mean to give drinking lessons. I just hate hangovers. I try to avoid them, but I find them often. Or they find me. Either way. I cause them, but it is not a conversation though. They might be my only friend, but they are a pretty shitty friend. They lead me into the abyss. Let me languish there until I can barely keep my shit together. And then when I come back they say, "See, I told you so." I suppose I don't know though. Maybe I am singular in this viewpoint? The government goons telling me I am a sociopath, maybe that means my hangovers are sociopathic too? Maybe other people just feel kind of lousy when they drink too much. They take a nap, drink some water, and everything is just fine again? It is possible. It wouldn't surprise me. I might be unique. Maybe that is why my jokes are so funny? Maybe I am missing something? Like I am really smart, and everyone else is just a big fat moron?

I got out of bed. Went into the bathroom. Drank some water from the sink. I looked in the mirror. My Hitler good looks were tarnished. I looked like Hitler if his face had been melded with a hound dog. My eyes were red. I was as sad as could be. I looked like I was whining. I smiled my banana Laffy Taffys at the mirror. Took another drink of water. Slinked off to bed again. My body was tired and hot. I looked out the window. It seemed like early morning. I was hungry. I wished I had a different option to eat than to go to Shandy's to eat the Juicy Lucy. I was in no mood to see Shandy or JayJay. I wanted some pizza or something. A bowl of soup. To take the day off. To just lie around and recover. Read a book. If I had a book. Which I didn't. Turn on the television. Which I wasn't even sure worked. That wasn't an option though. I had two options. Either go to Shandy's to eat, or not eat at all. I chose the third option. Or maybe it was the fourth option. Which was falling back asleep while I was deciding.

I woke up a while later because there was a knock on my door. I felt better. Less hungover. My teeth seemed sharp. I needed to brush them. I got out of bed. Opened the door. Naked. It was Pink Eye Randy. I focused on his shirt. Just below his face and neck. I was not in the mood to see his eyes. I could see a little spittle on his chin. He needed a shave. His shirt had a collar. The shirt seemed like it was made out of something plastic. Something a wrestling coach would wear. I didn't say anything.

"Mr. B, can we talk?"

"Yes, Randy."

"Can you put some clothes on? Your wiener makes me uncomfortable." I sighed. The idea that I was making him uncomfortable was egregious. After last night's mayhem I didn't see him as a bit-player in the scheme of things anymore. He knew what he was up to. At least a little bit. But I would have thought that he would have the self-awareness that his eyes were a point of contention. I shut the door. Put my clothes on. Made sure I had my wallet and car key. Squirted a couple drops of pink eye medicine in both my eyes, just in case. Opened the door again. Shut it.

"Come with me."

I got into the yellow Rabbit. Pink Eye Randy got into the passenger seat. I could smell him. He smelled like cleaning fluid. He seemed sober. He tried to make the seat go back further. I told him that the seat couldn't go back any further. He just sat there. Looking straight ahead. I reached over, opened the glove box. I knew I had some sunglasses somewhere. I didn't find them there. I shut it. Then I felt around under the driver's seat. Nothing. Then I got back out of the car. Looked in the hatch. I found them underneath the gallon of antifreeze that I never managed to put into the engine. I should do that.

I took the sunglasses and antifreeze out. I handed the sunglasses to Pink Eye Randy. Told him to put them on.

I popped the hood. Looked around for what I thought would be an antifreeze thing that would tell me what to do. But then I realized that I should pour the stuff into the radiator. I took the cap off. There was liquid all the way to the top. I put the lid back on. I slammed the hood down. Put the antifreeze back in the hatch. Stood there for a second wondering what I was thinking. Then I realized I had confused antifreeze with windshield wiper fluid. I didn't have any windshield wiper fluid. I shut the hatch. Got back into the Rabbit. I looked over. Pink Eye Randy was wearing the sunglasses. Looking foolish and cool. It helped. I started the car. Sighed. Turned around and drove out of the parking lot.

Pink Eye Randy really enjoyed the sunglasses. I don't think it had ever occurred to him that his vision would be less sensitive. Maybe Tricky Houdini was right. Maybe it was in his genes. Pink Eye Randy's genes. He looked at stuff with aplomb the whole way to Shandy's. Pointing at things, gasping, in shock sometimes. I suppose maybe he just hadn't left the racist Motel Mumbo Jumbo for such a long time that he was seeing the world for the first time in forever, or maybe he just wasn't overwhelmed by light, but it was kind of nice to see somebody being so positive for once. Plus it was nice to not have to process his snotty eyes while talking to him. I didn't say anything as we drove. Pink Eye Randy narrated:

"Look at that cow! Oh my god! That tree! You see that, Mr. B!" I smiled. "Those birds! Mr. B! Those birds!" I was almost in tears when we got to Shandy's. He was pulling on my heart strings. I don't think it was just the hangover talking. I was open. He was breaking my heart. I parked and kind of waited for a second. Regaining my feelings. My guess now was that Pink Eye Randy was living the night-life because he couldn't get out during the day. That this was all new to him. I let him have a gander. Letting him check out the scene. There was a red car. He said, "Red that doesn't burn! Mr. B! Are you seeing this!"

I lost it. I burst into tears. I didn't know what to do. I just sat there crying.

"Mr. B! Are you seeing this! Are you seeing this!" I ate all my tears as they flowed down my face and into my mouth. "Mr. B! You have to look at this!"

"I am, Randy, I am."

I sat there blubbering like the wimpy worm that I was. Not sure what had come over me. I suppose it was the hangover. Or maybe I had developed a deep connection with Pink Eye Randy that I wasn't aware of. I was quite fond of the guy, but it wasn't a burst into tears when he could finally see the world as it was because he could finally see because of sunglasses kind of relationship. Apparently it was, though. Maybe deep down I was just a great big softy. The government goons could eat one. If only they could see me now. I looked into the diner. I didn't see them sitting down. Maybe they were up on a hill nearby with a pair of binoculars. I mean, it was special. Poor Pink Eye Randy. Going through life the way he has. Too sensitive for this world. Drinking his pain away. Only feeling comfortable at night. I suppose maybe I just identified with him. All those time feeling sorry for myself, and to never think it could actually be worse. That maybe there was a simple solution to my problems as well. Like maybe there was a pair of sunglasses that could see through all the damaged baggage that I was carrying around with me. Like some pair of sunglasses that would make my childhood go away. Or make my father drop dead before he learned how to beat me senseless. Or all the years traveling around the country being a two-bit jokester with all the charm of a Bazooka Joe bubble gum insert. Whatever it was, whatever was causing all this emotion, it was hitting me pretty hard. I wept and wept and wept until I didn't think I could weep anymore, then I wept some more.

Pink Eye Randy never noticed. He just kept pointing out things that he was looking at. Telling me to take a gander. We sat in the parking lot until I ran out of waterworks. I looked in the rearview mirror. My eyes were as red as Pink Eye Randy's. I wished I had a second pair of sunglasses. Not the hypothetical ones I was just wishing for in my moment of tenderness. There was nothing I could do about it. I knew I didn't. I didn't know why I was feeling self-conscious. I had been coming into Shandy's for, I don't even know, weeks now? Just days? With bright red eyes because of the pink eye. What difference did it make that my eyes were red because of tears this time? Who could tell the difference? Either way, it bugged me. I got out of the yellow Rabbit and went around to the hatch. I opened it. I poked around. I found a ball cap. It said, Funny Bones Tulsa. It had a picture of a dancing skeleton. It was a cheap black hat. With a Velcro adjustment on the back. I put it on. Took it off. Adjusted it. Put it back on. Pulled it down over my eyes. Pink Eye Randy was waiting for me.

"Nice cap, Mr. B! Funny Bones, that's funny."

"Thanks, Randy."

We started walking to the door of Shandy's. I remembered I left the keys in the car. I said, Hold on a sec. Ran back. Opened the door. Grabbed them. Shut the door. Scanned the area. I really did think the government goons might be on some hillside with binoculars peeping on me. If they were I couldn't see them. I ran back to Pink Eye Randy. We walked inside.

The diner had a few people sitting around. None of them recognized me. Or if they did they didn't act like it. Or maybe my ball cap was giving me a disguise. Shandy came out of the kitchen. Came over.

"Bouillon! I almost didn't recognize you. Nice cap! Funny Bones, that's funny. Have a seat anywhere."

"Hi, Shandy."

I led us all to the back booth in the corner. The one where I could keep an eye on the yellow Rabbit. I slid into the booth. Pink Eye Randy did the same on the other side. I turned a coffee cup over. Pink Eye Randy did the same. Shandy handed us menus. Took two of the paper place mats away. Poured some coffee and left.

I didn't bother looking at the menu. Pink Eye Randy picked his up. Started reading it out loud. I said:

"Randy, you don't need to read it out loud, I know what I want."

"I just, I'm sorry Mr. B, I just, normally I can't read things when it is daylight. I was just testing it out."

"No shit, well, forget what I said, sock it to me."

"Sides. Hash browns. Two dollars and fifty cents. Bacon. Four dollars. Oatmeal. Plain. Three dollars. With maple flavor. Three dollars and fifty cents. That doesn't seem like a good deal, fifty cents for maple flavoring. Sausage. Four dollars." Shandy showed up with the coffee.

"Sounds like a real nail-biter, haha! Let me know how it ends." She poured coffee. Pink Eye Randy didn't know she was joking.

"Oh, I am just reading the menu, ma'am. But it looks like it ends with the kid's menu." Pink Eye Randy had turned the menu over.

"Randy, she is joking."

"Oh, okay." I looked at Shandy. She was smiling.

"Shandy, do you know Randy? He owns the Motel Mumbo Jumbo."

"Don't think we met. Good to meet you. Whatool you guys haves?"

"I'll have the Juicy Lucy with hash browns and bacon. Over easy."

"A man after my own heart. White bread, please."

"Randy? White toast?"

"Yum!"

Shandy reached down to get the menus. I didn't move fast enough. She brushed my arm with her hand. I jerked back. Bit my lip. Fireworks exploded down below. I tried to hide it. Shandy looked at me. Either she was used to it by this point, or it only half-registered because she didn't ask me if I was okay. Pink Eye Randy seemed indifferent. He was looking at other stuff that he could look at. Pouring milk into his coffee. Turning the sugar jar with the metal flap in the sunlight to make rainbows. Shandy walked away. I watched her buns. She was wearing black synthetic pants. Without pockets. Her buns cleaved in half. I remembered I had a pair of her panties under my pillow. I felt dirty thinking about it. Cum was dripping down my leg. I took my napkin and discreetly shoved it down the front of my pants. I was starting to think I should be wearing diapers when I came here. When I came here. When I cum here. My mind started working on a joke. I cum here so often I need diapers. I should write that down.

We sat there in silence. Me, making sure the yellow Rabbit was okay. Looking out for the government goons. Pink Eye Randy playing with the sugar jar.

"Does that happen every time she touches you, Mr. B?" He noticed.

"It does, Randy. Every time."

"Do you think it is love?"

"I am not sure, Randy. It's complicated, I think."

"It seems like love."

"Yeah, I don't want to talk about it. You grew up here? This town?"

"Nah, not really, I grew up at the motel with my dad."

"Who's your dad?"

"What do you mean?"

"I mean, who's your dad?"

"The man that runs Comedy Smithereens."

"Tricky Houdini? That's your dad?"

"Tricky Houdini?"

"Duncan is your dad?"

"He is."

"And you grew up in the motel?"

"I've lived there my whole life. What's the big wow?"

"I don't know, Randy. Duncan doesn't act like your dad, I guess. I mean, I don't know. He never said you were his son, I suppose. It just, I don't know."

"My dad is sad. For a long time now. Since my mom left. I think he is lonely. But it is nice having you here. It makes him happy. And all the others now too."

"When did your mom leave?"

"Oh, I don't know. She got sick and left. Then it was just me and my dad."

"I'm sorry to hear that."

"So am I, Mr. B."

That was it. The end of our conversation. I took my ball cap off and put it on the table. Felt the come dripping down my leg. Looked out the window. Keeping tabs on the yellow Rabbit. Scanning the hills for the government goons. Shandy brought our Juicy Lucys. We ate them. I must have bummed Pink Eye Randy out because he didn't seem to have the same gusto for looking at things anymore. We finished breakfast. Walked up to the counter. Paid. I forgot my ball cap. Went back. Grabbed it. As I was walking back Shandy stopped me. She was standing in front of the window that looked into the kitchen. JayJay was slinging hash. His sideburns glistening in the wind. He looked up at me. Glared. I tried not to make a face. He was trouble. I could feel it. Shandy whispered to me. Right there, in front of JayJay. She was trouble too. She whispered:

"I am coming tonight. And I am wearing fresh panties."

Shandy! She tried to reach over and touch my arm. Like in a friendly way. I jumped back.

"I got a whole new set!" I lied. My voice cracking.

The napkin in my pants dropped down my pant leg. I shook it out as I made a dash towards the exit. Pink Eye Randy was milling around, looking at stuff. I grabbed his arm and pushed him out the door. We got to the yellow Rabbit. Got in. I started it. Sighed. Drove back to the racist Motel Mumbo Jumbo as quickly as the little thing could go. My society time was starting to rub me the wrong way. I didn't have it in me to give Pink Eye Randy the grief about last night. About the green room and the structure of the evening. I just wanted to be alone. Take a bath. Read a book. I didn't have a book, but maybe I could read the rest of the newspaper I had. Brush my teeth. Do some laundry. Everything about my daily life was kind of falling apart. I needed some structure. I wasn't sure where to find it. I pulled into the parking lot of the racist Motel Mumbo Jumbo. Got out. Pink Eye Randy got out too. I said:

"Thanks for the breakfast, Randy."

"Thank you, Mr. B. You want your sunglasses back?"

"They're yours now, Randy. See ya tonight!"

"Thanks, Mr. B!" Randy wandered off looking at things.

I ran into my room. My guts were now on fire. I hopped on the toilet and let my butthole boil like some whistling tea kettle. When I was done I thought about calling the Better Business Bureau to rat on Shandy's. They were really pushing things too far. But then I remembered my hangover, so I let it slide. I ran a bath. I put the newspaper on top of the toilet. Lid down. I got naked in the room. Looked outside. Watched Ruth Gator Bait Ginsberg walk by. She looked in. Saw me naked. Laughed. I shook my wimpy dangler at her. She shook her head. I went back into the bathroom. Eased my way into the hot water. Stood up again. Reached over the newspaper. Dripping water on it. Grabbed a washcloth. Slunk back into the bath. Soaked the washcloth. Folded it, and put it on my forehead. Closed my eyes. I let the water run until it reached my nipples. I bent forward and turned it off. I submerged myself again. My knees were out a mile, but the rest of my body was under water. I reached over and scratched my butthole. A fart came out. The smell was fast because of the steam. I stayed there soaking. Feeling okay. Listening to the faucet drip.

The bath got boring after a while. I sat up. Let the washcloth fall into the water. Picked it up. Squeezed it out. Scrubbed my face and my ears. My eyes. My teeth. I cupped some water into my hand and put it in my mouth. Rinsed it around. Spit it out. I dangled the wash cloth on the faucet. Picked up the newspaper from on top of the toilet seat. Tried to read it. I couldn't. I was too distracted. Plus it kept getting into the water. Soaking the bottom. Before long it was a wet soppy rag itself. I wadded it up and threw it onto the counter. I stood up. Took the bar of soap. Got it wet. Did a suds maneuver on my butt and wimpy worm and wimpy beans, my armpits. Put the soap down. Dipped back into the water. Rinsed off. Stood back up. Dripped for a few moments. Got out. Grabbed a towel. Dried off. Drained the tub. Threw the towel on the counter and went into the room. Gator Bait Ginsburg was walking back by. I guess whatever business she had going on the other side was done. She stopped. Looked at me. Shook her head. I waved my wimpy worm at her. She yelled through the window, "You fishing for minnows?!" Then she threw her head back and let out a cackle. Continued walking. What a jerk. I got dressed. My clothes stank. I really needed to do my laundry. One of these days I would figure it out. My pants itched. In the crotch area. I panicked for a second. Thinking I had scabies. But then I realized that I had about a billion sperms collected down there. Fucking Shandy. I thought about her panties. Under the pillow. I wasn't in the mood. Then I thought about what she had just said at the diner. About wearing fresh panties. For tonight. Now I was in the mood, but I didn't want to be in the mood, considering she might give me some freshly soaked panties after my set tonight. I was in quite the pickle. Shoot a load now while I am sober with a crusty pair of panties, or wait for tonight when the panties might be fresh, but I would be drunk. I wasn't sure I could do both. I decided to see what my body thought.

I went over to the pillow. Took the panties up and smelled them. They smelled like Shandy's perfume and also piss. My worm was poking a hole through my pants. I walked over. Shut the shades. Pulled my pants down. Got on the bed. Put the panties on my face. Thought about Shandy in those synthetic pants she was wearing today. The whole operation took maybe ten seconds. I put the panties back under the pillow. Stood up. Waddled to the bathroom with my pants around my ankles. Took the washcloth off of the bathtub faucet. Wiped my loins clean. Put the wash cloth back on the faucet. Pulled my pants up. Zipped them. Buttoned the button.

I went back into the room. Opened the curtains. I looked out onto the parking lot. There was no action. I thought about going over to Ruth Gator Bait Ginsburg's room to tell her she was a jerk, but then I thought about her walking by my window. I realized she had been carrying a plastic sheet. This made me laugh. She had the bed bugs too. I wondered how her eyes were feeling. This was quite the operation Pink Eye Randy and Tricky Houdini were running. I wondered how long anyone would last. I had lasted a while because I didn't have anywhere else  to go. I knew nothing about the other comics aside from Ruth Gator Bait Ginsburg maybe being from southern

California supposedly. Maybe she was just as listless as I was. Just the action of getting a plastic sheet meant she was in it for the long haul. I hadn't seen the Harbinger Of Chaos. Maybe he had already ditched. I suppose his real name was Seth. Or that is what somebody yelled when he was on stage. Maybe he had a following? Possibly he was from around here? Maybe he didn't need to stay at this lousy infested motel. Or he had another gig somewhere down the line. I kind of wanted to find out, but I found myself feeling indifferent about investigating. What good would that information do me? He either left or he didn't. And I didn't want to find myself in some long boring conversation with the guy if he was still here. I could care less about what his actions were. Where he came from. Who he was. I wasn't in the market for new friends at the moment. That breakfast with Pink Eye Randy reminded me what emotions feel like. I wasn't in the mood. I suppose if Shandy knocked on the door, I would let her in, see where that went, but some dude that tells Egypt jokes on the Bazooka Joe Circuit, not interested. Why waste my time with some guy when I could get the same satisfaction from just chewing on a chunk of bubble gum?

Ruth Gator Bait Ginsburg did seem interesting. She was cranky though. She reminded me of my ex. The Lizard. I had heard my ex say that same line a million times before. The one about fishing for minnows with my wimpy worm. I don't understand women. They can make a joke about your penis a million times in a day like nothing means anything, but the second you call their tits flapjacks, whoa boy! Third World War! I remember this one time I came home. Half drunk. My show had gone like shit. The Lizard, sitting on the couch. The tiny little thing. Curly black hair and huge jugs. She was tanked from Gin. Watching some dumb show about an idiot bunch of kids that were having issues in school. I walked into the kitchen to make myself a drink. She yells from the other room, over the top of the sounds coming from the television:

"How'd it go?" I yelled back.

"Fine."

"What?"

"Fine!"

"Speak up, I can't hear you!"

"Fine!"

"What? The television is on, I can't hear you!"

"It went fine!"

"What?!"

At the time I was on a cold vodka kick. Vodka in the freezer. Lots of ice. I took the bottle out. The ice trays were empty. I stood there, angry. Why couldn't she just refill them? I slammed the door. Poured ice cold vodka into my glass. Walked into the living room. I looked at her drink. Ice to the brim. I said:

"Why can't you just..." She looked over at me.

"How'd it go?"

"How's your drink?"

"What? Hold on, the television is too loud." She turned the television's volume down with the remote control. "What?"

"How's your drink?"

"Oh! Nice and cold, the way I likes it." She took a drink. Held it up. Smiled.

"Yeah, me too." I held my drink up. She noticed there was no ice.

"Where's the ice?"

"You tell me."

"Oh, great, here we go again."

"Why can't you just refill the fucking things? It's not that hard."

"Give it a rest will ya. I told you to buy ice, but nooooo, we got those things to make ice. It's pathetic."

"Don't be a bitch. You think ice just grows on trees? I work my fingers to bone so you can just sit there drinking ice cold gin watching your dumb ass shows, no cares in the world?"

"You work your fingers to the bone? Ha! You take turds on stage, and then come home all butt hurt because we don't got no ice. You're pathetic, Bullion."

"Okay, well, what the fuck do you do to keep these good times going? Watch the tee-vee? Suck the postman's dingaling?"

"Well, at least he has something to suck on. With you it's like flossing teeth."

"Yeah, I am sure. My question though is, does he think he is coming to IHOP when he gets here? What with the flap-jacks you are serving up? Does he ask for a side of bacon smothered in Brillo pad? A pad of butter? Maybe he thinks he is at the gym, about to do a round on the speed bags?"

"You fucking son of a bitch!" She lurched at me. Knocking the coffee table over. Her drink included. I watched the ice fall out and spread out on the carpet. I held my drink above my head. She was small. There was no danger of injury. She scratched my face and yanked at my genitals. "See what I mean! I can't get nothing, there is nothing there!" I pushed her back with one hand, still holding my drink above my head. She was drunk. She landed on the couch. Crying.

"What the fuck is your problem? You give me shit all day about how my dick doesn't do you right, and the second I take a shot at you, suddenly I am the bad guy?"

"You don't know shit about women, buster. You don't know shit about shit. Leave me alone. I don't want to talk to you."

I left her on the couch. Went back into the kitchen. Sat down. I could hear her picking up the coffee table. Putting the empty cup on it. She turned the television back up. Before long she was snoring. I didn't know what to do. At the time I thought it might still work out. I felt bad for her. Her tits were fine. Jugs even. I mean, I didn't have any feelings one way or the other. I was just sick of her giving me shit about my penis. I really think she was sleeping with the mailman. I kind of wished she was. It would have made her happier. I think. Maybe she wouldn't get drunk every night, sitting on the couch, watching her stupid shows. Passing out. Waking up with a pants load of shit. Stumbling into bed around dawn. Stinking the place up. I suppose, thinking about it now, the relationship was quite toxic, but at the time I thought she might find me agreeable again, maybe come to my shows like she did in the beginning, try a little harder. But this is how it was. So be it.

It has been nearly a decade since these fun times happened. Which is why I found it so surprising that Shandy had awakened something in me. Maybe it was Shandy's sobriety that got me? She was level headed. Had a job. A business even. I suppose she would even laugh at my jokes about flap-jacks. I mean, she had big honkers too, but they weren't flappers, so she might not be so insecure, but that wasn't the point with The Lizard. The point with my mx was that she hated herself, and I hate myself too. Our relationship was symbiotic because of this. A couple of asshole drunks feeding off each other. Toxic and angry and abusive and co-dependant.

I thought this through. Deciding that going over to Ruth Gator Bait Ginsberg's room and telling her her boobs were floppy wasn't the same as her standing in my window telling me my dick was so small that I could only catch minnows if I used it as bait. That it would be a bad idea. Because on one hand, it was an asshole move, and on the other hand, she would probably just kick me in the balls and be righteous for it.

I paced around for a while. Trying to think of new jokes. I was getting nothing. I wanted to go for a walk. To get away. This new reality was feeling crowded. I had too many people to think about. They were everywhere. My right. My left. Inside. Outside. Bed bugs. Pink eye. Dirty pants. I was feeling trapped. The scene was expanding too rapidly. I left the room. Went around the front of the

Comedy Smithereens. Walked through the parking lot. Up the hill. I looked around. Thinking I would find the government goons peeping at me from a distance. I saw nothing. I pushed up the hill. Through trees and branches. I was walking without a trail at first, then I came to a trail. I followed it. It went up, and up. I was walking slowly. My lungs sucked. I couldn't remember the last time I had any exercise. I was breathing heavily. The trail was small. Like a deer trail or something. I had to grab branches to keep myself going. To pull myself along. Eventually the trees gave way. The sun came out. I was on top of whatever mountain that was above the Comedy Smithereens, above the racist Motel Mumbo Jumbo. It was kind of pretty. A cliff. A cliff that looked over the interstate. Rolling hills. Trees. Forest. Cars screaming by. Going as fast as the signs would let them. There was empty beer bottles and cans. Empty spray paint cans. The word, BUTTS sprayed on  the rock cliff. DANNY DOES DOGGY. LEGLE WEED. There was a poorly painted marijuana leaf and a giant boner with balls. I was guessing it was a teenage hangout. I kicked a can of spray paint. It seemed full. I picked it up. Depressed the nozzle. There was something in it. I walked over to the wall of rock. I was going to write QUEEF, but instead I only got out QUE before the canister ran out. BUTTS, DANNY DOES DOGGY, LEGLE WEED, QUE. I threw the spray paint can on the ground. The confusing message was now even more confusing. I scrambled up the last little bit of trail. The sun was out. The vistas were sweeping. I sat down. My legs dangling over the cliff. I laid back. The sounds of cars on the interstate. The smell of dirt. Grass and pine needles and rock. Spray paint. I listened to birds. My shoes heavy, hanging on my feet. I squinted the sun away from my eyes. My face was now warm.

I don't know if I fell asleep or I just got bored, either way, I stood up again. My feet were needles. They had fallen asleep. I stomped around for a while. Trying to get the feeling back. I unzipped my pants. Took a leak over the edge of the cliff. Looked down. About a hundred feet away I saw some motion in the trees. I squinted. I saw a head peeking through a branch. A pair of binoculars attached to the face. I sighed. The government goons were in fact spying on me from a distance. I unzipped my pants and waved my wimpy worm at them. Then waved with my hand. There was a sudden movement and the face with the binoculars was gone. These fuckers were obnoxious as hell. I started plotting a way to get down to them. Maybe sock them in the guts when I caught up to them. There wasn't a trail though. By the time I caught up with them they would be gone I decided . I flipped them the bird in their general direction and started walking back to the racist Motel Mumbo Jumbo.

When I got back to the parking lot I saw the Harbinger Of Chaos going into his room. He was holding a plastic sheet. I laughed. I guess he wasn't going anywhere either. So much for my theory that he had better gigs somewhere else. He was just as big a loser as the rest of us. I don't know why, but this cheered me up. I wasn't happy that he was a loser or whatever, just that him being a loser made me feel like less of a loser. You know what I mean? If I couldn't figure out a way to get the hell out of this shit-hole, and Ruth Gator Bait Ginsburg couldn't figure out a way to get the hell out of this shit-hole, and now the Harbinger Of Chaos couldn't figure out a way to get the hell out of this shit-hole, maybe collectively we weren't all bad losers, it was just bad circumstances that was keeping us all down. Society or whatever. Forces bigger than ourselves that were conspiring against us. We were victims, not losers. No matter how hard we tried, the Man would always be able to kick us down a notch. No matter how hard we worked we would never get ahead. The system was rigged. And it was rigged against us.

I went into my room. Shut the curtains. Paced around making greasy footprints on the carpet. I needed new material if I was going to get Shandy to cream her panties again. I wondered what she was doing. What she was up to. What JayJay was doing. What he was thinking. I couldn't tell if he liked me or hated me. I suppose he glared at me earlier, but maybe he was just in a bad mood. He seemed like the kind of guy that would get into a bad mood and take it out on everyone else. Or maybe he just thought my hat was stupid. I don't remember if I was wearing the hat when he glared at me though. Maybe I was making the whole thing up. Maybe he smiled at me, and because I was feeling guilty from getting an arm job from Shandy I put expressions on his face that weren't really there? I hoped he wasn't coming tonight. That Shandy wears a skirt. That instead of giving me her wet panties after my set, instead she says something like:

"I need to show you something, Mr. Funny Bones, can we go back to your room? It's private."

Then, zoinks! A wham-bahlam! Hummina-Hummina. Wheet-whoo! Aaaa-OOGA. This thought became my muse. I was feeling ripe, and fresh. My brain was spitting out jokes both stupid and brilliant. I thought of a duck joke. A joke about mayonnaise. A joke about a cow that I wasn't sure if I had already thought up before, but was good. A joke about abortion. Retirement. A joke about a haircut. I was all over the place. Unstoppable. I should have written the things down, but they were coming so fast, and I was in such a fantastic headspace there was no way I could forget them. I meditated for what seemed like hours. In the end I felt like I was at the very top of my game. I hadn't been this fertile in years, decades even. I was ready. I opened the curtains. It was dark out. It wouldn't be long. I went into the bathroom. Washed my face. Combed my hair. Brushed my teeth. It had been a long time. I spit quite a bit of blood out. I really needed to take better care of my teeth. I smiled my banana Laffy Taffys in the mirror. Admired my Hitler good looks. Blew myself a kiss. Shut the light off. Went into the room. Felt my pockets. Making sure I had my wallet. I felt the pink eye medicine. Took it out. Squirted a couple drops in both my eyes. Put the bottle back in my pocket. I was ready to go. I shut the light off in the room. Opened the door. I walked across the parking lot of the racist Motel Mumbo Jumbo and went into the Comedy Smithereens back door.

The place was on fire. Brimming with people. The energy was electric. There was a line out the door. People begging to come in. It seemed like standing room only. My bar stool was occupied. The dandruff soaked Hitler Youth was working overtime. There was a new bartender too. My stupid brain called her The Nubian Princess. Probably because she was Black and very pretty, but also because I heard her say, Whatool you haves in an English accent, which, I don't know why this made her Nubian, but then the Harbinger Of Chaos was on stage telling Egypt jokes, so all these things combined to make my idiot mind create a universe where I reduced her to being a figment of my imagination. I kind of wanted to go apologize for thinking the things I was thinking, but she seemed really busy. Also, that seemed like a really stupid idea. To apologize for a thought you had. However, I still thought of her as The Nubian Princess even after I castigated myself.

I looked around for Shandy. I couldn't see over the crowds of people. I hoped that she was sitting in the front row like last time. I looked around for the government goons. I couldn't see them either. I hoped they had gone back to whatever lousy hotel they were staying in. Comparing notes, or whatever the hell it is that they did. Calling The Lizard to give her an update on their stupid progress. I really wanted them to go away.

I was annoyed that my seat was taken. I didn't know what to do. I remembered the green room, so I walked around the back side of the horseshoe bar and looked for a door. I didn't find a door, but I did find a curtain. There was a piece of paper safety pinned to the curtain that said, "Talint" written in black marker. Oh, Pink Eye Randy, you break my heart. I pushed the curtains to the side and walked in.

——◆——

The green room was amazing. I suppose it was shit, but it was amazing because it was an actual green room. The walls were painted green. With couches. Mirrors. A bar. A fridge. Baskets of fruit. The place was a dank greasy mess, but it was something I didn't expect. Ruth Gator Bait Ginsburg was sitting on a couch. Smoking a cigarette. Pink Eye Randy was there for a second, but then he disappeared behind a curtain. I assumed he was going somewhere else, but knowing him, he might have just gone back there to hide out for a second. To take a break. There was a coffee table in front of Ruth Gator Bait Ginsburg. She had a drink. Next to her drink was lines of what looked like cocaine, there was a rolled up dollar bill next to the lines. She said:

"Well if it isn't King Rex himself. Pour yourself a

drink and come have a little hoose-gow." She must have been having the same problem I had earlier. Naming the bartender The Nubian Princess. The Harbinger Of Chaos's set seeping into her mind. I could hear it coming in through tiny speakers mounted near the ceiling.

I walked over to the bar. Poured myself a rum and Sprite, easy on the ice. Took a giant drink. Poured myself another. Walked over and sat down next to her. Her legs were crossed. She slid the drugs over to me. I picked up the tooter.

"Hate to see it go to waste." Snorted a line of cocaine in one nostril. Then switched. Snorted a line in the other nostril. I let out a yelp. "Damn!" Put the rolled up dollar bill back. Slid the drugs back to her. Ruth Gator Bait Ginsburg did a line. Rubbed her nose. I said, "What do you mean?"

"What do you mean, what do I mean?"

"King Rex."

"Oh! You're all gussied up buckaroo. Slicked back hair. Teeth like shiny butter."

"It's a big night." The drugs were kicking in. I think I might have done too much. I sucked my drink down and stood up and poured another. I sat back down. I looked at Ruth Gator Bait Ginsburg's cigarettes on the coffee table. I gave her a look. A look that meant, "Do you mind?" She nodded. I lit the smoke. It went straight to my guts. That and the booze and cocaine. She could tell something was up. She pointed to a door I hadn't noticed before. It said Toilet. I got up. Said, "Excuse me." Walked fast. Opened the door. The room was just a toilet. With a roll of toilet paper. I turned the light switch on. A very loud fan was sucking air. I thanked god for such a tiny miracle of both a fan and a loud fan to boot. I undid my pants. Sat down. I listened to the fan as my ass flapped wet things and abrupt farts out. The white noise was hypnotic. I stared at the door. Chewing on my chin. Taking large drags from the cigarette I was smoking. I opened my legs and ashed between my knees. My mind was boggled. I hadn't been this high in a long long time. I blasted out a few more turds. Took the last drag from the smoke. Dropped it between my legs. Heard it sizzle. Wiped until I got bored. Stood up. Did my pants up. Looked down at the toilet. Frowned. Flushed. I would have washed my hands but there was no sink. I walked out of the toilet room. I left the light on, the fan on. Shut the door behind myself. Ruth Gator Bait Ginsburg said:

"Everything come out alright?"

"Yeah, it did. Slick and juicy as ever."

"You were in there for a while."

"If I've learned anything from the bible it's that quality things take time."

"I was about to call the fire department, get them to bring the jaws of life, ya know."

"Yeah, I'm sure you were."

"Seriously, did you start writing a novel in there? You can name it Moby Shit? Call me Charmin, that's a good first line."

"It was the burst of times, it was the stinkiest of times…shit, I got nothing. Now I remember why I don't do this shit, it makes me stupid."

"I half expected you to have a beard when you came out."

"Don't you have a set to get ready for?"

"I thought I did, but then the health inspector just showed up and told everyone to go home because somebody reported a gas leak. And that gas leak was your ass!"

I sucked down my drink. Made another. Trying to ignore Ruth Gator Bait Ginsburg roasting me. She was annoying, but her jokes were funny. I needed to stay focused. I was kind of getting freaked out. I could hear the Harbinger Of Chaos finishing his set. This sucked. It meant that he would be coming into the green room in just a second. I wasn't ready for such a change of energy. As annoying as Ruth Gator Bait Ginsburg was, I didn't mind her vibe. I could easily sit there all night drinking with her, doing lines and smoking cigarettes, but something told me the Harbinger Of Chaos wasn't the kind of guy that just hung out. Something told me he was hard to get along with.

"You ready, or what?"

"Ready as ever. You want more of this blow? Seth is straight-edge, I need to hide it. The dude's a dick."

"Oh, you know him?"

"You want some or not?"

"Sorry for livin'!" I did a line. Handed it back. Ruth Gator Bait Ginsburg did the last line. Wiped the thing with her finger. Rubbed it on her gums. Put the thing under the couch cushion she was sitting on. Held out her cigarettes. I took one. She lit it. I stood there. Smoking. Half-cocked. Or fully-cocked. I didn't know. High and not looking forward to the Harbinger of Chaos's bad attitude.

"Wish me luck!"

"Good luck!"

The crowd was clapping. I could hear it through the speakers. Ruth Gator Bait Ginsburg disappeared behind the curtains just as the Harbinger Of Chaos came through the curtains. He was sweaty. His eyes were bright. They were also very red and also very crusty. He was holding his top hat in his hand. I was surprised that he was bald. But bald just on the top. The hair around his head made him look like a monk.

"It's cooking out there, fool!"

"You kinked the bone?" I felt ancient saying this. I hadn't heard that phrase in almost 20 years. The coke was dredging up memories.

"Huh?"

"You killed it?"

"I guess, I wish you guys wouldn't smoke in here. Where's my water at? Oh, there it is!" I said nothing as I took a drag from the cigarette I was holding. "Okay! Off to meet my adorning public! Later loser!"

The Harbinger Of Chaos put his top hat back on and ditched through the talint curtain. Going to meet his adorning public. Good riddance. The intense vibes dissipated the second he left. I was glad he was gone. I heard Pink Eye Randy introduce Ruth Gator Bait Ginsberg from the small speakers hanging next to the ceiling:

"Birds and hawks, drop your socks and grab your cocks for Ruth Gator Bait Ginssssssbeerrrg!"

"Thank you Randy! You are a gem! Give it up for Randy!" The crowd cheered. "Listen, you ever put a tampon in and forget about it for like two days? I know I have, and I find it shocking! Toxic-shocking, I mean."

I sat there on the couch. Trying not to listen to her set. Trying to focus on my own set. I wished I had more cocaine. I looked at the cigarette I had been smoking. I must have ignored it too long because it wasn't smoking anymore. Pink Eye Randy came into the green room. He was looking drunk. Swaying. He was still wearing the sunglasses. He looked cool. I asked him if he had a lighter. He did. He lit the half-smoked smoke.

"I got more blow, Mr. B." He handed me a bag. I didn't know what to make of it. I put it in my pocket. Next to the pink eye medicine and my wallet. He also handed me a pack of cigarettes. And a lighter. I put those in my other pocket. What was happening? Why was Pink Eye Randy giving me drugs and cigarettes? I didn't mind because I wanted both of those things, but it seemed inappropriate. He asked me if I was ready to go on when Ruth Gator Bait Ginsburg was done. I said I was. Then he was gone again.

I stood around drinking rum and Sprites, easy on the ice. Pacing. Listening to Ruth Gator Bait Ginsberg's set. Knocking back bumps and smoking cigarettes. I had forgotten all my jokes from before. I knew I had a set, even if it wasn't new jokes, but I was kind of freaking out. I kept licking my lips. Drinking. Snorting cocaine. Smoking. Things weren't good. I was gonna tank. I could feel it. Fuck. What good was a greenroom when you can't relax? Ruth Gator Bait Ginsberg's jokes started slithering into my ears like hilarious snakes.

"And when the money got into my account I had to send it back! Because, because!"

Then she went into this whole thing about anal sex that really threw me off. I mean, it wasn't even a joke. It was just about her shitting on some guy's dick. And the guy was like, "You win some, you lose some." Which sent me down a dirty road. My ex. Shitting her pants all the time. Sitting on the couch. Drinking rum. And here I was drinking rum. Almost no ice. As some sort of rebellion? I didn't know. I couldn't take it. I was about to run out of the room. Through the curtains. Hop into the yellow Rabbit, and get the fuck out of town. But instead, Ruth Gator Bait Ginsberg came back into the greenroom. Sweaty and smiling. Her eyes, bright red. She looked me up and down. Laughed. Said:

"What the fuck, man?. You gonna be alright?"

"Suck it, Ruth."

"Yeah, I don't know. I left you a fun crowd, I'd hate to see you blow it."

"I'll be fine."

"You don't look fine. Take a drink, man. You got eyes like baby teeth."

"I'm fine."

"Seriously." She made a drink that was just rum and ice. Handed it to me. My mouth became uncontrollable. She shook her head. "Drink it."

I could hear Pink Eye Randy introducing me.

"I gotta go." She saluted me like I was an astronaut. I must have been very confused because she sighed and took the cigarette out of my hand.

"Good luck, wild man."

I waded through the curtains. Not knowing where I was going. I found myself on stage. Pink Eye Randy was talking into the microphone:

"Listen, if you need to take a piss, go outside, there is trees and bushes, if you need to drop a deuce, I hate to tell ya, you are out of luck. The toilets are all clogged." I stood there frozen. Trying to stay hidden. Someone yelled, "Bullion!" Pink Eye Randy turned around. He looked cool with his sunglasses. He went back to the microphone. "But seriously, nobody shit in the toilets anymore. They don't flush. You are just making things worse." The crowd booed. Someone yelled:

"Quiet down, Randy! Let Bouillon get some!"

"Somebody has to clean that shit up!" Pink Eye Randy was very upset.

"Nobody cares!" The crowd yelled.

"Yeah, well, I care. I have to clean it up and it's gross."

"So what?"

"Chicken butt!" Pink Eye Randy yelled.

"Let Bullion do his thing!"

"Fine! I hope your turds go right back up your butts!" Pink Eye Randy stormed off the stage. I watched him go to the bar. Yell something. The Nubian Princess handed him a plunger. He shook his head. Pushed through the crowd. Disappeared. I felt bad for him. But what could I do? I had a job to do myself. I walked up to the microphone. Tapped on it. Took a drink from my rum and ice.

"Is this thing on?" The crowd went wild. Shandy was indeed in the front row. Wearing a skirt. I could see right up it. She wasn't wearing any panties at all. It was nothing but bush and bacon strips. I nearly fainted. She was smiling. Clapping. JayJay wasn't there. The crowd, aside from the few people sitting down in front, at tables, meaning Shandy and a few others, the crowd was standing. I didn't know that so many people could be in this room. I peeked around. The government goons were there. With their clipboards. Off to the side. I sighed. Took a sip from my drink. Put it down on the stage. Chewed my jaw for a second. I was high as hell. All I wanted to do was just dive into Shandy's crotch and eat her out for hours. Stick a finger in her butthole and maybe play with her nipples. But I had a show to do. I collected myself and started talking. "Now it has come to my attention that we got ducks hanging out at the bar, some of them you should worry about, I mean, they don't speak, like they might be dumb, and they might give you a disease, but if you ask me, I just think they are anti-Quackers." I was just as confused about the nonsense coming out of my mouth, but the tone must have been correct because the audience slurped it up.

I was doing good. Nailing it. Knocking them down. Despite my booze soaked ham-colored flesh and Hitler good looks. All the cocaine rolling around my bowling ball brain. I was focused and astute. I managed to remember all the jokes I conjured up earlier while waiting to get drunk. I even pulled the cow joke off. Even as I was saying it I swear I had done it before, or even heard it recently. Is that a cow in your pants? Because I can sure smell your dairy-air. Shandy seemed to be enjoying it. I watched her knees billowing. A peek of chestnut pubes every now and again. Either piss or cum dripping down her chair. I wasn't worried about popping a boner. The cocaine had done away with that idea. As turned on as I was upstairs, down below I was more wimpier than ever. I chewed my jaw. Grunted out a few more yucks. I really had the crowd going with me. Then something happened that I didn't expect. Usually the stuff that came out of my mouth was just a long list of dumb jokes. The trick was to keep remembering them as they came to me. You tell enough crappy jokes in a row people tend to get distracted and mistake consistency for brilliance. You do something long enough eventually it feels like you have always been doing it. The future seems inevitable. Nobody remembers how things start. Just how they are going, and how they end.

I don't know if it was the cocaine or the cigarettes or the boredom or the government goons looking at my dangler through binoculars earlier, but my yuck-arama turned serious. Suddenly and without warning. And because I was so used to just going with the flow while standing on stage, I opened my mouth, as wide as it could get, and just let my thoughts fall out, like wet hot diarrhea.

"You know what gets me?" The crowd all yelled, "What?" "Now hold on, I don't mean it that way. Listen, I'm serious." "How serious are you?" "Seriously, shut up." Hahahaha. They thought that was the joke. I didn't blame them. Like what I said before, the future becomes inevitable. "What gets me is that there is no universal truth. Not in the way we think about it. There is just too many of us. All living different lives. There is no one thing that can define us. What gets me though is that there can be a universal Lie. I mean, think about it. All this shit that is supposed to be true, about society, about life, it is all just a bunch of bullshit. I mean, I got these goons following me around these days telling me I am different than I think I am. And you know what I think of that?" "It stinks!" The crowd must have remembered a fart joke I did a few days ago. "Yes! It stinks. I mean, who the fuck are they to tell me who I am and who I aint, right? I mean. you, the guy in the tank top, the one that says Podbody's Nerfect, what do you do? Like for a living?"

"Me?"

"Yeah, you."

"I drive trucks."

"Okay, what if I told you you don't drive trucks, I seen you drive a car, so that makes you a nurse. Does that make sense?"

"No!"

"Okay, good. I mean, that is stupid, right? I can't go around telling people what they do, but all these assholes with their Ivy League diplomats writing magazines about college and the stock index telling us we drive cars instead of trucks so therefore we are nurses not truckers, that is bullshit. I don't get it. Where the hell do they get off?"

This went on for 20 minutes. I was dropping screeds left and right. About society and the nature of collective understanding. Getting the crowd really riled up. Jumpy even. They were getting angry. Frankly, I was too. A man in the back yelled something really offensive to every single person in the crowd aside from himself. This broke the hypnosis. There was a sudden silence. A glass broke. The sound of a door being opened. The sound of a sack of meat hitting the ground. Then a loud cheer. I guess the guy was thrown out. This made me rethink my hot wet diarrhea. I stopped the rhetoric and went back to telling jokes. But something inside me was different. For the first time in my life I really felt understood. My loins regained the inertia from the cocaine. Shandy's billowing wet bush sent a lightning bolt to my groin. I was hard as a rock. I didn't care. Nobody could see it. I assumed. I wasn't packing much luggage, so it wasn't like the van's doors were busting loose. I wasn't about to lose a couch on the interstate, if you know what I mean. But I felt free for the first time in forever.

I rolled with it. I did another 30 minutes of material. Ended with a joke about cunnilingus. I must have been thinking about eating Shandy out. I said:

"And when I woke up the next day, I had to go to the dentist to get a haircut! Thank you! Good night! Tip your bartender!" The crowd erupted. I was parched. Sweaty. I worked my way back into the green room. Through the curtains. It took a while to figure it out. Nobody was in there. Thankfully. I could hear the crowd chanting my name over the tiny speakers next to the ceiling. I made myself a drink. Rum and Sprite, easy on the ice. I took it into the bathroom. Sat down on the toilet. I didn't think I had to go, so I kept my pants up. But then I thought about it again. I wasn't sure. I stood up. Pulled my pants down. Sat down again. Reached into my pocket. Pulled out the little baggie of cocaine. Dumped some on the webbing between my finger and my thumb. Sucked it up my left nostril. Did the same thing with my right nostril. Zipped the bag closed. Bent over. Picked up my drink. Took a drink. Grabbed the cigarettes while I was down there. Lit one. Stared at the door while smoke filled the room. Let out a few squirts and some farts. Wiped until I got bored. Stood up. Looked down. Frowned. Pulled my pants up. Zipped them. Did the button. Made sure I still had the drugs and my wallet and my cigarettes. Bent down again. Picked up my drink. Left the bathroom.

Pink Eye Randy was now in the green room. With his cool sunglasses.

"Damn good set, Mr. B. You really nailed it tonight. You have a visitor if you want."

"Thanks, Randy. Who is it?"

"The girl from the diner. Should I let her in?"

"Of course, of course."

"Mr. B."

"Randy?"

"You should maybe wipe your nose."

"Thanks, Randy."

I was wiping my nose as Shandy walked into the room. I was high again. My wimpy worm regaining its inertia. I felt really self-conscious. I tried to hide it. My eyes felt like they were connected to Slinky coils. I pretended I was making a drink in an attempt to seem relaxed and cool. Shandy smiled at me and sat down on the couch. She had something on her mind. This was good. Maybe she wasn't paying too much attention to me. I asked her if she wanted a drink.

"You got a whiskey? Straight?"

"Knob's?"

"Whatever is fine." She really did have something on her mind. I poured her a whiskey. Made another Sprite and rum easy on the ice for myself. Brought it over to her. Sat down on the couch. "Can I get one of those?" I handed her a cigarette and lit it for her. She smiled. Took a drag. Kind of looked at the cigarette. Held up her glass. "Good one tonight. Cheers." I clanked her glass.

"You okay? You seem concerned."

"I am concerned, Bullion. Really concerned. I don't know if you noticed, but I wasn't wearing any panties tonight."

"Oh, I noticed."

"Okay, good. I don't mean to be forward, but it wasn't any sexy thing or anything, it was more of a flag. I mean, I don't even know how to say it. Oh, Bullion, I am so confused." She went all blubbery. The water-works started flowing out. She collapsed back into the couch. I wanted to embrace her. To make her feel better, but the way I was sitting I could see her naked crotch. I kind of didn't want to move. I felt dirty about this, but I wasn't sure where she was going. So I hedged my bets and stayed where I was. Catching glances as her chestnut mound sat glistening.

"How can I help?"

"You can't help! That is the problem, you will only make things worse. That is why I came here. This needs to stop."

"What needs to stop? The yucks at the Comedy Smithereens?"

"No! You idiot, you and me. JayJay found out that I gave you my panties. I don't know how he got it out of me, but he did, and he forbade me from wearing panties tonight because of it."

"That is ridiculous. How is sending you out without any panties going to help anyone?"

"I don't know, but JayJay is a real jealous dude, Bullion, I think he might have killed a man before, you should watch your back."

"But I didn't do anything."

"He knows you get a thrill when I touch your arm, he says he's seen it. I told him he was crazy, but I don't know,

I think you know what I am talking about."

"Me? Noooo!"

"Yeah, I don't know." Shandy reached for my arm. I pulled back just in time.

"See! Now I can't even touch you! It's not sexual, I swear! Maybe you can go talk to him? Mano y mano? Clear the air?"

"You want me to go talk to JayJay about whether or not I get feelings when you touch my arm?"

"I know, it sounds crazy, but I don't know what else to do. He is so jealous."

"Yeah, okay. I guess. I mean, I don't really, I mean, okay. Are you going to be there?"

"He says he wants to meet you behind the diner at noon tomorrow. Just you and him."

"That doesn't sound so good."

"Bullion, you have to do this. For me. Please!" She reached over. Caught me unawares. I launched a load to the moon. It was so very intense my asshole cramped. "Are you okay?"

"I'm fine."

"So you will be there?"

"Tomorrow? Noon?"

"Yes, please. It is the only way."

Shandy got up. I watched her walking out. She threw the cigarette onto the ground. Didn't bother stamping it out. My crotch was wet. Slimy. This was getting old. I really did need to start wearing diapers around her. Either that or get an extra pair of pants. High noon with JayJay. How insane. There was no way in hell I was going to that meeting. What would be the best outcome? He beats my brains out? What was the worst outcome? He murders me? There was no good outcome. I suppose if he needed to find me, he could come find me. He knew where I lived. Where I was every night. This whole interaction seemed fishy. I was starting to wonder what Shandy was up to. I mean, she touched my arm on purpose. She knows her powers over me. What the hell. I sat there thinking for a few moments. The sound of tinkly music was coming in over the speakers next to the ceiling. Then it abruptly stopped. The club must have been shutting down. I stood up. My wet loins annoyed me. Fucking Shandy. What next? I got up. Grabbed the bottle of rum. Walked out of the green room. Out the back door of the Comedy Smithereens. Walked over to Ruth Gator Bait Ginsberg's room. Or at least I hoped it was. I knocked on the door. The lights were on, but the curtains were closed. I half-expected the Harbinger Of Chaos to show up. I sighed when it was Ruth Gator Bait Ginsberg. She said:

"Oh! It's you, come on in. I was about to rub one out, wanna watch?" I shrugged. I went inside. Shut the door. She took off her clothes. Got on the bed. Proceeded to rub one out. I sat on a chair, drinking rum from the bottle. Doing bumps of cocaine off the webbing between my index finger and my thumb. There was something very unsexual about the whole experience. She had a huge black bush. Squirted a few times. Then that was it. She put her clothes back on. We shared the rum and the cocaine. Talking about life on the road. Comedy. How insane the racist Motel Mumbo Jumbo was. Bed bugs. Pink eye. I gave her a hug around four in the morning when the rum ran out. Stumbled back to my room. Kicked off my shoes. Slid into bed. I got back out, took a piss. Went right back. Got back out. Went into the bathroom. Took a drink from the sink. Got back in bed. I was going to regret tomorrow. And now that JayJay wanted to beat me up, I wouldn't even be able to go to the diner. Typical. I had the best night on stage in my entire career, and now everything else around me was falling apart. I took Shandy's panties out from under the pillow. Smelled them. Hoping to get a boner. I was too high and too drunk and too tired. I just held them by my nose like a security blanket. Like something comfortable. Squeezing them. Before long I was in Snooze City. Population, Moi.

I woke up feeling deeply ashamed. Fragments of the night coming in and out of focus. I vaguely remembered the political rant I did. I kind of remembered talking to Shandy after that. That JayJay wanted to beat me up behind the diner at noon. I remembered that she wasn't wearing underwear. And I vaguely remembered getting a peek at her bush in the green room. I remembered watching Ruth Gator Bait Ginsberg rubbing one out in front of me. I remembered all the cocaine. But mostly what I remembered were the cigarettes. Every single one of them. What the hell was I thinking? My brain felt as dry and vapid as an off-brand soda cracker. My jaw hurt. My teeth felt bent. My eyes were swollen. I tried to look out the window to see what time it was. All I could see was white. There was a pain behind my right eye. I could feel it coming. I didn't want it to come. But it was coming. I held my eyes closed for as long as I could. Trying to move the pain away with my thoughts. It wasn't going anywhere. I laid there motionless. Trying to think of anything else. It was coming. It was coming. I tried to resist. I really did. I tried to roll over. To get more darkness. But my nose came into contact with a stink that was either saliva or dog shit. That did it. I ran to the bathroom. Making it just in time. The vomit splashing disgusting toilet water on my face. This added to the painful thrusts my body was making. Yellow bile coming out. Mixed with what looked like coffee grounds. I was surprised there was so much vomit. Where was the liquid coming from? All I had to drink in the last who knows how many hours was rum and a handful of water. I remembered taking the drink of water before I went to bed. I suppose none of that mattered. I wasn't really asking those questions. I did wonder where the liquid was coming from. But not in a logical sense, more like, I didn't understand. Why wasn't I vomiting sand at this point?

I puked until I couldn't puke any more. I stood up and went to get a drink from the faucet. As I stood there taking in a few little sips, waves of nausea hit me again. I was back at the toilet. Puking my guts out. This time I was really done. I could feel it. There was nothing left. I stood up. Wiped my mouth. Flushed. My headache was gone. Kind of. The migraine was gone. But my head still hurt. I was very dehydrated. I could tell because my right calf was about to cramp up. I stretched it out as I tried to put as much water back into my body as I could. I didn't get too much in before I gave up. I needed to think of other ways to get my fluids. I went back to bed. Closed my eyes. Pulled the blankets up. I was hungry for a soup or something. I kind of wanted to just lie in bed. Watch a movie or something. Even the television seemed like something to do. To keep me distracted from my thoughts. By my thoughts I mean my shame. I was roughed up. I had pushed it too far last night. I needed a day off. What I really needed was a different life. One where things like last night didn't happen. I felt like I knocked five years off of my life. Not that it mattered at this point. It was all downhill now anyway. I was trying my hardest to fall back asleep when there was a soft knock on the door. I managed to get up. Draping the blanket over my shoulders. I wasn't in the mood to feel more vulnerable than I was already feeling. I opened the door.

Pink Eye Randy was standing there. Wearing his cool sunglasses. He was holding a paper bag. A bottle of what looked like soda water. A bottle of rum. A white coffee mug slung around his thumb that said World's Best Cat Mom written in cursive on the side. I moved to the side. He came in. Put the stuff on top of the bed. Said:

"You sick Mr. B? It smells like sick in here."

"I'm fine."

"Good. I brought you some stuff."

"Thanks, Randy."

"I noticed you didn't go to the diner like normal. I was worried about you Mr. B."

"Thanks, Randy."

"Are you okay?"

"I'm fine."

"Okay, good. I won't keep you then."

"Randy."

"Yeah, Mr. B?"

"Everything go okay last night? I feel like I had a weird set."

"You did great! Oh! Here!" Randy reached into his pocket. Pulled out a very large wad of cash. "Your earnins'." He started to hand me the wad of cash. It smelled like the inside of a funeral parlor. I didn't want to touch it. I might throw up again. I had him put it next to the television. Next to the box of toilet paper. "Okay, then."

"Okay then."

"Very well."

"Very well, then."

"Okay."

"Randy!"

"Sorry, Mr. B, I came here to give you this stuff but now I can't remember what I was going to do next."

"Do me a favor and remember outside, please."

"Sure thing." He stood there still.

"Randy!"

"Sorry, Mr. B, but I am remembering. I was supposed to tell you something. My dad said, tell Mr. B that..."

"Your dad said you should tell me that...?"

"I should tell you that..."

"Randy!"

"I should tell you that...Oh! I remember. My dad told me to tell you that the Harbinger Of Chaos quit and said that you can all go suck an egg you filthy loadies. Also, he hopes you all rot in hell."

"All of us, or just me?"

"I guess all of us."

"Thanks, Randy."

"Sure thing, Mr. B! Hope you feel better. See you tonight!"

Pink Eye Randy left. I shut the door. Closed the curtains. I had to turn on the lights because it was so dark. I almost opened the curtains again because the light was so awful coming from the ceiling. I looked at the pile of money. Frowned. It looked like thousands of dollars. I frowned because I wanted to count it, but I was too sensitive to do so. I walked over to the paper bag on the bed. Dumped it out. It was a sandwich or what looked like a sandwich that said "Turk" on it. I hoped it was a sandwich that came from Shandy's and Pink Eye Randy didn't make it. Also in the bag was two more bags of cocaine. Two packs of cigarettes. A bag of chips. And a pickle wrapped up in a paper towel. I found my pants and took my wallet out. I put the bags of cocaine in my wallet. I reached back into the pocket my wallet came from. The bag of cocaine was still in there. From last night. I guess we must have been doing Ruth Gator Bait Ginsberg's cocaine. Or something. This new thing about Pink Eye Randy being a pusher was getting out of hand. I'm not saying I was minding it so much, but I didn't understand what he was up to. I put the other bag of cocaine in my wallet as well. I opened the soda water. Took a drink. It hit the spot. I took a bite from the pickle.

I was hungry. I opened the sandwich. It was a turkey club. With bacon and mayo and tomato and lettuce. I ate half of it standing next to the bed. The blanket still wrapped around my shoulders. I took a few more bites of the pickle. I didn't open the potato chips though. They seemed too loud for me at the moment. I took another drink of the soda water. Moved all the things off the bed and onto the night stand. Got back into bed. Closed my eyes. I played with a piece of bacon stuck between my teeth in the back. After a while I fell asleep.

I felt a little bit better when I woke up. I laid in bed eating the other half of the sandwich and the rest of the pickle. Taking drinks from the bottle of soda water. The room was depressing. The light shining from the ceiling throwing angry shadows on greasy slime. I got up. Opened the curtains. It was late afternoon now. I looked out on the parking lot. There wasn't any activity. I walked to the door. Opened it. Looked out. The Harbinger Of Chaos's car was gone. Ruth Gator Bait Ginsberg's car was still there. I put my clothes on and walked over to her room. Knocked. She answered it the same way I answered my door when Pink Eye Randy knocked on it. She looked ill. Her eyes were swollen. I could see her black bush peeking through the opening of the blanket she had wrapped around her shoulders.

"What the hell do you want?"

"Nothing. Just came to see you were doing alright."

"I'm fine."

"You hear about Chaos?"

"Yeah, good riddance."

"Yeah."

"Yeah, okay." She shut the door. I went back to my room.

I was feeling good enough now to not feel stupid. I was still deeply ashamed of myself. I decided to count the wad of cash that Pink Eye Randy brought me. The smell was still disgusting. Did he rob a funeral home? How do you get money to smell like that? Especially thousands of dollars? It was three thousand dollars. I tried to figure out the math of what that amount of money meant, but it was too arbitrary. I would need to know how much money the Comedy Smithereens had taken in. How many days I had been staying at the racist Motel Mumbo Jumbo. And then figure out what the percentage of my cut would be. I had no idea about any of these things. But for me it was a lot of money. I looked around to find a place to hide it. I tried to put it under the television, but that just made the television look weird. Tilted. I thought about putting it in the tank of the toilet, but that was stupid. The only real option was to put it in the yellow Rabbit, or under the mattress. The mattress seemed like a better idea. Something told me the yellow Rabbit wasn't long for this world. I suppose what told me that was the fact that the thing was ancient, had hundreds of thousands of miles on it, and every time I started it I had to pray that it started. One day it would get towed away from me and the idea of leaving thousands of dollars inside made my stomach itchy. I walked to the far side of the bed. The furthest distance from the door. Put it under the mattress and tried to both remember about it and forget about it at the same time.

There was nothing to do now but wait. My hangover was grotesque. My body was sore and tired. I just wanted to sleep. To have some time alone. To sleep for a few days. Regain my strength. But I had a show to do. Or at least that is what I told myself. Maybe I would have a little bump. Drink a little rum. Smoke a cigarette. Something to pass the time before it was the staging hour. I poured some rum into the World's Best Cat Mom mug. Topped it off with some soda water. Took a sip. Took my wallet out. Took out a baggie of cocaine. Walked over to the television. Wiped it down with my hand. Dumped some coke on it. Took my wallet out. Made some lines with my driver's license. Went to get a bill out to roll up. To snort it. I was out of bills. I walked around the bed. Reached under the mattress. Pulled out a bunch of stinky bills. Put them in my wallet. Save the one I rolled up. Snorted a line of cocaine. It smelled like a funeral home. I thought I would just do one, but I suddenly felt different about it. I did another line. In the other nostril. I put the rolled up bill down. Next to the lines of cocaine. Took a drink of rum and soda water from the World's Best Cat Mom mug. Reached into my pocket. Found myself lighting a cigarette without even really thinking about it. My hangover was on the outs. My shame was still there, but was different now. Somehow justified. I opened the door and walked out of the room. Smoking in the room seemed gross. It must have been later than I thought because the light outside was twilight. Receding yellows that were coughing up blue and black orange. I was feeling excited for some reason. Thinking tonight would be a good night. Remembering the night before in a different way.

I thought about Shandy. What she was up to. Why she had come to me with her waterworks and lame story about JayJay wanting to meet me behind her diner. I remembered that I was supposed to meet him at high noon. Whoops. Did that mean he would come find me? Was Shandy just fucking with me? Was JayJay going to show up tonight and punch a shit through my guts and out my butt? The guy was huge. A big gorilla with big sideburns. And I was just a wimpy worm that crawled out of a slimy mud hole. I didn't stand a chance. I finished my cigarette. Went back inside my room. Sat down on the toilet. Squirted a few anxiety shits out my asshole while looking at the wadded up newspaper on the counter. Annoyed with myself that I destroyed it. Even if you don't really read something when you are taking a shit, it is nice, however, to have something to read on the toilet. I wiped until I was bored with it. Stood up. Frowned at the toilet. Flushed. Zipped my pants up. Did the button. Rinsed my hands in the sink. Admired my Hitler good looks in the mirror. Smiled my banana Laffy Taffys at myself. Went back into the room. Sipped from the World's Best Cat Mom mug. Trying not to get too drunk before I could get actually drunk. I wondered if Tricky Houdini had gotten a replacement for the Harbinger Of Chaos. I was interested enough about it to decide to go to the green room early. To find out. I did another line of cocaine. Drank the rest of my drink. Went back into the bathroom. Combed my hair. Brushed my banana Laffy Taffys. Spit out a bunch of blood. Took a drink of water from the faucet. With my hand. Shut the bathroom light off. Made sure I had my wallet and my smokes. Turned the room light off. Thought about locking the door. Turned the light back on. Now I had things to worry about. I hesitated. Which made me suck down another line of cocaine. My eyes got wide. I reached into my pocket. Pulled out the pink eye medicine. Squirted a couple drops in both eyes. Put the medicine back. Looked for my key. Found it next to the lamp. Next to the unopened bag of potato chips. Put the key in my pocket. Turned the light back off. Looked back at the room. Everything seemed fine. I left. Forgetting to lock the door behind myself.

⚬

I walked through the back doors of the Comedy Smithereens. When I got to the bar I could see the place was packed again. I couldn't tell if Shandy was in the front row or not. I hoped she wasn't. I wasn't in the mood for her mind games tonight. I looked around for the government goons. I couldn't see them. That didn't mean they weren't there. It just meant I couldn't see them. The Nubian Princess and the dandruff soaked Hitler Youth were quite busy. The Bouncer was doing her thing. Tinkly music played on the speakers. Nobody was on stage yet. I went around to the back. Through the curtains that led into the green room. The curtains that had the paper that said "Talint" safety pinned to them. Ruth Gator Bait Ginsberg was sitting on the couch. Looking like something death dragged in in a suitcase. She was trying to drink a drink. But she was having troubles with it. She would hold it up to her mouth, and then put it back down on the coffee table. A very large and very loud person was sitting next to her. Yelling at her. Not in an unfriendly way. Just boisterous. The both of them looked at me when I came in. The loud one stood up and said:

"Hi! I am Bex. They, them. If you give two shits." They held out their hand.

"I'm Bullion. He-him. And I do give two shits." I shook their hand.

"Good to hear it. Great vibes you got here. What is this a hangover sanitorium? Everyone around here looks like death is playing tonsil hockey with your ass cracks."

"You missed a good one last night."

"I don't think I missed anything. Unless missing something means getting run over by the Butthole Express." They were funny. Much funnier than the Harbinger Of Chaos.

"Save it for the stage, you jerk." Ruth Gator Bait Ginsberg said.

"Save a jerk for the stage? I don't got no dick, don't you know that? Trigger warning, bitches."

I went over to the bottles of booze. Made myself a rum and Sprite easy on the ice. I turned around. Bex was sitting down again. Their drink was full. Ruth Gator Bait Ginsberg's drink hadn't moved. I was about to sit down in a chair when Pink Eye Randy came in. Wearing his cool sunglasses.

"Bex, you are on. Hope you are ready."

"I've been ready since first call, Randy. Let's roll!"

"Great! I'll introduce you." Pink Eye Randy disappeared through the stage curtains. Bex kept talking.

"See, that is from PeeWee's Big Adventure. When he finally finds his bike in California. And the little kid and the nuns are shooting that movie and then PeeWee gets his bike back."

I heard Pink Eye Randy over the small speakers by the ceiling.

"Worms and Germs. We got a special treat for you. Straight from your step-mom's drunken angry couch-soaked mouth! Bexxxxxxx!"

"Oh shit! Gotta go!" Bex ran out. We could hear them starting their set:

"Well, hello. I see you guys, the question is, do you see me? Have you ever been to Ohio? What the hell am I talking about? This is Ohio. The real question is, have any of you ever left Ohio? I know you haven't, you look like a pepperoni wrapped in a tortilla made of American cheese. I mean, if that is food-fusion, I don't even want to know."

Bex was off to a good start. I wanted to listen but I was kind of concerned about Ruth Gator Bait Ginsberg. I also wanted to take a shit and do another line of cocaine. Maybe smoke a cigarette. I stood there trying to make a move. But then I realized that Ruth Gator Bait Ginsberg was just hungover and I didn't need to worry about her. I guessed I had some weird connection because she had rubbed one out in front of me the night before. There was no reason to feel nostalgic about it. I made myself another drink. Took it into the bathroom with me. Unbuttoned my pants. Unzipped them. Let them fall to the floor. Sat down on the toilet. Listened to the fan run as I stared at the door. I kind of wished I was out in the audience at the moment. Something told me that Bex was the true Harbinger Of Chaos, not the Harbinger Of Chaos himself. That dude was just meat-head fun-times telling jokes about things that happened 4,000 years ago. Good riddance is right, like Ruth Gator Bait Ginsberg had said. Bex, however, seemed like bad news incarnate. And I was sad I was missing it.

I sat on the toilet listening to the fan. Drinking my drink. Nothing was coming out. No piss. No farts. No shit. I thought I wanted to do more cocaine. But then I didn't. I was feeling shaky all the sudden. I was beginning to wonder why I even went into the bathroom in the first place. If I wanted to be alone I could have just gone back to my room. Maybe I was just processing something that had come up that I wasn't aware of. Like a shift had happened and I needed to make sure I was okay with it. But that didn't seem right. I suppose I just came over early to check out the new talent and instead I was sitting in the bathroom. On the toilet. My naked butt flapping in the breeze. Drinking a rum and Sprite easy on the ice. I suppose there was only two reasons I was there. To take a shit, or to do more cocaine. And the shit was stuck on the inside. I reached down and took my wallet out of my pants. Opened it. Took a bag of cocaine out. Opened it. This took a while. I had bitten my fingernails off at some point not noticing and I was shaky as hell. I dumped some powder on the webbing between my forefinger and my thumb. Sucked it up my right nostril. Did the same again with my left nostril. Made a yacking noise. Zipped the bag back closed. Put it back in my wallet. Put my wallet back in my pocket. Picked up my drink from the floor where I had left it. Took a drink. Put the drink back down. Stood up. I could smell my butt. Even though nothing came out. I pulled my pants up. Did the button. Zipped them. Bent down. Picked up my drink. This time I farted. I wondered why bodies were so gross. All the farts and turds and cum and spit and puke and smells. I flushed the toilet for no reason. Walked back out into the green room.

I could hear Bex really socking it to the crowd. I could tell they were making people uncomfortable just by the reaction from the crowd. Nervous laughter mostly. It sounded like there was an audience participation thing going on. "Do you mind if I sit in your lap?" Nervous laughter. "Don't worry, I won't molest you." Nervous laughter. Muffled yelling from the back. Then somebody yelled, "Get that fucker outta here!" Then something like bedlam. Shuffling or something. It was hard to tell. A scream. "Nah! You don't know shit man!" What sounded like broken glass. "Give it back! I said give it back!" And then silence. Then Bex again. "Well, that was special. I guess I aint in Brooklyn no more." This led to actual laughter. They went back to their set. "The nice thing about getting molested is that you are never lonely, right? I mean, as a kid, I never knew where I would be sleeping, but I always knew somebody would give me special attention, even if just for a second. There is no dearth of child molesters in the world."

I listened to the Bex while standing in front of the bar. I had lit a cigarette. I was feeling kind of annoyed at Pink Eye Randy. Being a pusher and all. I had stopped smoking years ago, and now I couldn't get enough of them. And the cocaine was going right to my blackened soul. I felt like a wet mule eating oats again after being put in some barren and rocky pasture. Something didn't seem right about it. First Class treatment for a third rate hack. I looked over at Ruth Gator Bait Ginsberg. On the couch. She looked like she had fallen asleep. Her drink had about a half inch of melted ice on top of it. Which meant she hadn't touched it in some time. I wondered if I should wake her up. I suppose she was about to go on stage. Or maybe not. She looked ghostly. Even as she slept. Her skin was really white. Translucent. I think she had told me she was part Chinese and part Italian the night before. Whatever that means, but with respect to her being really white at the moment. I guess what I am trying to say is that she was looking really white and I don't know if that was such a good thing. For her. I mean, she wasn't Scandinavian is all I am saying.

I stood there wondering if I should wake her up. In theory she was about to go on stage. I suppose that was the right thing to do. But I felt bad for her. She was not in a good state. As I contemplated what to do Pink Eye Randy showed up with his cool sunglasses carrying a clipboard.

"Ruth! You're on next. Get your bees in a bonnet." Ruth Gator Bait Ginsberg woke up. Startled.

"Wah?!"

"You're up. Chop-chop."

"Did you just seriously tell me to chop-chop, you gummy-eyed creep. Get the fuck out of here before I shove that clipboard up your ass." Pink Eye Randy ran back to where he came from. "What the fuck, man. Did that really just happen?" I shrugged. "How long I been out? Damn, last night was brutal, dog. You got anymore of that hoosegow? I am feeling a little peaked."

I took my wallet out and handed her a full bag of cocaine. Said, "Keep it." She dumped a pile on the coffee table. Looked around. I handed her a card. She made a bunch of lines. Looked around again. Handed me the card back. I handed her a stinky bill from my wallet. She said:

"Damn! This smells like a funeral home. It stinks!. What the hell?"

"Yeah, I don't know, ask Randy."

"That fucker?" She did two lines. Handed me the rolled up bill and winked at me.

"Don't mind if I do." I did the other two lines. I left the bill rolled up and put it in my wallet. Ruth Gator Bait Ginsberg zipped the bag of cocaine closed. Put it in her bra. Ran her index finger along the white dust left behind. Rubbed it on her gums. Took a drink from her drink. It must have just been the melted ice.

"Damn, that is some weak ass shit. Top me off?" She handed me her glass.

"What's your poison?"

"What's my poison? Ha! What is this, the 40's? Tell the Chinese girl chop-chop, and now you with your, What's my poison? You understand this is why America can't have nice things, right? It's all white guy rhetoric. We are never getting nowhere at this rate."

"Sorry, what is your drink of preference you self-important asshole?"

"Ha! Now there you go. Get me a G and T, if you don't mind."

"What about the rest of this?" Her glass was half full. I held it up.

"That's up to you, my friend." As a lark I drank what was left in the glass. It was brutal. Straight tequila. Ruth Gator Bait Ginsberg laughed. I poured her a gin and tonic. Easy on the ice. I handed it to her, "Thanks, guy."

"You got it, doll face."

"Ha! Cheers." She held up the drink. I held my drink up as well. "Last night was something else. I hope I didn't freak you out with my bean ticklin'."

"Ah, nah, par for the course."

"How is that par for the course, that sort of shit happen to you all the time now? You get a little bit of success and all the ladies rub one out in front of you for funsies?"

"No, not at all, I mean, you get a bunch of blow and a bunch of booze, things happen, you know?"

"Yeah, I guess. All I am saying is that I am sorry, I hope

you weren't too skeeved out, is all."

"Fine by me. You can squirt a load in front of me anytime you want. I got nothing to do these days."

"Oh, I squirted?"

"Lots."

"Shit."

"Seriously, it aint nothing."

"Yeah, okay. If you say so. I feel embarrassed as shit."

"Don't worry about it. We can do it later again if you need proof. Ya know, just to take the edge off."

"Bullion, are you hitting on me?"

"Maybe. I don't know."

Just then Bex came back into the green room. The crowd was cheering. I could hear it through the tiny speakers near the ceiling. They were sweaty and glassy-eyed. Saw that me and Ruth Gator Bait Ginsberg were in a moment.

"Get a room, you creeps. What is that cocaine?" The dregs of the drugs we just did were apparent. I shrugged. Ruth Gator Bait Ginsberg reached into her bra. Took the bag out. Bex shrugged. I shrugged. I reached into my pocket and took out my wallet. Handed a card to Ruth Gator Bait Ginsberg. She dumped some cocaine out. Made some lines. I took the rolled up tooter out. I handed it to Bex. Ruther Gator Bait Ginsberg handed the card back. I put it in my wallet. Bex smelled the rolled up bill.

"What the hell? Did you find this in the dumpster behind a funeral home?"

"Right?" Ruth Gator Bait Ginsberg said.

"Ask Randy." I said.

"That fucker?" Bex did a line. Handed the bill to Ruth Gator Bait Ginsberg. She did a line. She offered it to me. I declined. I was feeling very high at the moment. The tooter went back to Bex. Then Ruth Gator Bait Ginsberg again. Then back to me. I put it back in my wallet. Bex walked over to make a drink. Pink Eye Randy came back in. Sheepish. He wasn't carrying the clipboard anymore, but he was still wearing his cool sunglasses.

"Are you ready, Ruth?"

"Why yes, Randy, I am ready, thanks for asking."

"Well, okay, I am glad to hear it. Shall I introduce you now?"

"Yes, you shall."

"Okay then, I will see you out there. Good luck."

"Thank you, Randy."

"You are welcome, Ruth."

Pink Eye Randy disappeared through the curtains. The tinkly music stopped playing. I hadn't even noticed it was on. Such were the vibes at the Comedy Smithereens. Pink Eye Randy came over the little speakers next to the ceiling.

"Cunts and Blunts, put your hands together for Ruth Gator Bait Ginssssssbeeeerg!"

Ruth Gator Bait Ginsberg sighed. Stood up. Waved her drink at me and Bex. I said:

"Break a dick!"

"Suck a donkey dick out there!" Bex laughed at their own joke. Then mumbled, "Suck a donkey dick out there? What the hell? Stupid!"

Ruth Gator Bait Ginsberg made her way through the curtains and onto the stage. Her set started.

I sat down on the couch. Bex stood next to the bottles of booze. Perusing them. I listened to Ruth Gator Bait Ginsberg's set with my eyes closed. Bex doing commentary.

Ruth: "But then the guy picked up the dog shit with a paper bag. A paper bag! Who picks up a dog shit with a paper bag!"

Bex: "I'll pick up her dog shit with a paper bag."

Ruth: "I looked at him and said, what happened to the popcorn? I guess you left the movie before the credits?"

Bex: "I got a movie you can watch."

Ruth: "Did you lose your ticket, how is that even

possible? Curb your dog, bitch!"

Bex: "How about you and I do it doggy style later, hmmm?"

Bex was very odd but funny. They finally decided on a drink to make. Something green, apparently, but what was green on the bar was unknown to me. They sat down next to me and remembered something or something occurred to them because they ran out of the green room without saying anything except, "Shit! No, no, no!" Leaving their drink behind. I was so curious that I waited for a second for them to come back. When they didn't I took a sip. Absinthe? Really? Pink Eye Randy was something else. I was expecting apple vodka at best. But Absinthe?

I was up next. I rubbed my legs and tried to get in the mood. I wasn't feeling very funny, and I was high as hell. The sound of tinkly music came over the tiny speakers next to the ceiling out of nowhere. I must have spaced out because it did not feel like half an hour had gone by since Ruth Gator Bait Ginsberg had gone on stage. I was sitting there feeling stupid when she came back through the curtains looking sweaty and pleased. I asked how it went.

"Fantastic! Aren't you on next? You ready?"

"Fuck! I'm ready."

"You don't look ready."

"Thanks, that's quite helpful."

"Anything for the cause."

"Where's Randy?"

Pink Eye Randy never came back. I didn't know what to do. Five minutes turned into ten minutes. I could hear the crowd getting restless. Someone yelled loud enough for the speakers next to the ceiling to pick it up, "Where the hell is this idiot? C'mon!" I made myself a rum and Sprite. Easy on the ice. Did a couple bumps of the cocaine. Ruth Gator Bait Ginsberg was in the bathroom otherwise I would have had her introduce me. Or Bex, wherever the hell they went in such a hurry. I worked my way through the curtains and onto the stage. I tapped on the microphone. The crowd cheered. "Is this thing on?" Typical laughter and clapping and cheering. I felt like the idiot the peanut gallery heckler had portended. "Hey barkeep, cut out the tinklys!" Nothing happened. "Hey bartender, can you cut the music?" The dandruff soaked Hitler Youth yelled something. A moment later word got to me from the crowd, "They don't know how to!"

"Fucking Randy! What the fuck!" I was instantly over-dramatic. "Does anyone know sound shit?"

A voice came from the very back, followed by a telephone of helpful audience members. "The bouncer does!" The music turned off. I went to speak into the microphone. Nothing came out.

"Now the mic doesn't fucking work!" I yelled at the

top of my lungs. My nose was dripping. I wiped it. I looked at my sleeve and then at the audience. They were standing there staring at me, grim faced and stupid. "The mic doesn't work! Tell her!" The crowd telephoned the words back to The Bouncer. There was a murmur that made it back to the stage.

"Try it now!" One guy yelled.

"Check, check." There was sound. "Okay. We are good now! Wow, thanks, guys! And congrats everyone! We solved the world's most stupidest unnecessary pointless problem!" The crowd cheered. I shook my head. Someone yelled, "Cinco de Mayo!" I took a drink from Rum and Sprite easy on the ice. "Really? Is it really Cinco de Mayo?" Someone yelled, "No shit, Sherlock!" I pretended to look at a watch on my wrist. "How long have I been living here now? That's insane that it is May now. Wait, no! Hasn't it been May all month? What the hell is going on? Somebody give me a margarita! I can't even think straight." A minute went by. For some reason I did a bump of cocaine while standing on stage. It was messy and I turned my back to the crowd, but I did it. Then I lit a cigarette. Then, instead of doing my usual things I decided to improv what at the time seemed like the stupidest thing I could possibly say.

"Cinco de Mayo. You know in Mexico, Cinco de Mayo is like a celebration, I think it is like the fourth of July here, but down there, like down there in Mexico or whatever, but down there if you say happy fourth of July they understand what you mean because everyone understands what the fourth of July is, because America is the best and everyone else can suck it..." The idiotic crowd went ballistic with this statement, somebody handed me a margarita, "...but up here, in America, if somebody says, like, happy cinco de Mayo, that means that you are happy they just put a jar of mayonnaise in the sink, right? Who the fuck celebrates that? How does sinko-ing the may-o-naise garner any sort of good times at all? Put that shit in the fridge, you son of a bitch! Not only that, but down in Mexico they put mayonnaise on corn. Mayonnaise on corn? Why not just rub it in dog shit and roll it around in cat litter, right?"

The rest of my set was pure nonsense. More nonsense than before. More nonsense than normal. It didn't make a difference. The audience ate it up, hook, line and stinker. Maybe it was the drugs and the booze, the incredible luck I had been having or even that I was still alive after all these years, but I was starting to become very paranoid about what was happening at the Comedy Smithereens, what was happening at the racist Motel Mumbo Jumbo, what was happening at Shandy's, in Drei Ecken, Ohio. A lifetime of slinging half-funny knock-knock jokes did not deserve the welcome this audience was giving me. Sure, I had put in my hours along the way. I calculated it once. I don't remember the exact number of hours I had spent on stage, but it was over myriad. But once I got on stage I could bullshit my way through hours of material and improv, but I knew that I was not as funny as these fools were thinking I was. They were starting to make me angry. As somebody that both loathed and needed an audience to make art, I had always had a complicated relationship with the audience, but this was becoming absurd. As a test, I went on a full bodied political screed to end all screeds. Raising my voice, screaming at the top of my lungs about this or that. Constantly wiping my hair back, adjusting my posture. Had anyone been able to mute my voice and put me in a military uniform, change the colors to black and white, I would have been a propaganda video for the Third Reich. It wasn't comedy I was doing, it was a political rally. And those fuckers, the fickle assholes that had made me try my hardest for decades just to put a tiny morsel of food in my mouth, the audience I mean, they loved it so dearly, so fondly that they were banging on tables and screaming at the tops of their lungs when I finished my set.

I was pissed. I hated their guts. I looked down at the

stage. The drink I had walked in with was sitting there, full as it was when I walked in, sitting on the stage. I kicked it into the audience like a football. It hit some poor sap in the guts and he doubled over. This only drew more admiration from the crowd. They were chanting my name when I split the curtains that led into the green room. It wasn't a normal chant. It wasn't a chant where they just wanted more. They sounded worked-up. Riled-up. Energized. They had lost their minds. Some guy got on stage and yelled, "Sieg Heil! Sieg Heil!" through the microphone. The crowd joined in. Soon the Comedy Smithereens was shaking. Wavering. Shifting. Creaking. It sounded like a riot was breaking loose. Bottles being smashed. Tables being broken. I grabbed the bucket of ice, two glasses and the bottle of tequila and ran out the back door. I was scared. It was scary. I could have sworn I heard a gunshot, but I wasn't sure.

I ran the bottle of tequila and ice and glasses over to Ruth Gator Bait Ginsberg's room. I kicked the door because my hands were full. She opened it, naked. "Oh! Tequila!" I put the stuff down and peeked out through her curtains. Making sure nobody followed me. Making sure the riot wasn't spilling out into the parking lot. Ruth Gator Bait Ginsberg made herself a drink and was immediately annoyed with me. "C'mon, man, what the fuck?"

"Dude! You don't even know! I think there's a riot over there!"

"Wait, what? Let me see!"

I turned off the lights and we opened the curtains. Suddenly the back door of the Comedy Smithereens dropped to the ground. A very small man rolled off of it and stood up, dusted himself off and ran back inside. A very large man came out, shirtless. He was carrying a beer keg over his head like Donkey Kong. He threw the keg at the yellow Rabbit. "Not my car!" The very large man lurched back inside. With the door knocked down we could see some of what was happening inside. The crowd was going insane. There was a fire that we could clearly see. I clearly saw the dandruff soaked Hitler Youth and The Bouncer throwing bottles of booze into it. Flames erupting with each new bottle thrown. The Nubian Princess ran into the parking lot looking scared and holding a knife, but instead of running away she stabbed my back left tire and ran back inside. "Not my tire!" Then, like some gossamer ghost, Tricky Houdini scudded out of the missing back door of the Comedy Smithereens in a white robe carrying a scuttle of what I assumed was gasoline. After he dumped most of it on the corner of the building and then around the corner towards the front, he lit a match and the Comedy Smithereens went up in flames.

Tricky Houdini jumped through the flames and back into the club. His robe was on fire as he ran towards the fire we could clearly see inside. Nobody came into the parking lot to give my car more suffering. We watched Bex load their stuff into their car in a very quick manner, and then drive away. A look of grim panic on their face. Ruth Gator Bait Ginsberg saw this and said, "Shouldn't that be us?"

"Yeah, I don't know!"

She started packing her suitcase. I poured myself a drink and lit a cigarette. I watched the flames climb the walls of the Comedy Smithereens. I felt like a dick, but I was more worried about my car than I was about the club. I became worried that the flames would melt it. "Be right back." I ran out to the yellow Rabbit. Looked at the damage Donkey Kong had done. Frowned. Looked at the damage The Nubian Princess had done. Frowned. I got in. Started it. Sighed. Backed up and slowly drove it away from the fire and parked it in front of room seven where Bex had ditched from. I walked back to Ruth Gator Bait Ginsberg's room and tried to turn the knob. She had locked the door when I was gone. I knocked. She let me in.

"What's going on out there?"

"Not much, really, just the fire, I guess."

"Is it a riot, or whatever? Are the cops coming? The fire, you know, department?"

"Oh, I don't know. I was worried about my car is all. Sure the hell seems like a riot!"

Ruth Gator Bait Ginsberg walked outside. Naked. The fire-light bouncing against her youthful naked body. As she stood there listening to the riot, or whatever, as she had called it, Pink Eye Randy showed up.

"Randy! What the hell is going on?"

"Hi, Ruth, great set tonight! I was just coming to tell you, there is a fire and you should be careful."

"Yeah, but there is a riot, Randy! Shouldn't we call the cops or at least the fire department?"

"My dad says we shouldn't call the cops or the fire department until tomorrow. Is that Mr. B? Hi Mr. B! Great set tonight!" I waved through the window. "Thanks, Randy!" I could have gone outside but I didn't. The door was open and I could hear their conversation from where I was. For some reason I thought it was a great time to do a few bumps of cocaine. I watched Randy walk back towards the office and Ruth Gator Bait Ginsberg walk back into the room. She yanked the drugs from my fingertips and said, "Give me that!" A few seconds later she was in the bathroom with the door closed. I heard her lock it. I walked outside and listened. I wanted a cigarette and remembered I had lit one just a little while ago, I had no clue where it was. For all I knew it was in the yellow Rabbit. That would be great. Donkey Kong and his beer keg, The Nubian Princess with her knife, and after all of it, I burn the car down with my smoke? I looked down and realized I was still smoking the cigarette I was worried about. I lit a new cigarette with the tip of the last one that I had forgotten about. I watched the fire burning for a few puffs, but then I noticed the light in my room was on. I was going to ignore it, but then a shadow slid across the sidewalk. The shadow was curly and the gait was something I knew. I sighed. I shut Ruth Gator Bait Ginsberg's door and walked towards my room.

I attempted to open the door to my room. It was locked. I reached into my pocket and found the key. My ex was sitting on the bed counting the funeral home cash I had hid under the mattress. She didn't look up. Just looking at her tight little mouse-like face concentrating on the money, her curly black hair sticking out in all directions, her very gigantic breasts sagging with her incredibly awful posture, her legs crossed, wearing a brown-green skin tight body skirt. Just looking at her aroused so many disgusting emotions I almost strangled her, thinking I could drag her lifeless body over to the Comedy Smithereens, throw her into the flames and nobody would be any wiser about it. Still counting the money she reached over to the night stand, took a glass filled with what appeared to be my rum and an exorbitant amount of ice and drank on it, "There's ice in the sink." The sound of her voice sent shockwaves through my guts and made my penis as hard as a rock.

Like the fool that I am, instead of turning around and getting in my car and getting the hell out of Drei Ecken, I took the World's Greatest Cat Mom coffee mug into the bathroom, put a few cubes of ice in it, took it back into the room and made myself a rum and soda. I dropped my cigarette onto the greasy carpet and stamped it out.

I lit another one and found another bag of cocaine in my wallet. I did a couple of bumps and put it back. I opened the curtains further so I could get a better look at the fire. Soon it would jump from the club and over to the motel. Whether the racist Motel Mumbo Jumbo would burn to the ground as well was unknown, but nobody was coming out the back door of the Comedy Smithereens any longer. I was curious enough about what was happening in front of the club that I almost left Liz where she was, leaving her to steal my money and do whatever it was she had come to do without me, but the curiosity of why she was here was stronger than the curiosity of what was happening with the riot.

Watching her counting that money, drinking that drink, sitting that way, looking the way she looked, it reminded me of when the government goons had showed up and I had treated them to the tasty treat of my dirty naked hairy butthole. She was fucking with me. She was fucking with me and it was working. Every ounce of self-respect and self-preservation in me was screaming that I should walk back out the door and never look back, yet there I stood, hard as a rock, staring at the Lizard, counting my money and showing me her dirty naked hairy butthole. When she finished counting she put the cash in the turquoise colored leather purse with foot long tassels that was next to her on the bed, "It's not much, but it'll do." She took another drink from her iced rum, "Now, where were we? Oh, right, the slimy wimpy worm and his greasy, bed bug infested, cum soaked motel room. Did you think I wouldn't find these?" She pulled Shandy's panties from under the pillow. Smelled them. Whipped her head back like they stank. Looked at me with her giant, brown and vacant eyes. She looked very upset. Like somehow, after over a decade, me having a pair of some other woman's panties under my pillow was akin to me cheating on her. And it worked. I suddenly was filled with such great shame and guilt that I apologized.

"I'm sorry, I didn't know th-th-th-that, you were c-c-c-coming over." I couldn't believe it. I was even stuttering. I never stuttered before I met Liz and I never stuttered after we were finished, and here we were again.I could see myself from outside of myself watching myself behave like this and I was powerless to stop it. "Well, you are going to have to make up for it then." Liz uncrossed her legs and pulled her skirt up to her stomach, she slid back and spread her legs. Like a zombie I was right there again. The repulsive smell. Like a burst ingrown hair mixed with rotting garbage and raw ground beef accidentally left on the counter all night. The prickly, close shorn pubic hairs, the chunks of toilet paper stuck to various places. I gagged as I licked. She said things like, "Slurp it up, you wimpy, slimy worm. That's right. Now lick my butthole, you scummy wimpy faggot, lick it now and don't be stingy." I was hypnotized. I had no idea what I was doing. At the same time I had dropped my pants and was playing with my rock hard erection. I looked over at the window, the fire burning the Comedy Smithereens to the ground. Something exploded and sent a ball of flame out the back door. I went back to gagging on my ex's vagina and butthole. Liz grabbed my hair and started whacking my face against her crotch. It hurt my nose and I stubbed my cigarette out into the greasy carpet. Her facial assault must have broken something loose, because out of nowhere I sucked a huge string of snot down my throat and with it there must have been three lines of cocaine because I went from being a hypnotized robot to complete autonomy in a matter of seconds. I stood up and without having to do much of anything I launched a load that seemed to spin and float in the air forever, like an actual rocket in space, Liz was starting to say, "What the fuck are you doing, you slimy worn, get back down there!" The load slipped past her lizard lips and her lizard teeth and into her lizard mouth. I had never seen her move that fast once she realized what had happened. She jumped off the bed and ran into the bathroom, spitting into the toilet yelling, "You fucking son of a bitch! I'm gonna fucking kill you!" I pulled my pants up and grabbed her purse and ran back to Ruth Gator Bait Ginsburg's room. The door was open and the lights were on, but her car was gone and there was turd floating in the toilet. I frowned at the turd and flushed it. I felt  jealous of her youthful bowls. I didn't know what to do. Ruth Gator Bait Ginsburg would have known exactly what to do. But now she was gone and soon my ex would find me and there was nothing I could do about it.

I ran to the tequila and ice. I took it into the bathroom. One of the glasses as well. The turquoise leather purse with the funeral money. I locked the door. I made a drink and lit a cigarette and did a few bumps of cocaine. I stood there staring at myself into the mirror. At my Hitler good looks. Smiling my banana Laffy Taffys. My eyes looked like broken light bulbs. Like a string of Christmas lights wrapped around a stick of black licorice. I was looking gaunt. Undernourished. Outside the bathroom I could hear my ex looking for me. Banging on doors. Yelling my name. Telling me to expose myself before she found me otherwise there would be hell to pay. Soon her voice was accompanied by three other voices. They sounded like the government goons with their fake accents and their phony credentials. I was trapped and there was nothing I could do about it. I wanted to make a break for it. Run to the yellow Rabbit and hit the skids, but the damn Nubian Princess had stabbed my tire. Why did she stab my tire? Of all the tires to stab? Why mine? Could she read my mind? Did she know that I called her the Nubian Princess? Or was she just caught up in the moment and stabbed the first tire she saw? And what about Donkey Kong? Was it just luck that my car was right there, or were people out to get me? I was doing more bumps of cocaine to try and solve the mysteries in my head when I heard the motel door break open.

"We know you're in here, Mr. B, don't even think about what you're thinking about doing." What was I thinking about doing? Was Maurice reading my mind? What I was thinking of doing I was already doing. I had removed my shoes and put half the money in one shoe and half the money in the other. I put the shoes back on. I tried to buy some time as I tied them.

"I was gonna take a shit, if that's okay!"

"Ms. Liz! We got him!" A few moments went by.

"Where's that fucking motherfucker at?"

"Bathroom. He says he needs to take a shit."

"Fuck that, knock the door down."

The bathroom door broke open and Maurice smiled at me. He was missing two teeth on the top that I hadn't noticed before. He grabbed me by the front of my collar and drug me out of the bathroom. He threw me on the bed. I saw their cruiser outside. The lights were off, but the engine was running. Rona was sitting in the driver's seat and Cor was standing next to the motel room's open door. I could hear the fire blaring and what seemed like screams coming from the distance. Possibly a gunshot or two. Liz walked into the room like she was in a Hollywood movie. She was twirling Shandy's panties. Walking slowly. Her face was as grim as a bag of brown rice. Her body skirt bulging below her giant sagging knockers. Her nips poking loose. Maurice walked into the bathroom. Came back holding her turquoise leather bag with the long tassels.

Liz must have left the room and came back in for dramatic effect because I could hear her clearly inside the room before. That or she went back to get Shandy's panties from my room. Either way, her movements were odd and she was really hamming it up.

Maurice and Cor were making me nervous. They didn't even pretend to be from the government anymore. Cor had a gun in his pocket that I could see bulging out, and Maurice held his hands in fists the second he dropped me off on the bed, even though now he was holding Liz's purse. I waved at Rona sitting in the cruiser. She waved back. Rona seemed okay. I wanted to ask her how she got mixed up in all this nonsense, she did seem like a decent person, she had been honest at the diner before. Which was nice and odd. But she was also mixed up with these goon jerks. I really wanted to know how that happened. Instead Hollywood Liz grabbed the turquoise bag from Maurice and looked inside.

"What happened to the money, you dickless fuck?"

"What's your obsession with money, Liz? You gotta live your life, man."

"Search him."

Maurice did me a great rub down. It had been a long time since I had been touched like that. I felt sleepy and relaxed for the first time in years afterwards. I was about to thank him when he said, "Nothing."

"Check the bathroom." Maurice went into the bathroom. He came back out and shrugged. Cor walked into the bathroom and shot the toilet. Everyone recoiled except for Rona because she was in the cruiser. "Was that necessary, Cor?"

"Yes."

"You're an idiot."

"At least we know for sure now."

"We know you are an idiot, that is for sure."

"That's not what I meant!"

"Maurice, check the room. Cor, do me a favor and get lost."

"Okay, Ms. Liz, I'll be waiting outside."

"Great."

"Just let me know when you need me."

"Okay, Cor."

"I'll be right outside."

"That's great."

Cor was just as bad as I was. I assumed that he and Liz had something happening. Going on. He was a totally different person than before. Before he had been level headed and almost reasoning with me to be reasonable about whatever scheme this gang of goons had going on. Like he knew it was nonsense, but soon it would all be over. But now he was a different person. Insecure and needy. I felt bad for him.

Maurice tore the room apart finding nothing. He took his frustration out on me. It was like the sound guy in Oberlin all over again, except this time instead of making hilarious jokes he just beat me until I fell down onto the greasy carpet. Not nearly as roughed up as I should have been. I think it was because I was drunk and high. Like my body took the blows easier. Like how sometimes drunks survive car crashes. Either that or I was just numb. As I was lying on the ground Maurice pulled my pants down to check if the money was in my pants somehow. Up my ass crack. He kicked me and mumbled something about checking the other room as he left. Cor came back in, "Everything alright?" Liz ignored him and stood over me.

"Where is it?"

"Where's what?"

"Don't play stupid, idiot, we know you have it, now cough it up."

There was a gunshot outside. Liz and Cor ran out to check what was happening. I struggled to get up, but I managed. I pulled my pants up and did the zipper and the button. I was curious about the gun shot myself, so I went outside. Maurice was lying in the parking lot motionless. Pink Eye Randy was pointing a gun at Cor who was pointing a gun right back at Pink Eye Randy. It was a dangerous sight. The Comedy Smithereens had caught the racist Motel Mumbo Jumbo on fire. The light from the flames made wavering shadows of Cor and Pink Eye Randy. Liz was kneeling next to Maurice screaming. Begging him to get up. Rona was backing up the car. She looked terrified. I thought she was going to haul ass out of there, but instead she parked and got out. She opened the back door of the cruiser and she and Liz dragged Maurice's lifeless body into the back seat. Liz bawled her way into the car. Rona shut the door behind her. She got into the driver's seat. Cor kept aiming his pistol at Pink Eye Randy while he circled around to the other side of the cruiser. He fired a shot at Pink Eye Randy before he got inside. The bullet missed by a mile and struck the number four on the door of my room. The cruiser peeled out and then they were gone. I walked over to Pink Eye Randy. On accident I looked him directly in the eyes. He wasn't wearing his cool sunglasses anymore. It took me a second to recover.

"What happened, Randy? You okay?"

"I'm okay, Mr. B." I checked his body for bullet holes. "Mr. B, stop that, it tickles!"

"Sorry, Randy, just checking for wounds. Whose gun is that? It's not yours is it?"

"Oh, no, it belongs to that guy."

"How did you, what did you, what happened?"

"Nothing happened, I was packing your things for you because the fire is spreading and the guy came in and pointed the gun at me and then I don't know, I thought he was going to shoot me, but he got distracted by something on my face and I took the gun from him and then it went off. I hope he's okay."

"I don't think he's okay, Randy."

"I don't like that, Mr. B. I'm sorry the gun went off."

"I know you are, Randy." I put the gun in my pocket. Then I took it out again and walked closer to the backdoor of the Comedy Smithereens. Wiped our fingerprints off it for some reason and threw it into the flames. "Randy, we have to go. Can you grab some clothes and stuff?"

"Where're we gonna go, Mr. B? I don't want to leave my home."

"I don't think your home is going to make it, Randy."

"But that is where I live, Mr. B."

"I know, Randy. This is urgent."

"Okay, Mr. B, what should I grab?"

"I don't know, clothes, whatever, anything, anything you think you need."

"Okay, Mr. B."

I ran into room number four and grabbed the suitcase that Randy had so thoughtfully packed for me. I looked around the room to make sure I had everything. There was an explosion and the lights went out. I ran my suitcase to the yellow Rabbit and threw it into the hatch. I ran over to the office to check on Randy. He came out from the back with his cool sunglasses on and a leather bomber jacket. He was carrying what I can only assume was a lamp in the shape of a goose, or it was a goose sculpture with an electric cord. He was carrying a suitcase as well. It was dark and hard to see, but by the firelight it looked like something from a cartoon. Like there were stamps on it from traveling. I asked him if he had everything. He said he did. I said that was good and we had to get moving.

I don't know why, but I thought somehow the flat tire would have fixed itself when Pink Eye Randy was packing. It didn't. I sighed at the sight of it. I removed some things from the hatch and confirmed what I already knew would be true; the spare tire was flat as a pancake. I took it out and bounced it just to verify what I already knew. It didn't bounce. I put it back into the hatch as well as the suitcases and the lamp and the other things I had removed. I sighed. Shut the hatch. Thought for a second. Looked at the flat tire. Sighed again. Then I let out a very deep sigh. I was drunk, I was very high, the Comedy Smithereens and the racist Motel Mumbo Jumbo were on fire, Pink Eye Randy had just killed a man and my back left tire was flat. If we started driving now and a cop came around I would get pulled over. And if I got pulled over, that would be it. I would never leave jail.

"You okay, Mr. B? You seem upset."

"We're fucked, Randy. Royally."

"Because of the tire?"

"Yes, the tire, and about a million other things. You can't drive, can you?"

"Not a car, Mr. B."

"What can you drive, Randy? Me crazy? Just joking. I don't think a lawnmower is going to get us out of this mess."

"I don't know how to drive a lawnmower either."

"I know, Randy, I am joking with you." I lit a cigarette and watched the fire burn. The office was now on fire. The riot was still happening out front, or at least it sounded like it. I was resigning myself to my fate. Absently I asked Pink Eye Randy, "Well, what do you drive then?"

"I can drive an airplane."

"Can't we all?" I did not take him seriously.

"We have a plane even, just up the road. My dad says I am very good at it. I even have a license, see?" Pink Eye Randy took his wallet out and handed me his flying license. I tilted it into the direction of the flames and saw that indeed, Pink Eye Randy was a licensed pilot.

"No shit! That is fantastic, Randy! Good for you! How long did it take you to get that?" I didn't understand what Randy was implying when he showed me the license. I was prematurely defeated. I wanted another drink and a few more bumps of cocaine. I started walking to room number seven. Where the tequila was. I picked up a glass and put some ice into it that was melting on the greasy carpet. Maurice, may he rest in peace, made quite a mess of things looking for the money. I located the bottle of tequila. The lid was nice and tight, luckily. I poured a few fingers of the yellow stuff and twisted the lid back on. I took a sip and dumped a couple bumps of the white stuff on my thumb. Randy had been talking about learning to fly this entire time. It was very fascinating stuff.

"And now I can fly on my own and we have a plane over at the hangar just down the road." Either the cocaine triggered something in my brain or the tequila, or maybe I just got smarter all of the sudden, but I finally understood what Pink Eye Randy was saying.

"Are you saying that there is an airplane a couple miles away that we can fly away from here with, Randy?"

"We can go anywhere, Mr. B, I have a license even, I showed you."

"Well, what the fuck is the hold up?!"

"There is no hold up, Mr. B, you just need to do your cocaine and drink your tequila. I have been ready since you asked me to grab some clothes and stuff." Pink Eye Randy, maybe though, not on purpose, I suppose, really knew how to deliver quite the knock-out. Or maybe it was on purpose and he was the most sincere straight man the comedy business had ever seen. I shook my head, he had zinged me so thoroughly, "Brutal, man." I slammed my drink and we walked to the yellow Rabbit. I put the bottle of tequila in the hatch and got into the driver's seat. Pink Eye Randy got into the passenger seat. I turned the ignition and sighed when the car started. I told Pink Eye Randy to lead the way. Soon we were clomping down the road with a flat back left tire. I was drunk and high and certain a cop would come by and see us limping away from the burning Comedy Smithereens and racist Motel Mumbo Jumbo. That they would pull me over and that would be that. I was a goner. There was nothing I could do about now. I turned the headlights to bright and swerved my way down the highway at a brisk 12 miles an hour.

The rear left tire clumped as we drove. Clump-clump-clump. As the tire clumped the car would bounce a little. I thought it was hilarious, "We're really in it now, Randy!" Things were going great. The directions Pink Eye Randy was giving me were simple. The only problem was that at the speed we were traveling it was going to take us forever to get there, which I did not mind. I was enjoying the drive, but the longer we were on the road the more likely it was that a cop would come by and shut our operation down. About ten minutes into the trip I could see headlights in the rearview mirror. Had I been smart I would have pulled over and I don't know, ran and hid in the ditch? The stupidest thing I could have done was keep driving. But I was drunk and high, so I kept driving. The headlights approached quickly and then instead of passing us, the car stayed on our tail. I turned the flashers on hoping they would go around. The car looked like a police car even though I couldn't tell because their headlights were blinding me, but as it approached I thought it looked like a police car. I rolled my window down and stuck my arm out trying to wave the car by. Instead of the car going by, a gunshot went off and snipped off the tip of my cigarette. I pulled my arm back in and rolled up the window, "Wow, the cops around here really don't like smoking."

"I don't think they're cops, Mr. B."

"I know, Randy."

"Turn here."

"Okay." Thump-thump-thump. There was a very visceral noise, a thunk that meant the tire had broken free from the hub. And then the steering became slippery. The car wanted to pull to the left but I wouldn't let it. I asked Pink Eye Randy to take the wheel so I could light another cigarette. I rolled the window down again making sure I didn't stick my arm or my elbow or my fingers out. The cruiser pulled up beside us. Liz was sitting shotgun and Cor was driving. He was holding his pistol in his left hand. For some reason my mind thought, "He is either really good at shooting or he is left-handed." We were driving so slowly that Liz didn't have to yell.

"Pull over, fucko." She looked very sad. She looked like she had been crying. I didn't see Rona in the back. I could only assume that Maurice was not in the back either. There was dried blood on Liz's face.

"Make me." I don't know why I thought being defiant

was somehow going to change the situation, their car was about three times larger than mine and I only had three tires. Liz tilted her head towards Cor and Cor pushed us to the side of the road. I put the car in park and looked up ahead. There was a flashing red light. High in the air. The airport. We were so close. Cor parked so close to the yellow Rabbit that me and Liz were almost sitting next to each other like in a movie theater or something. I could smell her breath. It was uncomfortable and unpleasant. I asked Pink Eye Randy to get out. He did. I left the car running and the lights on and dragged my way across the console and out the passenger side door. I watched Liz kick Cor as she did the same thing. She called him a million humiliating names and I was glad not to be in his situation. When he got out of the cruiser and walked around to the front of the car I could see that he had been crying too. He was holding his gun like it was nothing more than a heavy hand-sized rock that he had been put in charge of. He seemed listless and beaten down. Feckless. Broken. Liz came around to the front of the cars, she stomped between the headlights, and got up into my face. She immediately started screaming smells up my nose.

"I know you think you're funny, you limp-dicked faggot, but nobody is laughing anymore, and not only that, but Cor is going to shoot you in the chops and that will be the end of it! Hand it over or else!"

"I don't got your stupid money, Liz. I never did. Either Cor took it or Maurice took it, or I don't know, you took it yourself, Liz, that's my guess."

"I know what happened!"

"She didn't take the money, man!" Cor suddenly was up to the task again. He pointed the gun at me and walked in front of Liz. I put my hands up. Pink Eye Randy snuck away behind me. Into the shadows. I assumed he was going elsewhere to hide or run away. Which is what I would have done if I was him.

"Alright! Relax! I'm not saying she took the money, I am just saying I don't have it. Can't you point that thing somewhere else? I really don't think anyone else needs to die for three thousand bucks."

"Three thousand bucks? No, he's mistaken, Ms. Liz, right? I thought it was…I thought, wasn't it? Mo died for a measly three thousand bucks, what? No! You said it was more, lots more. This whole time? What the hell was I going to make? Oh, Mo! Poor Mo!"

"Oh, shut the fuck you wimpy slimy worm of a scumbag cunt, go sit in the car and wait until I tell you when you can come back out again." Cor whimpered back to the driver's seat of the cruiser. Liz followed him back and opened and closed her hand a few times indicating she wanted his gun. He gave it to her. She came back into the headlights and pointed the gun at me.

"You sure know how to pick em', Liz. Don't listen to her, Cor! I have the money still! You don't have to live this way! You can have it all! Just come do what you know is right!" Cor was bawling in the driver's seat. He kept banging his head against the horn. Every now and again a bleep would squeak out. He was bellowing, "Maurice! Noooo! I'm so sorrrrry!" Liz ignored him.

"Shut up, you stupid scumbag! You're not funny as you think you are, and you have never been funny, so don't even try! Give me the money and we'll let you alone."

"What money? I don't have the money. And even if I did have the money, is it really worth somebody dying for it? Have you lost your ever-loving mind?"

"The money is irrelevant, but Maurice would have wanted it this way."

"What way? You pointing a gun at me?"

"No, he would have wanted justice."

"What justice? There is no justice. This is all some sort of set-up, right? You're just fucking with me, right? This whole thing is just a fuck around, right? It just got out of control, right?"

"No, No. No. No! Not at all! I'm gonna shoot you. I'm gonna shoot you you slippery limp-dicked wet pumpkin pie! I can't believe Mo is gone!" Just then Cor wailed from behind the steering wheel, "Maurice!" Liz started hitting me on the chest with her fists and the gun. I was afraid she was going to accidentally shoot me. I hugged her to keep her from shooting me. "You didn't have to kill him. He was a good man. Oh, MoMo!" She started crying. The gun fell to the ground, but instead of letting her go I kept hugging her. As awful as she was, she was still a human and she was hurting. I started crying myself, not about Maurice, he was a menace to society as far as I was concerned and it was maybe for the best he was gone, but I was crying in general. In general about the state of the world. About poor Pink Eye Randy and the end of the Comedy Smithereens and the racist Motel Mumbo Jumbo. About life and how complicated and painful it was. Instead of saying anything comforting to Liz I felt like I needed to set the record straight.

"I'm sure he was great when he wasn't beating people up, but I didn't kill him, he was going to kill Randy, and instead something else happened, what the hell does that have to do with anything? Why did you, what, what are you, why did you, how come there were, how come you sent three rubes to keep an eye on me just so you could steal three thousand dollars from me? I think you've lost your mind, Liz." I let her go and picked up the gun. I wiped the fingerprints off for some reason and threw it over the fence that was next to the ditch that was next to the road. I heard it plunk into the water. I could see Pink Eye Randy lurking behind Liz. In the shadows. I shook my head. He looked like he was about to tackle Liz. I didn't want him to tackle Liz.

"I didn't lose my mind, I fell in love, you asshole! And now he's gone! I can't believe my little MoMo is gone! Why did you have to kill him?! He was so good, such a good person!  and you're such a fucking wet fart of a loser!" Cor wailed again, "Maurice!" Liz yelled, "Shut the fuck up, you stupid faggot!"

"I loved him too, Liz! You can't take that away from me! Your grief doesn't cancel out my feelings!"

Liz walked over to the open cruiser door and kicked Cor. She yelled at him to scoot over. She put the car in drive and turned it around. They sped off into the silent distance. Into the night. I stood there confused about what had just happened. Why they had gone wherever they went to drop off Maurice's dead body and Rona and then had come back to hunt us down only to shoot the tip of my cigarette off and then have a pointless conversation about nothing next to a ditch while confessing a love for a very violent and angry man and lamenting about a few thousand measly dollars that they were going to steal from me. Money I had earned fair and square. Money that I had hidden in my shoes. Underneath my feet. But it was such a small amount of money. It wasn't worth killing somebody over.

I felt bad for Pink Eye Randy. He was such a sensitive soul. I was afraid that he would be scarred for life about what happened with Maurice. But the money was in my shoes and I was drunk and high and confused and emotional and I couldn't believe it, any of it, and now I had sympathy for Liz and Cor and Rona, I could only assume whatever the hell it was that they were up to had some greater purpose, but instead of getting somewhere with it, Maurice was dead and there wasn't any money coming to any of them. Pink Eye Randy came back from out of the shadows.

"Those guys are jerks!"

"They really are, Randy."

"I don't like 'em."

"I don't like 'em either, Randy. Should we go?"

Pink Eye Randy got into the yellow Rabbit. I did too. We clomped a few hundred yards until we reached a chain link gate with curly barbed wire along the top. Pink

Eye Randy got out and unlocked the padlock that was holding the chain in place. He waved me in and locked the gate behind me. Pink Eye Randy got back into the car. I drove to the hangar thoughtless. I was distracted with what had happened a few moments ago. I sat there staring at the hangar with the yellow Rabbit's headlights spilling onto the giant metal door. Pink Eye Randy walked in front of the yellow Rabbit. Still wearing his cool sunglasses. His leather bomber jacket. He unlocked a door and disappeared. Soon the hangar door opened. The lights were on. A two seater plane came into focus. Pink Eye Randy picked it up by its tail and pushed it forward. The words, "Not Self, But Others," were written on the side of the airplane in cursive. It took me a moment to read and understand the words. I either needed glasses or the part of my brain that could read cursive had been melted away by all the years of abuse. Either that or I was just so drunk and high that I couldn't read. But that didn't explain why I couldn't read Shandy's diner sign. I had a notional moment about getting my eyes checked, but instead I wondered what the words, "Not Self, But Others," meant with respect to Pink Eye Randy and Tricky Houdini. I came up with nothing. They seemed like nice enough words to name your airplane.

I turned the yellow Rabbit off. I switched the lights off. I dropped the key on the passenger side seat for the next person who would own the little guy. Or the police officer that would probably be driving it to the dump or the impound lot. It was a sad moment for me. The car had done me a lot of good for as long as I had been slinging yucks around the country. I thought about removing the license plate for both a souvenir and to keep the cops off our trail, but I didn't have a screwdriver and I basically forgot about it the second I thought of it.

Pink Eye Randy went back into the hangar and shut the huge metal door. A moment later he was helping move our suitcases and his goose lamp into the airplane.

I lit a cigarette and felt very drunk and very high and very stupid. In order to combat this, I did a few bumps of cocaine and took a slug of tequila I was holding by the neck of the bottle.

I stood there smoking, thinking about what had just happened, about what the words, "Not Self, But Others," could possibly mean. Was Tricky Houdini and Pink Eye Randy Bulshoviks? Marxists? Commies? I really needed more Communist jokes in my set, I decided. Nobody takes them seriously anymore. But they are hilarious as hell.

I looked up at the stars. It was a beautiful night. Randy was doing things to get the airplane ready or something. I didn't know. The second I looked up at the stars I got dizzy. I thought, "Whoa! I am wasted." I laughed and laughed and then I threw up. A moment later Pink Eye Randy helped me into the airplane. He told me to get rid of the cigarette because there were no windows and the smoke would cloud his vision. I dropped the cigarette into the pukes and smiled at Pink Eye Randy.

"Randy, you know what? You're okay. I don't know if anyone tells you that enough. You're a good kid and I love you, I hope you know that."

"Thanks, Mr. B. I love you too. Now let's get you buckled up." Pink Eye Randy buckled me into the seat and put headphones over my ears.

"Is this Freedom Rock, Randy? Turn it up!"

Pink Eye Randy got into the pilot seat and buckled himself in. He took his cool sunglasses off and put a leather flying cap on. Buttoned it under his chin. He put headphones on. He started the plane and soon we were taxiing to the runway. The plane stopped and Pink Eye Randy did a cross check. I could hear him through the headphones checking things. I watched the propeller spinning. Nothing made any sense to me. As far as I was concerned Pink Eye Randy was putting me to bed.

"Everything is a go. Are you ready, Mr. B?"

"I'm ready, Randy. Red-aye to rock a bye-bye. Let's do this shit!"

The plane accelerated down the runway. I could feel the gravity pulling on my body. I could see the stars in the night sky looking like cold milk. The moon looking like a hairless coconut. I blinked and pulled my head forward trying to pay attention. My efforts didn't last very long. I passed out before we were airborne.

*Thanks:*
George Truman
Jason Stark
Miette Gillette
Tina Satter
Scott Gillette
Michael Jung
Jack Warren
Jess Barbagallo
Agustin Maes

## About the Author

Joey Truman is a writer.
He is the inventor of the Tickler, the Cubby Bubby,
and Dykes on a Stick.

## About the Publisher

Whisk(e)y Tit is committed to restoring degradation and degeneracy to the literary arts. We work with authors who are unwilling to sacrifice intellectual rigor, unrelenting playfulness, and visual beauty in our literary pursuits, often leading to texts that would otherwise be abandoned in today's largely homogenized literary landscape. In a world governed by idiocy, our commitment to these principles is an act of civil service and civil disobedience alike.